ISLAND *of* REFUGE

LINDA HALL

ISLAND of REFUGE

a novel of suspense

Multnomah®Publishers *Sisters, Oregon*

ISLAND OF REFUGE
published by Multnomah Publishers, Inc.

© 1999 by Linda Hall

International Standard Book Number: 1-57673-397-1

Design by Kirk DouPonce

Cover photography by Geof Du Feu/Photonica © 1999

Multnomah is a trademark of Multnomah Publishers, Inc. and is registered in the U.S. Patent and Trademark Office.

The colophon is a trademark of Multnomah Publishers, Inc.

Printed in the United States of America

MULTNOMAH PUBLISHERS, INC.
POST OFFICE BOX 1720
SISTERS, OREGON 97759

05 06 07 08 09 10 — 10 9 8 7 6 5 4 3 2

To Rik

Then the LORD said to Joshua: "Tell the Israelites to designate the cities of refuge, as I instructed you through Moses, so that anyone who kills a person accidentally and unintentionally may flee there and find protection from the avenger of blood."

JOSHUA 20:1

SUNDAY, JULY 16, 1978

FROM THE JOURNALS OF MARTHA MACGREGOR

It wasn't Andrea's death that caused the church to shut its doors for good. No, I can't in all honesty place the blame entirely on that event. There were others factors too. Andrea's death was merely the beginning of a long chain of questions with no answers. Or the answers given did not satisfy.

There were only six of us who came to church on this windy Sunday morning in July; only six of us to decide the fate of a church that has been standing since my great-grandparents came to this island. Jules didn't come this morning. Neither did Walt or Bill or Shirley or Alexis or Sam or Mary. And of course, Colin hasn't come since Andrea. I don't know why I persist. Perhaps I feel some kind of historic obligation, since it was my own great-grandfather who founded this church. Maybe that's why I keep coming. In spite of everything.

It is afternoon now as I sit here at my writing table. It is pleasant here and I can see far out over the cove. Behind me, to the right, is the mainland. I can't see it from where I sit, but I know it's there. To the left extend the thousands of miles of ocean. Jack is down at the wharf, I see, along with Lenny and Alexis. Mary is there, too. It's so very calm on this side of the island. The sun has even come out. It looks like Alexis and Mary are heading my way. I will invite them in, I'll put the tea pot on, and we will chat. The subject of the church, of course, will never come up.

It isn't so pleasant on the other side of the island where the church is. It never has been. It was exceptionally gusty there this morning. Sometimes when that happens, the church bell rings all on its own without warning. That occurred this morning. We were huddled in the pews, and I was wishing I had lit the woodstove just to take the chill off. We talked for a few minutes, maybe twenty, about what we should do with this building and was there any hope of a minister ever coming back here.

"We've been down that road before," said Will. "We just don't have the money to support one."

A few heads nodded.

So that was that. When Dob's father, Jake, got up and said, "Well this is it, then. This is the final time," the bell began to ring. We all looked at each other, all six of us. I thought of Andrea and began to shiver. No one said anything then, and no prayers were said at the closing of the church. We just got up silently and filed out.

For more than a century this church has stood high on this windy hill, a sentinel facing the wind, a fortress against storms. But the life went out of it this morning; we all heard the death rattle of its bell. Now it is simply a corpse, a tumbledown shell. The islanders will have to find their sanctuary elsewhere.

ONE

PETER GLASS AWOKE TO SOUNDS; the summer morning sounds of people talking, a dog barking, birds, a child's laughter. He had been sleeping on his side, curled up, stiff and uncomfortable on the bench seat of his truck. He forced open his eyes, groaned slightly and sat up, straightening his legs, running long fingers down his dirty jeans. At twenty, he felt old and tired, as if the bulk of his years were already behind him. Out of the passenger window pale gray rocks were scattered across the hillside like bleached bones. To his right was a cemetery where the tombstones were all leaning at the same angle, as if blown that way by wind.

He yawned and rubbed his eyes in confusion. He hadn't remembered driving in here. It had been a night like dozens of nights before it in his running.

Again he heard sounds. A squealing child's laughter, a woman's murmuring voice. He looked around him, saw no one. Was he alone here? Was this noise a part of his madness? Chasing him here, even? Would he never escape? He lay back down and stared at the ceiling of his truck's cab and thought back to the night that he had decided to run.

Leaving like he had wasn't something he planned. It was one of those things that just sort of happened. The afternoon had been overlaid with a damp, drippy fog when he had left his apartment on foot to pick up a carton of milk, a box of Cheerios, and maybe rent a video or two from the convenience store on the corner. Then it would be back to his apartment to spend that evening like he had spent every other in recent months, with the phone off the hook, the doors double locked, and a chair hooked under the knob like he had seen on television.

The only vehicle in the parking lot was a rusting green pickup with a Montana license plate. He thought about that, about someone getting in a truck and driving all the way up here to Edmonton, Alberta, Canada, from someplace in Montana. What was stopping him, he thought, from getting into his truck and driving down there? What was preventing him from even going past Montana, just getting on the highway and not stopping? Eventually he would find a place, wouldn't he, where the ghosts didn't batter his nights with dreams? Where he didn't wake up shivering and afraid?

As if in a dream he had calmly done just that. He went home, packed his clothing into two large duffle bags, threw his sleeping bag into the cab of his truck, packed up a few books, drove to the bank and withdrew all his savings (the $1200 he was saving for school), and then without leaving anyone a note, he headed south.

He raised himself and looked out the window again. The voices had quieted, perhaps they had been a part of his dreams after all. He ran his hands over his hair and stubbly face. His stomach hurt, as it had for many days now, and it seemed more than hunger that gnawed at him that morning.

The need to relieve himself finally made him reluctantly open the door and climb out. He squinted in the bright sun and stretched. His legs still felt stiff and his left shoulder was asleep. He rubbed it absently as he stumbled toward a stand of trees behind the cemetery, feeling grimy, grubby, and sick. He had worn these same clothes for days, and he couldn't remember the last time he had had a decent hot shower with a real bar of soap and a bottle of shampoo. In the old days, his other life, that would have been unthinkable. Every morning he would shave, then shower, then put on a clean shirt and pair of pants. After a glass of grapefruit juice and a bowl of raisin bran he would board the bus to West Edmonton Mall where he worked in a bookstore.

He gazed beyond the cemetery to an old church which stood on stone blocks, some of which were missing, a gap-toothed smile. One long window on the side facing him had been boarded over.

As he stood there hidden in the tree's leafy arms, a woman opened the back door of the church and stood in the doorway. She wore a pale skirt which fell to her ankles and her feet were bare. She was looking at his truck, he saw, but he was too far away to read her expression. A small child skittered out from behind her skirt and laughed swinging chubby arms. It was this child's laughter that had awakened him.

He made his way back to the truck, a curious embarrassment overtaking him should that woman in the long dress see him so disheveled. At the passenger side of his pickup, which faced away from her, he found a bottle of tepid water on the floor of the cab, filled no doubt at one of the last gas stations. He found his toothpaste and brush and managed to squeeze out a small bead of the paste though the tube was virtually empty. After he brushed his teeth, he rubbed a handful of the water over his face and through his hair. His bath for the day. It would have to do. He drank the rest of the water in the bottle. A few days ago he had run out of food, but he knew from his mountain biking experience in his other life that water was important. He made himself drink bottles of it every day, even when it gagged him and made him sick.

If he had to do it again, he would be more careful with his vehicle. It was in Minneapolis that someone broke into his truck and stole his wallet plus all of his clothing and his good sleeping bag. All he had left were the clothes on his back and three hundred dollars he had placed in an envelope under the floor mat. He was going to use that money to start his new life. Now he needed it to buy gas. He began watching the homeless people. He would sit on a bench and watch where they slept at night, how they found their food, what words they used when they begged for money. He consoled himself that maybe it was good he lost his identification, since he was going to start a new life anyway. Maybe this was just fate. Or part of his punishment.

After that he scavenged in dumpsters behind grocery stores for limp lettuce leaves, soft oranges with patches of blue, and moldy bread. He ate the mold without question; he had read someplace that they made penicillin out of mold.

Outside of a McDonalds (was it in Toledo?) he won the lottery; he found a Happy Meal consisting of three-quarters of a burger, an entire bag of fries, a small orange pop still covered with a lid, and a cookie. No doubt some whiny child had demanded it, and then some exasperated mother had trashed the whole works when the child didn't finish it. At the very bottom of the bag he had even found a little Disney character which he had propped on his dashboard. Maybe it would bring him good luck.

But that was a long time ago.

"Hiya." Peter looked over. At the front of his truck was that small child, a little girl, he saw. Her faded dress, printed with big yellow sunflowers, was too big for her and hung loosely to the ground. Her hair was honey colored and baby fine and her feet were bare.

"Peekaboo," she said covering her eyes with her hands.

"Hello."

The child held something toward him in chubby fingers. "Wanna apple?" she asked.

He took it. "Thank you," he said. She ran, laughing, towards the front of the truck again. He ate it quickly. It tasted wonderfully good. Some of the juice dribbled on his chin and he wiped his face with the sleeve of his sweatshirt.

"Peekaboo!"

"Is that your mother?" Peter pointed at the woman who had added a large straw hat to her ensemble.

"Mama," said the child yelling loudly and running back toward the woman. The apple had settled oddly in his stomach, and he hugged his arms around him and leaned against the truck waiting for the nausea to pass.

The woman caught the running child and picked her up. She was still looking at him, he saw, the child squirming in her arms. He ought to walk over there. Probably he should apologize for parking on church grounds. He started toward her.

Next to where she stood, he saw a couple of rakes, a shovel, and a wheelbarrow. Beside the cemetery was a large garden patch. Perhaps this woman was the church gardener. Maybe she was the wife of the minister. Maybe all of them—this woman, the child and the minister—lived in a little house beyond the church that wasn't visible from where he stood. He looked at her. She had long, thick hair, the color of wheat. The weave of her straw hat cast crisscross shadow lines on her face, and her skin bore that ruddy look of long healthy hours working out of doors. She stood almost as tall as he. To Peter, she looked like a goddess standing there, ringed with the sun. In another place and another time he would think about her and her garden until a poem came. But there was no more poetry. Running had replaced long contemplative hours of solitude. His apartment with its locked desk which opened up to a world of poetry and journals and dozens of half-finished chapbooks was far from this place.

She spoke first. "Are you okay?"

"I'm sorry for parking there," he stammered. "I didn't realize I was on private property. I'm just passing through."

"You don't pass through here. There's no place to pass through to." She had a soft southern accent, not harsh, not drawing attention to itself, but gentle, her voice like liquid.

"Oh."

She continued, "You can't go anyplace from here. Except back. This is east, about the farthest east you can be."

He looked nervously around him. The little girl had squirmed down from her mother's arms and scampered into the cemetery.

"What is this place?" he asked. "Where am I?"

"You don't know?"

He shook his head.

"Lambs Island."

"An island?" He ran his hand through his hair, looked around him.

She gazed at him curiously. "The only way onto this island is by ferry. You would have had to come here by ferry. Do you remember doing that?"

Dim, sleep-starved memories flitted in and out of his thinking: A dark road, hands unsteady on the wheel. Gripping it. Afraid of sleep, of what new terrors it might bring. And so hungry. So tired. Driving east, always east. Hungry. Sick. Away from Alberta. He remembered, but only faintly, a car ahead of him driving down onto a ramp. He had followed keeping his eye on its tail lights. And then a clunking, the sound of water. He had driven onto a boat? Where in the world was he? He had looked out, but saw nothing in the blackness. At some point he must have driven off the ferry and then to this cemetery and this church.

The woman was peering at him more closely. "You really don't know where you are, do you?"

He swallowed, shook his head.

"You're in Maine. Lambs Island is off the coast of Maine."

"I'm, uh…" He paused and looked down. Her feet were sturdy and slender, brown from the sun and soil, the toes long, the nails evenly cut. He looked at his own big feet crammed into scuffed Nikes.

He cleared his throat. "I've sort of run out of money." His voice broke. "I notice you have a large garden. If you would let me I could work in it. I'm a little…short of cash. And then I could get going again. Be on my way."

"You came here for a job?" She looked at him incredulously.

He cleared his throat, swallowed, nodded. The little girl was sitting at the edge of the garden digging with her mother's trowel and talking loudly to a group of imaginary friends, ordering them about.

"You're hungry," she said. "And when you're hungry you don't need money, you need food."

"You need money to buy food."

"We can give you food, but we can't give you money."

He pointed to the church. "Are you the gardener for the church?"

"I live there."

"In that building?"

"My name is Naomi," she said stepping toward him. "This is my daughter, Zoe, and yes, we live here. Come inside and I'll fix you something to eat."

"Your daughter gave me an apple." He could picture it in his stomach, a lump of chewed fruit flesh. He still felt slightly nauseous.

The room they entered ran the entire width of the back of the church, and was cut off from the main sanctuary by old and graying dry wall. It looked as though this may have been at one time a part of a building project—make a kitchen in the back. They probably had fund-raising suppers, maybe even had one of those giant thermometers out front. But somewhere along the line the project was abandoned, and all that was left was this dented, graffitied dividing wall. In the center of the room a collapsible wooden folding table, the kind churches use for potluck suppers, was surrounded by folding metal chairs. At one end of the room was a large woodstove and next to it a very old refrigerator which didn't look like it plugged in anywhere. Against the wall by the door were a couple of folding cots with blankets. She told him to sit at the table and she would fix him a sandwich. He watched her gather a few things from an ordinary cardboard box: a loaf of dark bread, a ripe, round tomato. He watched her fingers slice the red fruit with a large knife. She wore a thin silver band on the ring finger of her left hand.

"You and your husband live here?" he asked.

She turned sharply, knife held high. "My husband's not here now." She paused. "He'll be back soon."

"Oh."

She handed him a sandwich. Between two slabs of dark bread was a tomato, thick-sliced and seasoned with a sprinkling of some kind of herb, no doubt from the garden out back. She had also cut up an apple and placed it decoratively around the edges of the plate. She placed in front of him a large plastic tumbler and a jug of water.

He ate hurriedly, washing the sandwich down with glass after glass of cold water.

Naomi watched him. "When was the last time you ate?" she asked.

15

"I don't remember. Couple days ago, maybe."

She sat beside him, frowning. "I shouldn't have given you all of this. Not on an empty stomach. Not all at once."

"I'll be fine."

A few moments later he was stumbling out of the back door toward the stand of trees behind the cemetery where he leaned against a willowy tree and vomited. Naomi had followed him and was wiping his forehead with a damp cloth.

"I'm sorry," he said. Peter was embarrassed, mortified that this woman had watched him be sick. "I'm fine," he kept telling her.

Naomi was shaking her head. "I should have known that you hadn't eaten in a while. I should have been able to tell from your face. The coloring." She was stroking the back of his neck with long fingers. "A tomato was the worst thing for you."

"I'm okay."

"And then an apple before that...."

She looked at him, touched his forehead. "You are sick. You're feverish. No wonder you don't remember coming here. You need rest and good food. In small doses until you're stronger."

He stood up shakily and wiped his mouth with the sleeve of his shirt. "I'm fine," he said.

"Can you walk? Do you have bedding in that truck of yours? Why don't you get what you have and come with us? Stay at our place for a while."

"Thank you," he said, his voice barely above a whisper.

At his truck he gathered together his meager possessions. He had found a blanket and some clothing in two plastic bags outside of a Goodwill.

"Is this all you have?" she asked gathering his things.

He nodded, looked away from her.

"Well, we all make do, don't we?"

His head hurt and when she led him to one of the cots in the room, he lay down. She pressed cool fingers above his eyes.

The last thing he remembered was this goddess looking down at him with her wheat hair, frowning slightly, stroking his head. He fell asleep then, and in his dreams she held him tightly to her, warming his cold and injured soul.

TWO

WHEN PETER AWOKE A FEW HOURS LATER, it was to singing; a soft voice, feathery, and a song he thought he recognized. For a brief drowsy moment he was home and a child, and his mother was singing to him the song she always sang,

> Speed bonnie boat like a bird on the wing,
> Onward the sailors cry,
> Carry the lad that's born to be king,
> Over the sea to Skye.

No, that wasn't the song he heard now. He opened his eyes. A girl with large, brown eyes and a heart-shaped face was sitting cross-legged on the other cot, a chubby baby in her arms. She was rocking it and singing softly. She looked so young. When she noticed him looking at her, she said hello.

"Hi." He stared at those eyes.

She laid the sleeping baby on the other cot, so close to him that he could have reached out and touched it. On the floor was a cloth bag stuffed with baby clothes and diapers.

She said, "Would you like some tea?" Her movements were soft, fluttery, her hands in midair when she talked.

He cleared his throat and wondered who she was. Naomi's sister? "I don't want to be a bother. I'll be leaving soon."

"Oh, it's no bother. I'm going to have some myself." She talked while she worked, filling the kettle from the plastic jug on the floor. Drops of water smacked the top of the hot stove like wet kisses. He felt warm, sleepy.

"I'm Jo," she said, plunking down next to the baby.

"Peter," he answered.

"A name from the Bible."

"I guess. I don't know."

"*Saint* Peter."

"I'm not exactly a saint."

She was very tiny and had soft brown hair which curved gently on her shoulders. Strands of it glinted in the sunlight that came through the windows. A tiny blue ribbon was tied to one side and held it off her face. It was her smallness and her eyes that made him originally think of her as much younger. But closer to her, talking with her, she seemed closer to his age. She wore patched jeans and an oversized man's white shirt with the sleeves rolled up above the elbows. And those eyes. He couldn't keep from looking at those eyes.

"Do you live here too?" he asked.

"Yes."

He made an attempt to swing his legs over the side of the bed, but nausea forced him down again. He rubbed his eyes and groaned slightly, hoping she wouldn't hear.

She looked over at him. "Naomi said you were sick."

"I'm okay now."

She jumped up. "Oh, the kettle's boiling." She hummed while she worked, then turned to him, "Sing me something."

"What?"

"Come on. Sing something."

"Me?"

"Did you ever get a stupid song in your head and then you can't get it out? Here I am singing the song to *Sesame Street*. I was looking down at the baby and all I could think to sing to him was the song to *Sesame Street*. And now that stupid song will be stuck in my head forever unless I hear something different."

"*Sun*-ny day…" began Peter.

She put her hands to her ears and giggled. "Please, no."

"Sweepin' the *clo*-uds away…" He was laughing now.

"I hate you! Now, I'll be cursed with that song in my head forever!"

"On my way to where the air…is…sweet…"

"Stop it!" She cupped her hands over her ears and said loudly, "I can't hear you! I can't hear you!"

He put up his hand. "Okay, promise. No more 'Sunny Days.'"

She let her hands drop to her side.

"*Sun*-ny day," he began again.

"You're such a brat!" She stuck her tongue out at him. "I shouldn't be making tea for you at all, but Naomi told me I had to."

"Is Naomi your sister?"

"My sister? No, what a weird idea. No, she's a friend. She's been helping me." She handed him a cup of tea in a cracked, lined mug which read: Maine: The Way Life Should Be. There was a chip out of the top. He turned it so he could drink out of the unchipped side. She opened up a folding chair and sat next to him, cradling her own mug of tea in both hands.

The tea was the oddest tasting beverage he had ever put to his lips. He looked at strange leafy bits floating on the top.

"It's herbal tea," she explained. "Got ginseng in it, I think. One of Naomi's mixtures. She told me to make you ginseng tea, says it will get you up and about quicker. Give you energy. Naomi's into herbs. She also left this piece of plain toast. Said it would be better than fresh for you. And not to put anything on it." She handed him the thick piece of plain brown toast.

"Thanks."

The baby stirred and Jo gently rubbed his back.

"How old is it?" he asked.

"It's a he and his name is Curtis and he's eight months."

The baby Curtis mewed, pursed his lips for several seconds, cried out and then fell back to sleep. Apparently only a bad dream, maybe a bit of indigestion. Peter knew about both.

"Is he your brother?"

"You're so full of weird ideas. Curtis is my baby."

He took a bite of the toast and swallowed. When it stayed put, he took another. He ate and drank slowly until he could feel his strength gradually return. He wondered if he were strong enough to get up now, maybe even go outside for a bit.

"Where are you from?" she asked.

"Not around here."

"I figured that much, but from where, then?"

He paused.

She put her hands up. "Okay, you don't want to tell me. That's fine. I'm cool with that. Nobody around here talks about where they're from anyway. Why should you be any different?"

"I'm leaving soon anyway," he said. "Heading south."

She looked toward the door. "Do you want to go outside and talk? I was going to go outside after Curtis got to sleep."

"Yeah. I wouldn't mind. It's hot in here." He rose slowly from the cot. He felt much better, almost human.

"That's on account of the stove. Naomi's always cooking things."

Peter looked around him: at the cardboard boxes next to the wood stove, the plastic shopping bags of clothing, the boxes of food, the wooden folding table, the fridge that didn't plug in. It was as if everyone was here temporarily, evacuees from a natural disaster. Nothing looked fixed or nailed down. "Do you all *live* here?" he asked.

She laughed and her eyes danced. "Now you're sounding like Naomi, *y'all*. But you're not from the South, I can tell, Saint Peter."

"I'm not a saint."

"So you said."

Standing next to him, she came barely to his shoulder. "We live here. Me and Curtis and Naomi and Zoe and Colin and an old man named Jeremiah. Colin and Jeremiah sleep in the sanctuary. But Colin's away now." She motioned toward the inner door.

Peter followed her outside.

For the next half hour they each sat on a tombstone in the cemetery and talked. His tombstone read, *Gerald Coombs, Born 1843, Died 1891 in an accident in the Gulf of St. Lawrence. Rest in Peace, Loving Husband and Father.* Her tombstone read, *Andrea, beloved Island Child, 1950-1977.* Both grave markers were overgrown with weeds and grass.

She told him that she was escaping a boyfriend who regularly beat her up. She showed him a mark on her neck. She said she feared for her and Curtis's lives. She went into great detail about how he would beat her, until finally she had no choice but to run away.

"Weren't your parents able to help you?"

"My parents?" She looked past him; a strand of brown hair blew forward on her cheek. He wanted to touch it. "Get real."

He thought about telling her of his own journey, but instead he said that he worked at a bookstore and had completed three years at university and had planned to go back this fall. He also wrote poetry sometimes. He was here on vacation.

"Tell me one," she said clapping her hands.

"Tell you one what?"

"Tell me one of your poems, one of the ones you made up."

"I can't," he said. "It would sound stupid."

"I bet it's not stupid. I bet it would be nice."

He looked down at his Nikes. "Well, maybe if you're interested I could show you my books sometime. They're in my truck."

"You have books?"

"Well, not published books, just my own poetry in binders."

"Oh, I would love that!"

She climbed off her tombstone and twirled in the sunshine in front of him a couple of times. "I wanted to be an actor. That was my dream. I wanted to go and study drama. Everyone said I was a natural—"

"But then you got a boyfriend, and Curtis came along, but your boyfriend wasn't what you thought."

She picked a stray flowering weed, sat back down on her tombstone and began plucking away at the wisps. There was silence, the only sounds were the occasional laughter of Zoe, the digging in the garden, Naomi's low voice.

Then Jo said, "Do you ever wish life was a video, and you could rewind and erase the really bad parts, and with the really good things you could rewind them and play them over and over again, as many times as you wanted?"

He looked at her.

She continued, "That's why I want to be an actor. In movies you can do that. If the director doesn't like something, they yell 'cut' and you get to do it all over again." She smiled at him. "What are some of the good parts that you'd play over again?"

"I don't know. I'd have to think."

"With me it would be the last happy Christmas I had. I was little, and I wanted one of those Cabbage Patch dolls more than anything. Do you remember those? People were like crazy over those for a while. I sat on Santa's lap in the mall and told him. I prayed every night. And then on Christmas morning, the very first present I opened was a real Cabbage Patch doll! That was my last happy Christmas. Then my mom started getting her sickness."

"Do you still have it?"

"Have what?"

"The doll."

She shook her head. "I don't even know where it is now. Probably got thrown out in the garbage when my mom got in one of her moods. Now, it's your turn."

"Okay, well, let me see. I don't go to church anymore, not at all. But I think walking to church with my mom."

"That's it? Walking to church with your mom? Whew, I think you better get a life, Peter."

He combed his long hair back through his fingers. "Well, in the summer you can hear the birds, and everything is green and fresh and new. And the smells of things. I like the smells of things in the early morning."

"You *are* a poet." She cocked her head and looked at him. "What about your dad?"

"Don't have one. Never did. Well, I mean I did have a dad, everybody has a father, but he died when I was a baby."

"That's too bad."

"You don't miss what you never had."

She considered. "I guess not. Now what parts would you like a chance to rewind and record over?"

He looked down, his hands on his knees, his jeans thinning there. After a long silence he shook his head. Jo sat next to him, very close. He could smell the soft cleanness of her hair. She said, "For me, I'd rewind and erase the whole last year, the last two years. Only I wouldn't erase out Curtis. I wouldn't change that." She cocked her head. "If I could record over, I'd sign up for drama school and not look back."

"Maybe you'll have a chance to," he said quietly.

"And maybe you'll have a chance to be a poet, a really famous poet and a writer." Her eyes were amber in the sun. "First you'll go back to wherever you came from, finish college, marry your girl-friend…Do you have a girlfriend?"

He told her about Blair.

"So then you'll marry Blair and write terribly good novels about sadness and fears and running for your life and how everything turns out okay in the end after all. And people will cry and laugh when they read them.…"

As she talked, her hands moving expressively, Peter looked past her, down beyond the front of the church, down to where the ocean met the land in an irregular line of rocks, out to where the water shimmered in the sun like a piece of crinkled satin, knowing that the things she was saying would never come to be. Never.

THREE

BY THE END OF THREE DAYS Jo had memorized seven of Peter's poems which she recited to him with dramatic flourishes of hands and eyes and voice. He was sitting on the cement steps at the front of the church, and she faced him on the overgrown lawn. At one point in the recital she fell forward into the rusty For Sale sign which hung there, nearly knocking it down. She laughed as she steadied herself, righted the sign, and continued.

They had spent the rest of their first day together poring over his binder of poetry. He let her read his finished poems and even look at the ones he was working on. But he never thought she would memorize them and recite them with such flair.

When evening had come, he placed his binders back under the passenger seat of his truck and went with Jo to the back room of the church where they sat around the folding table and ate bowls of Naomi's stew. He met Jeremiah, a quiet, bearded man with wire-rimmed glasses which kept falling down his nose. Every so often he would push them up with the middle fingers of his left hand. Later Jo told Peter that except for trips to the outhouse, Jeremiah never left the church. He spent his days in the sanctuary sitting at a table writing in a book.

"He's a true hermit," Jo had whispered. "But how could anyone be afraid here. This island is the last safe place. For me and Curtis."

She was holding the big, sleepy baby in her arms, and she danced with him in the starlight, humming a tune he didn't recognize.

Peter had slept in his truck that night.

The second morning, Jo left her sleeping baby with Naomi and said to Peter, "Follow me. I want to show you something."

The front of the church faced a gravel road. Across the road the land sloped down to the water. They walked toward the gravel road, trudging through red weeds that crunched when they walked on them. Jo held her arms slightly away from her body when she walked, palms down, fingers slightly splayed, as if balancing on a log. Yet, she was scampering through the underbrush faster than he was. Morning sunlight danced on the ripples of water in front of them.

When they reached the gravel road, they began walking eastward, toward the sun. The road wound inland, and for a few minutes the sea was briefly out of view.

"Where are we going?" he asked.

"A place worthy of a poem."

They passed fields of gray rocks and red weeds and small wind-blown shrubs. It was windy, and the chill of it penetrated Peter's thin sweatshirt. The road inclined slightly in front of them. At the top of the rise when they again saw the water, it was a breathtaking view. Ahead of them the Atlantic Ocean spread out before them like a rest-less blue blanket. On a point of land was a tall cone-shaped white and red lighthouse. They left the road, and Peter followed Jo through the underbrush toward it.

Past the lighthouse they stood on the edge. Far below, huge swells crashed against the rocks sending up a spray that Peter could almost feel, even at this height.

"Isn't it beautiful?" And Jo began to twirl. At the edge of the cliff with the wind in their faces Jo recited the first of his "Alberta" poems, the one about grains of wheat and shallow roots.

He told her he was embarrassed, and she asked why.

"I never thought you'd *memorize* it."

"Memorizing's easy for me. I want to be an actor. Actors have to memorize long passages. And sometimes they have only about half an hour to do it. I'm teaching myself some of the tricks of memorizing."

It was the following day that she had surprised him by reciting all seven in front of the church, tripping over the sign.

"You have to watch out for those For Sale signs," he said, laughing. "They're known to jump out and grab people."

Later they had walked to where Naomi was weeding her garden and talked to her for a while, then he and Jo went and lay on the soft overgrown grass in the cemetery and looked up at the cloud shapes. She had placed Curtis on a blanket between them.

"See that one up there?" Jo was pointing. "That one looks like a mother duck. See all those little clouds following. Those are the little ducklings. And that little cloud at the end, that's the littlest duckling and he's saying 'Hey, wait for me. Wait for me.'"

"To me it looks more like a fire-breathing dragon and those are the puffs from his fire-breathing mouth and that wispy end, that's smoke."

"No, everyone can see it's a duckling." She paused. "No mother should ever leave her duckling like that."

"Maybe the little duck's being a duck jerk. Maybe he's being a duck bully to all his duck brothers and duck sisters and that's why his mother's leaving him. Maybe he's being duck-punished."

Jo was hugging Curtis fiercely to her. There were tears on her cheek. "And how would you feel if you were the bad one that always got left behind? Tell me, how would that make you feel *Saint* Peter?"

He looked at her, at her small, defiant mouth, her brown eyes wide with anger or fear, at the way the wind caught the narrow ribbon in her hair, at the way Curtis's head was pressed tightly against her neck, her small hand covering the back of his head. The two faces together, the same brown eyes—looking more like two orphaned children than mother and son.

He reached out and touched her hair. "I'm sorry Jo. I didn't mean to upset you. I was trying to make a joke, and I guess sometimes I'm not very funny."

Her face softened. She let go, somewhat, her fierce hold on the child.

"Blair is lucky," she said.

"She wouldn't say that."

"You're gentle. You would never hurt her. You're a gentle person,

Peter." She looked at him. "Why'd you leave?"

"I had to."

"But why?"

"I killed someone once."

FOUR

THE FERRYMAN, JULES, LIKED TO THINK OF HIMSELF as the "protector" of the island people, their self-appointed guardian. He noticed things. He paid attention, keeping everything in his head until he had a chance to write it down in one of his scrapbooks. That was why when he saw the police car waiting on the mainland to come across, he told Dob who was down at the wharf at the time to go tell Walt in the coffee shop to get the word out.

The afternoon sun reflecting into the pilothouse where he sat almost blinded him. There were two cops in the car, he saw. Two was serious. Two meant business. There was a distrust of things mainland by anyone who lived on the island. He knew this. And his allegiance was always to the islanders. It had to be. He had known most of the Lambs Island residents since he had run away to this island as a teenager. He knew Martha MacGregor and her husband Joe before he died. When was that? Coming on to almost thirty years, must be. He knew Dob and his father, Jake, and his son, Scooter, he knew Matt, Simon, Lenny, Bill the boat builder, Manny, and then there was Walt who ran the island's only store. Maybe there was some trouble with lobster traps, some newfangled environmental law that the government had come up with, and now the lobstermen were contravening. No, then it would be fisheries guys waiting over there, not police. Maybe one of the kids is in trouble, he thought. He knew a few of the younger families on the island; most of them were born and grew up here and stayed here and married here. He knew the school children; he ferried them across to the mainland each day where the school bus waited for them.

He wondered if the police meant trouble for the "church people," as he and the other islanders called the little band of people who lived in the old church. Maybe this was something to do with Naomi and that little girl of hers. He thought of the others who lived there: Colin and Jeremiah the preacher. Used to be, mused Jules, that there were services in that old church. Used to be a minister came on alternate Sundays to give a sermon and communion. No more. Not for a long time now.

The water was calm. Flat seas made piloting the ferry something he could do in his sleep. Well, he should, he'd been doing this job coming on to forty years. When he was fourteen Jules had run away from his very large, very noisy family of eight brothers and two sisters and two loud and opinionated parents. Jules was sure that the god who was in charge of placing children into families had somehow put him into the wrong one. He just wasn't like the rest of them. He would retreat into the silence of his thinking when life around him got too loud. He would pretend not to hear, until gradually he really didn't hear. His brothers could be shouting in his ear, but if the part of his mind used for listening was switched off, he barely even flinched. When his parents took him to get his ears checked, he sat in the chair and ignored the sounds in the earphones. But it didn't work; they had some way of figuring out that he was faking and told his parents so. They were advised to take him to a child psychologist, but his father would hear none of that. Those were his exact words. "I'll hear none of that. No son of mine's going to a shrink!" he had shouted to the doctor in the waiting room.

He began by doing odd jobs for the fishermen. He got to know the island's eighty inhabitants. He liked the quietness of the place. No loud yelling. No blaring television or bright lights. He could concentrate on his job of knowing about people. Of listening and watching. Of paying attention.

Jules had paid attention when the girl Jo had walked onto the ferry in the middle of the afternoon three weeks ago, holding a baby, trailing the ends of a blanket behind her. He saw how she sat stiffly on the one gull-spotted bench provided for foot passengers. He watched her look down into the face of that baby. He saw her wipe the edges of her eyes with a corner of the blanket. When the ferry reached Lambs Island, he saw her walk slowly off, the blanket still trailing.

He had also paid attention when the skinny boy in the pickup had driven in last week behind Stu Philpot's Chevy. There was a slump to his shoulders, like he wasn't all there. Drunk? And New York license plates. He'd have to ask some questions.

There was also something else he remembered about that night too, something that he kept going over and over in his mind. Maybe it had something to do with the kid. Maybe it didn't. But when Jules was securing the ferry after the final run, he had seen someone in a dark coat and a black woolen cap with a white tassel rowing in the darkness across to the island. When Jules had called and waved, the figure had turned away.

When the ferry reached the mainland, he climbed down from the pilothouse and motioned for the police car to drive on. Then he ferried them across to the island, thinking.

FIVE

I KILLED SOMEONE ONCE. Words he had never said out loud. Not to his friends. Not to Blair. Not to his mother. Not at the trial. Not when the lawyer shook his hand at the end and said that he was free to go. Big smile. But the fact remained. *I killed someone once.*

He was sitting at the edge of the bay down at the front of the church skipping flat stones across the smooth surface. He closed his eyes, put his head between his knees as the days and weeks of the past month came to him in their enormity.

Once he had decided to leave Alberta he knew he had to move fast. If he allowed himself to think about it too long and too much, he'd change his mind for sure. His duffle bags packed, he had looked around his apartment, at his CD player, his vast collection of CDs, his mountain bike, snowboard, and computer. These he had to leave behind.

He had thrown what food he could into a plastic milk box; a half box of Cheerios, a box of granola bars, a carton of milk with some left at the bottom, a partial loaf of bread, some peanut butter. He didn't think about dishes, and it wasn't until he was halfway to Lethbridge that he realized that a bowl of cereal would be hard to come by. So he ate the Cheerios by handfuls and drank the milk out of the carton.

He had thought briefly of calling his mother in Red Deer, but decided against it. She would try to talk him out of it, and his mind was made up. He had to start over. When he finally did call her he would have a new name and a new identity. After all he had been through, he suspected she would understand.

Peter got up and began walking down the rocky shoreline, climbing over flat rocks and around tide pools. Ahead on the beach was an old green rowboat. So embedded was it in the rocks that it looked as if it had grown there. He lay down on the warm stones next to it gazing at the sky and the slow moving white clouds. A mother duck and her baby ducklings. He looked for them, but by now, they were long gone.

He heard voices and raised himself up on one arm to look over the top of the boat. Two cops were standing there, not more than half a dozen yards away from him facing each other. Carefully, quietly he lay back down on the rock and forced himself to remain perfectly still. How could they have found him here? How could they have known? He had crisscrossed all over the northern states, making sure that no one was following him. Along the way he had stolen license plates and kept changing them on his truck. The vehicle now bore a license plate unscrewed in the middle of the night from a junkyard in New York state.

The voices became quieter. They were walking away from him. He let out his breath. He wondered if there would ever come a time when he didn't look over his shoulder. Would he ever be able to ride his bike with his friends on the rocky mountain trails in the summer? Would he ever be able to snowboard down the mountains at Marmot Basin again?

He waited until the cops were specks far down the beach, then he scrambled back toward the church in a crouched position, keeping a watch for them. But they had gone.

The garden and cemetery were deserted when he returned. When he had left, Jo and Naomi, their children on their hips, were chatting in the garden. The place seemed so quiet now.

He pulled open the back door of the church. The room was empty. Completely empty. Jo and Curtis were gone. Naomi and Zoe were gone. The bags and boxes were gone. The loaf of bread on the table was gone. The box of food was gone. The bedding was stripped from the cots. He walked over to the wood stove. It was warm to the touch, and the kettle was still there, but the jars of leaves and herbs which rested on the shelf above it were missing. On the window ledge behind the stove he saw one of Curtis's baby bottles. He picked up the bottle and put it down again, feeling something akin to panic.

"Jo?" he called.

Silence.

"Naomi?"

Nothing.

"Jo!" More loudly.

Still nothing.

He opened the door to the main sanctuary. Dim light filtered in through long smudgy windows on the sides and revealed rows of straight-backed wooden pews. At the front of the sanctuary, which was really the back of the building, was a raised wooden platform with a railing, and behind it, floor to ceiling shelves were crammed with books. There was a small table there, too, a candle and some bedding folded neatly in the corner.

"Jo?" he called.

No answer.

"Jeremiah?"

Nothing.

There was a faint sour smell in the air which he couldn't quite identify. He walked down the center aisle, his Nikes squeaking on the floorboards.

"Jo?"

His voice echoed back to him in the sepulchral space. He heard a slight rustling from the back of the church, and he walked toward it. "Jo, is that you?"

On the very back pew lay a man half covered by a ripped and dirty sleeping bag. He was watching Peter intently, an amused expression on his face. Then he sat up, stretched, and said, "I'm not Jo, so sorry to disappoint you."

"Oh," said Peter, startled.

Peter was bad at judging ages, but figured this man to be somewhere in his forties. He was wearing a brown flannel shirt and a pair of grubby jeans, frayed at the bottom. Fine, brown hair, threaded with gray, reached just below his collar, and like Peter, he had about a month's growth of beard.

"Colin Workman," said the man rising and extending his hand. "Pleasure to meet you."

"Peter…Peter Smith. I'm looking for Jo. Have you seen her?"

Colin shook his head. "Nope. You seen Naomi anywhere?"

"I saw her earlier."

"And where's our beloved Reverend Jeremiah?" Colin yawned and stretched again, revealing a line of brown belly.

"I don't know. He's gone, too."

"Well, maybe all of them are together somewhere. Having a jolly tea party and they didn't invite us."

"It looks like everyone just packed up and left."

Colin grinned. "Oh, that's it then. Nothing to worry about, chap. Packing up and leaving. That's a common occurrence around here. Especially with that little girl of Naomi's. Every once in a while some mainland social worker gets a bee in her bonnet and decides to make this island her pet project. Decides Zoe would be better off with a real family in a real house with a swing set, a cocker spaniel, and a mini-van. When that happens Naomi leaves."

Colin scratched his belly. Their conversation was interrupted by loud voices and heavy-booted footsteps in the back. He looked at Colin, put his finger to his lips and then fell prone on the back pew. Colin grinned, gave him the okay sign, and walked to the front of the sanctuary.

Peter could hear the officers talking.

"She's been here. That much is for sure. See this baby bottle?"

"Bag it for prints," said the other.

Baby bottle? wondered Peter. *Jo?*

The policemen were now in the sanctuary.

"Workman, have you seen her?"

"Seen who, gentleman?" Colin answered.

"Joanne Sypher."

"Joanne Sypher? Never heard of her."

"We think she's the girl who's been here."

"Joanne Sypher? Oh, you mean Jo!"

"Don't be a smart alec, Workman."

"That's *mister* Workman to you. And why are looking for her?"

"She's a missing person. Got a call from someone on the mainland. They thought they saw a girl fitting Jo's description come over here a few weeks back."

"Oh yeah? Sorry, can't help you. Just got back myself."

Peter could hear the police officers walking toward him. It wouldn't be long before they found him. He pretended to be asleep, or drunk. He could sense them standing there, right above him. One of the officers prodded him. "You. Know where she is?"

"Leave me alone," said Peter. "I'm gonna be sick." He groaned.

"You ever see a girl here, about yay high, brown hair, pretty?"

"I just got here. I don't know what you want. Leave me alone."

"You never saw her here?"

"The lights are too bright in here. I'm gonna throw up!"

"That your truck out there?"

Peter almost said yes, then stopped himself. "What truck?"

"The truck out there. It's not yours?"

"Never saw it before."

After they left, Colin walked to where Peter lay dazed and uncertain in the back pew and said, "I wouldn't worry, kid. They're probably all at Martha's."

"Who's Martha?"

"She lives over at the townsite."

"You live here, too? In this church?" Peter asked.

"When I'm here. Off and on. I head north every summer. And you're from New York? I'm assuming that's your truck out there."

Peter nodded uncertainly. "I'm heading south."

This was the second time he had said the word *south*, and it was becoming familiar on his tongue. He wondered if all truths were merely lies told over and over again until they sounded right.

"South," the man repeated as if he didn't quite believe him.

36

"Well," said Colin walking over to the back pew where Peter had originally found him. "Time to unload my most recent finds." There were a number of plastic grocery bags which Colin untied and dumped out on the floor. He dumped out a shirt, a pair of worn gray wool mittens, a couple of bandannas, one red and one navy, a pair of suspenders. From another plastic bag Colin pulled out paperback books which he began carefully lining up side by side against the outside wall. He chatted rapidly and happily about his finds. Peter could read several titles; *Fodor's Guide to England,* the *Concise Oxford Dictionary,* and half a dozen on various aspects of wooden boat building. He also had quite a collection of biographies of explorers, people who had sailed across oceans in sailboats and rafts of various kinds, people who had sledded to the north pole, people who'd been to Antarctica. Covers featured fur-coated men beside dogs. He also pulled out some very old hardback books which were dented and spotted with mildew.

Colin picked one up and Peter caught a whiff of it. This was the sour smell he had recognized earlier.

"Classics, these are. *Through the Looking Glass,* and here's another one, *The Last of the Mohicans.* I shall read this one again. These are collector's items. Robert Louis Stevenson. And a leather-bound edition of *Snow White and the Seven Dwarfs.* You are welcome to read these while you're here, by the way. And some books for Zoe, *Winnie the Pooh, Charlotte's Web, Wind in the Willows, Where the Wild Things Are.* Now, I shall compete with Jeremiah."

"Compete with him?"

Colin pointed to the front of the church. "See all those books? Theological books. I don't have time for theological books, but Jeremiah's going through them. I have absolutely no idea why. Maybe he's writing book reports."

Their conversation was interrupted by Naomi who appeared in the doorway holding Curtis in her arms, a frantic look on her face. Zoe was clutching at the bottom of her skirt.

"Have you seen Jo? She's gone."

SIX

PETER LOOKED UP IN ALARM.

Naomi held the whimpering baby close and looked at Colin. "We have to find her."

"The police came," Peter said in alarm.

"What did you tell them?"

"As per usual, we didn't tell them anything," Colin said, "We're too drunk and stupid to know nuthin' from nuthin'. Unejecated welfare bums we are, you know."

Naomi sighed. "I promised Jo I would look after Curtis if anything happened to her."

"What do you mean if anything happened to her?" asked Peter his voice rising at the end.

She answered quietly, "That's what she said when she left."

"Left where?" asked Peter. "Where did she go?"

"We were over at Martha's. In her boathouse. Jules came here earlier and said that a couple of policemen were on their way over. Jo panicked, so we packed up and left. We were in Martha's boathouse. They wouldn't know to look for us there."

Colin said, "They were here in full regalia, I might add, and were their usual pleasant selves."

Naomi looked down at Curtis. "He's so young. She said she was going to be right back. I don't know why she left. She was frantic, wouldn't tell me where she was going. I waited and waited. Then I went looking for her. But I couldn't go too far, not with the two children. But she must have come back here, because the bottle's gone. I need to go find her. Perhaps she's still in the woods. But I can't take the babies...."

"The police took the bottle," Peter said.

"Oh." Naomi was biting her lip. "We've got to find Jo. We've just got to." She turned to Peter. "Can I leave Curtis and Zoe with you while I go and look for her? I have to find her. I know every place on this island. I know I could find her."

Peter looked at the children. "Uh, I don't know…."

"Do we look like a day-care service, Naomi?" Colin said. "Tell you what, Peter and I will look for her. We'll walk the length and breadth of this island until we find her. We'll mobilize a search party if that's what it takes."

"Don't do that," Naomi said. "No one from the mainland knows she's here. She's not supposed to be on this island."

"The police said she was a missing person."

"It's her boyfriend that got the police out looking for her," said Naomi. "That's what she told me. She's scared half to death."

It was windy when Peter and Colin left the church, and on their way down to the road Peter grabbed an old gray woolen coat from the back of his truck, one that he had found in the plastic bags he had picked up at the Goodwill. Dirty, it was still serviceable and provided some warmth. In the same bag was a pair of corduroy pants. They bagged on him, were too short, but his only other pair of pants were the jeans he wore most of the time.

"Nice coat," said Colin.

Peter looked at him, wondering if this was meant to be a joke. But Colin wasn't laughing.

"It keeps me warm," mumbled Peter buttoning it up to his neck.

Peter followed Colin, and they turned and headed up the road toward the cliff.

"Why are we going this way?" asked Peter. "Naomi thought she was in the woods."

"I want to give this island a thorough search."

"Where does this road go?" asked Peter. "I've never been on it past the cliff."

"All around the island. Out to the edge and back down to the town and then around to the ferry. This road heads down to the townsite.

The town is located on the lee side of the island. I have no idea why the church was built on the windward side as we who live therein have to endure all sorts of howling blasts in the winter. It's never warm enough in that building, as you will discover."

"I'll be gone before then."

"So you said. I just bet she's at Martha's. Right now the two of them are in the kitchen drinking tea and eating blueberry muffins, both of them surprised at all the fuss. We'll check along the coastline before we get there."

When they reached the cliff, Colin said, "Here we are; Deadman's Cliffs, Widow's Bluffs, or Suicide Ridge depending on your point of view," said Colin. "Listen to the waves. This is the farthest island out. From here all the way to Europe there are no more islands, no more obstructions."

Peter nodded. He remembered Jo standing right here, reciting his poem, the glints of sun in her hair, the ocean roaring behind her.

Peter held his coat closed but it flapped around him, and his hair blew across his face. As far as Peter was concerned Colin was standing altogether too close to the edge of that cliff. In his mind, he could see the lip of land giving way underneath Colin's muddy boots. Colin was looking down, pointing. "I was thinking she'd be down there. Maybe walking, even though it's dangerous at high tide, which is what we're experiencing now. But I don't see anyone."

Peter was standing a safe enough distance from the edge and had to strain to hear Colin's voice. "You can walk completely around the island at low tide. The sea is considerably calmer then, almost tranquil, and the rock formations are beautiful. But you better get around the point before the tide comes in. There's a story of a young woman who was out in her lobster boat trying to free a trap that had gotten caught. Thought she could race the tide. Guess what. She couldn't. The Coast Guard had to wait until low tide again before they could even retrieve the body. Messy sort of situation."

Peter wrapped his coat around him more tightly and shuddered.

He had grown up in landlocked Alberta. He had no experience with tides and currents and steep cliffs and an eastern ocean that showed no mercy. Funny, he thought, standing here with Jo the sea had seemed friendly, pretty. Now it was angry and harsh.

"You want to know what these cliffs are famous for? Shipwrecks," continued Colin. "This lighthouse has been here for centuries. It's been built and rebuilt many times. Used to be manned. Now it's all done by computers. There's a foghorn which is used in pea soup weather, which often happens, but that doesn't always help. In heavy fog, sailors can get disoriented. Sounds, like foghorns, can seem to be originating from the exact opposite from where they are really coming. Long ago, during really soupy conditions, they rang the church bell, too."

"They still do that?"

"The bell doesn't work any more. Clapper's been removed. Kind of like having your tongue cut out, I should think. But what you're looking at is history," said Colin, hands on hips, surveying the lighthouse. "Soon there won't be a lighthouse anywhere along the coast. Anywhere. All being cut back. It's all satellites now. You can captain one of those big crude oil carriers and you never have to leave the comfort of an easy chair on a warm bridge. Done all by computers, GPS, the works. Those who navigate by the stars and the seat of their pants are few and far between in this brave new world, my friend. Few and far between."

Peter, who didn't have a clue what Colin was talking about, felt considerably better when Colin moved away from the edge. They walked past the lighthouse, which was sending out a shaft of light at regular intervals.

"How far is it to Martha's?" Peter asked. They were walking away from the cliffs and the road was angling downward.

"Just another couple miles."

The rest of the trek was easy. They followed the road as it spiraled downward toward the lee side of the island. Evergreen trees and lush shrubs grew higher and more abundant on both sides of the road. Away from the sea, Peter felt warm in his coat as he kept pace with Colin. There were more signs of life as well; trailers, small houses and gravel driveways, people bending over in flower gardens and children kneeling in the dirt and playing with brightly colored plastic trucks.

"The town's up ahead?" asked Peter.

"Right up ahead. Martha lives down near the wharf."

"Who is this Martha everyone keeps talking about?"

"Martha owns this island."

Peter raised his eyebrows.

"Just kidding. Martha's lived here all of her life. Born here, grew up here, lives here now. So did her parents. So did her grandparents. Can you imagine? On this little five-mile island. She knows every inch of it, though. All her family's buried in the graveyard."

They were walking side by side down the center of the gravel road, and it struck Peter suddenly that few cars had passed. He said, "There's not much traffic, is there?"

"That, my young friend, is an understatement. The ferry only runs if you call Jules. And if Jules happens to be there, and happens to feel like powering it up, then you'll get across. Not a lot of tourists make it over here. This is certainly not Bar Harbor. There's not one hotel on the whole of this island. No camping spots, unless you want to camp on the beach. But then, there's no facilities. No flush toilets, no showers, no electricity or running water. And goodness me, here's the worst of it, there's no *cable!*"

Ahead Peter could see the water again, still and totally becalmed. He found it hard to reconcile this placid bay with the waves and spray on the point. The bay was packed with boats.

"People here like boats, I would say," said Peter.

Colin looked at him. *"Like* boats?" He winked and laughed. "Those, my friend, are work boats. No Club Med yachting here, pal."

"Oh."

To their left was a wooden dock that seemed to run the length of the town. Down near the wharf men in scuffed yellow pants called to each other. Peter saw haphazard stacks of rectangular metal containers made of thick screening. "What are those?" he asked.

Colin chuckled. "I am getting an idea you haven't spent a lot of time near the ocean. I find it difficult to believe you're actually from New York."

Peter shrugged. He would have to be more careful.

"Lobster traps."

"Oh. Yes, of course. I just couldn't see them through the trees properly. Lobster traps, of course."

Small clapboard houses sat on pilings or stone foundations and looked as though at any moment they could topple into the bay. On the hillside behind him, the buildings looked as if they were stacked one on top of the other. Many were done up in bright colors: reds, blacks, bright blues, shiny grays, with contrasting shutters. Peter was used to long, flat lawns of grass.

"That's Martha's," said Colin pointing to a small gray house. "The one at the far end."

The two of them headed toward the small building. They passed a man in a yellow slicker tying up an oily boat. Colin approached and helped, securing the thick rope effortlessly around a metal stanchion. The two talked as they worked; Peter stood to the side and watched.

"Heard you were back," said the man to Colin. "You seen Bill yet? He may have some work for you. Said he was wondering when you were getting back. Said I didn't know."

"I'll look in on him."

"You gonna get that boat of yours finished this winter?"

"Maybe. Maybe not."

"Yeah, that's what you say every year." The fellow winked. "Bill's over at Ray's right now. You might catch him there. Just saw him coupla minutes ago."

"I'll go see him."

"Some cops from the mainland been snooping around here, asking a bunch of questions. Thought you should know."

"Yeah, they were over at the church."

"They were asking about that girl. Naomi's friend. The one with the baby."

"As it happens, we're looking for her, too. She and Naomi were in Martha's boathouse."

The gray whiskered man said, "Oh yeah? Didn't see no one there." Then he looked at his boat. "Gotta do me a bit of fix up on the Mary Jane."

The name, *Mary Jane,* was scrawled in large script across the stern of the boat. The man looked over and seemed to see Peter for the first time. "Who's your scrawny friend?" he asked.

Peter cleared his throat. "I'm Peter Smith. Visiting. From New York State."

The man looked long at him. "Visiting?"

"He came at my invitation, Dob," said Colin. "He's an old friend. Staying here the winter. May work on the boat with me. Both of us may move on in the spring."

Peter stared at him openmouthed.

"Anyway," Colin was continuing, "we're going to head up to Martha's now. We're looking for Jo."

"Well, she ain't there," said Dob. "No one's there. Not even Martha."

"No kidding," said Colin. "Well, I would have put money, if I had any, on her being there."

"Maybe she left the island," Peter ventured.

"Nah, Jules would've said something. You can't come on or off this island without Jules knowing."

Even though Dob had said that Martha was out, the two of them headed over to her place anyway. Colin pulled open the door to her little house, stuck his head in and called her name. When she didn't answer, he walked in. Peter followed. There were two rooms in Martha's house: a large front room which faced the cove, and a smaller back room, separated by an open curtain. Against one wall was a wood cook stove and behind it, shelves of food, jars of things: dried soups, tea bags, dishes, plates, coffee mugs. A chair and a couch were covered in quilts and afghans and leaned against the other wall. A small table sat by the window. On it was a coffee can full of pens, some books, and a few framed pictures. A rag rug, worn and obviously hand made, was laid out on the smooth wood floor. Behind the opened curtain was a tiny back room with a neatly made up single bed.

"Martha," Colin called. No answer. Off her room was a small bathroom. The door was open.

"You stay here and wait while I nose around town a bit," Colin said, "Maybe go up to Bill's. See if I can find out where little Jo has gotten herself to."

"I can come."

"Martha and Jo may come back here. While you're waiting you can read through Martha's old magazines, lie down on her couch. Even have a shower if you want."

"A shower?" asked Peter running his hand through his greasy hair.

"Sure. It's right in there. Martha won't mind. You've probably been taking bucket baths like we do at the church. A hot shower is nice every once in a while."

When Colin left, Peter hesitantly ventured into the tiny bathroom. There was a shower there all right, a white metal cubicle with a big industrial bar of white soap and an immense plastic bottle of generic shampoo. Two minutes later he was soaped up and standing under the spray, which felt like hot needles on his grateful body. He washed away a month of road grime, a month of exhaustion.

After he had put his clothes back on, he sat on Martha's couch and watched the bay, his hair wet and glistening, his body clean and smelling of soap. His eyes felt heavy in the late afternoon, and he dozed, wrapped up in the clean quilt.

His nap was filled with voices; shrill voices calling over the wind, rustling voices in the grass by the church, sinister voices beckoning to him from beyond the cliffs. Accusing, vengeful voices chasing him from Edmonton, finding him here, making him go back, making him pay for what he'd done. *I killed someone once.*

The voice of Jo screaming as she tries to climb the cliffs and the tide races in behind her. She is there in his dreams, drenched with salt spray, calling his name as she reaches for a handhold on the sheer wet crag.

He groaned and struggled in sleep, limbs caught in the quilt which wound around his sweating body.

SEPTEMBER 28, 1978

From the Journals of Martha MacGregor

The clapper was removed from the church bell today. This morning it began to ring furiously out across the island, all on its own. Everyone heard it. It was a rogue wind that did it. I am sure of that, and try to tell Colin as much, but he refuses to listen to me. He insists that Andrea herself has risen from her resting place in the cemetery and has rung it. He is inconsolable about this. She died one year ago today.

When Andrea was a little girl she was the one who rang the bell every week. She would arrive at the church early on Sundays, and whoever happened to be there would let her in and walk with her to the bell tower where she would pull the rope.

When she was nine or ten, I can't remember which now, her birthday happened to fall on a Sunday. When she told this to the caretaker he said she could ring it once for every year of her life. That became a tradition: every year on her birthday she would ring the bell once for every year. Then she took to ringing the bell for friends' birthdays too, one pull on the rope for every birthday year. It got so that barely a day went by that the bell was not rung for someone.

But now, at Colin's insistence, we have removed the clapper. The bell, which would call people to assemble and warn sailors in the fog and tell the whole island of children's birthdays, will not ring again.

SEVEN

The pleasing, sizzling sound of food being cooked woke Peter up. Something keened in his memory. Pancakes and maple-flavored bacon sending little fingers of aroma—like on Saturday morning cartoons—streaming down the hallway, entering his room, and finally ending up in his nostrils as he lay underneath his Star Wars bedspread on a Sunday morning. He'd lie there listening to his mother singing softly as she poured the batter onto the griddle.

Carry the lad that's born to be king.

And then she would call him, "Peter, time for breakfast, get up sleepyhead. We've not much time."

Clad in pajamas, he would arrive at the table still smelling of sleep, and the two of them would pour Aunt Jemima syrup over thick pancakes. Later on they would walk to church.

Peter opened his eyes. Colin was standing by Martha's woodstove flipping pancakes, and outside it was night. One oil lamp on the kitchen table provided all the light for the room. There were no clocks in Martha's little house, and Peter wondered how long he had slept.

"Did you find Jo?" Peter asked sitting up.

Colin turned. "You're awake. I thought I was going to have to warn Martha about this strange man sleeping on her couch. I went up to Bill's, went to Sam's, saw some old friends. But so far Jo, like Martha, is nowhere to be found. And the power's out. That's another plus. Also means there's no lighthouse until they get the generator going."

"You looked for her?"

"Yes, I looked for her," said Colin forking a few pancakes onto a plate and setting it down in front of Peter. "After talking to Bill, I walked all the way back to the church. Naomi was there but not Jo. Then I came back here. Martha's gone, too. If you ask me they're off together somewhere. There's a couple shacks in the woods. I checked them once, but I told Naomi we'd check them again on our way back."

A niggling fear began to play at the corners of Peter's mind. He was hungry, but hardly tasted the pancakes. "I've got to go out and find her. We really should leave. If her boyfriend finds her…"

Colin pointed with his knife. "Sit. Eat."

Later when they finished eating and cleaning up, Colin said, "We'll borrow Martha's flashlight for our trek through the woods."

"This Martha doesn't mind if we borrow her flashlight and make pancakes with her flour and shower in her bathroom and sleep on her couch?"

"Martha? Nah. Martha's the closest thing we got to a hotel on this island."

"There are no stores here, either?"

"One fueling station down by the wharf for the fishermen. We passed it on our way here. There's a gas pump there for cars, too, added as an afterthought. There's a little bit of a store there with a cafe of sorts which is basically a row of stools behind a counter where coffee and fried eggs and gossip are dispensed with regularity. Guy named Walt runs the place, has for years. That's also where people come for their mail. Now where in the heck does Martha keep her flashlight?" He was rummaging in cupboards and in drawers. Finally, he found it, hanging by a plastic lanyard on a hook over the door. "Hah! The most logical place."

Peter followed Colin up from the wharf onto a winding dirt path. They made a turn into the woods into what looked like thick brush and walked past a small white house. Colin said, "Alexis and Lenny live there." They walked past the gray-headed couple's kitchen window and were inches from the two as they sat eating their supper at their kitchen table by candlelight.

"You know everyone who lives here?" asked Peter.

"I have a long history on this island."

What looked like underbrush with no rhyme nor reason became a path, although not as well defined as Peter would have liked. He kept tripping on roots and rocks trying to keep up with Colin's quick pace. They came to the cabins but found them empty.

By the time they reached the church, night had blanketed the entire island in thick darkness. The two made their way quietly through the back door of the church. The boxes and bags were back; the blankets on the bed and the jars of tea were on top of the stove once again. But no Jo. No Naomi.

Peter followed Colin through the door into the sanctuary and then out through the double doors at the front of the church, softly calling Naomi's name.

Naomi was sitting on the front porch steps of the church and didn't answer him. Beside her on a mat, asleep, were Zoe and Curtis, Zoe with a protective arm around the baby. Naomi was on the top step, elbows on her knees. The only light was the red tip of her cigarette. She didn't look up when they approached.

"Did Jo ever come back?" asked Peter.

She shook her head and swatted a mosquito on her ankle. Then she said, "She's still on the island. Jules never saw her leave."

She was smoking furiously. "And Martha's gone, too. And Jeremiah's gone. The power's out. That's not a good sign. And do you hear? Wind's coming up."

Peter watched as Colin took the cigarette from Naomi's hand, crushed it on the steps, and then flicked it onto the grass. He took her hands in his then and said gently, "Naomi, everything will be okay."

His look to her was so gentle, so tender, so private that Peter looked away.

That night as Peter lay fully clothed on the front seat of his truck covered by a threadbare blanket, he heard a cry, a piercing, keening sound, like the call of a solitary sea bird. He moved onto his back to listen more closely, but the sound faded. Maybe he had only dreamed it.

EIGHT

A STREAM RUNS THROUGH THE CENTER OF LAMBS ISLAND. In the spring it swells with run-off and winter melt and flows full and fat over the underbrush and among the evergreens. By autumn it is a mere trickle across rocks and tree roots. The spring-fed creek, named Alicia Stream on maps and navigational charts, is called simply "the creek" by islanders. It is the island's only supply of fresh water.

There are three tiny log cabins along the creek at various intervals, ski shacks built more than a dozen years ago when the state of Maine in a flurry of tourist-promoting activity decided that Lambs Island would be the perfect place for the entire eastern seaboard to go cross-country skiing. Maybe it was the location, too out of the way to be of much interest to rich Bostonians and New Yorkers, or maybe it was the aloofness of the islanders or the lack of services, but the idea never caught on. Now the cabins stand empty and ramshackle. Few people, even islanders, spend a lot of time at the creek, their work keeping them in fishing boats around the edges of the island.

But Naomi knows every meandering inch of the creek. It is to the creek that she comes after her husband, Philip, leaves, after he has promised that this time will be different, that this time he will stay. She comes to the creek after she watches him drive off, dust flying up from the wheels of his pickup, not looking back, not waving. At the creek she is cloistered and safe. The ocean with its storms and waves and unpredictable tides is far from this place. Sometimes she goes inside the first little cabin where she keeps a few glasses and some cutlery. Sometimes she makes a fire and has tea. Or sometimes she just sits on the broken steps of the little hut and watches fresh water dribble musically over colored stones. Often Zoe is with her and chases bugs and little ground squirrels. Naomi watches and smiles.

And it was to the creek that she went the following afternoon after they learned that Jo was dead, after they saw her body washed up on the shore down in front of the church. When the police cars lined the road, when they heard the commotion, voices, the yelling, all of them—she and Colin and Peter and Martha, who was there too—raced down to the beach, kicking up sand and stones behind them. They arrived in time to see someone giving her mouth to mouth resuscitation. But she looked limp and wet as a rag doll.

Peter, with the haunted eyes, had walked away and vomited into the bushes. Colin and Martha stood together staring down at the body. The sky was striated with red, Naomi noticed, when she turned and made her way back to the church, to the children she had left in her haste when they heard the news. Electrical storms, a front coming in, she heard Martha say to Colin.

A few hours later a social worker from the mainland had come for Curtis. They learned a lot about Jo from that social worker. She waggled her pen and told them that Jo's real name was Joanne Sypher, and that she had worked as a nanny for a family of doctors in Plattsburgh, New York. Curtis was not her baby but was the son of the two general practitioners, Drs. Kimberly and Randolph James, who had been frantically looking for Curtis and his nanny ever since the two had disappeared more than a month ago.

"It was all over the news," she said. "I'm surprised you didn't hear about it."

After Curtis left and after the ambulance had driven Jo's body away, a policeman had walked into the church without knocking and said he wanted to talk to all of them. He had said this while he walked around and around asking where Jo's possessions were. No one said anything. Peter sat slumped, his head in his hands and Colin was busily reading the morning news, which did not, of yet, carry the story about the death of Jo.

"We need her things," said the policeman.

Colin folded the paper and asked him if he had a search warrant and the man said that he didn't need one, since this church was public property and all of them were illegal squatters. And that if they didn't comply, if they made trouble for the police, they would be evicted. Sent off the island, too, for that matter.

"The church is not public property," said Martha. "This church is private property. These people are not illegal squatters."

"We're not bothering anybody, so why can't you just leave us alone?" said Peter, his face wet with tears.

The officer stood square in front of them and said, "In case you haven't realized, a death has occurred. We generally investigate deaths, especially suspicious ones. It's what the taxpayers pay us to do. That's why we need to look through her things."

"Are you saying this is a suspicious death?" asked Colin.

"Yes. That's exactly what we're saying. That little girl did not drown, she was murdered. Strangled."

Jeremiah entered the room, a canvas knapsack slung across his back, a surprised look on his face.

The police officer looked at him. "And where have you been all this time?"

Jeremiah smoothed his thick gray hair behind his ears, looked over the top of his little, bent wire-rimmed glasses and said, "I went away to pray."

"That's a good one."

"If the man said he went away to pray," said Colin, "he went away to pray."

The officer rolled his eyes. "Just tell me where her clothes are."

"Most of her things are hanging on that hook over there," Naomi said. "There's also a bag beside the cot."

"Thank you," said the officer turning.

"Not that coat. It's mine."

"This one?" said the cop holding up a long, many-colored quilted coat.

"Yes. That one's mine," said Naomi.

"Fine then." He hung it back up, took the small bundle of Jo's clothes and left.

In truth, the coat was also Jo's, but the police didn't need to know that. Naomi needed a coat. And what would the police do with all her clothing anyway? Naomi had always admired this coat which had come from a place called Margot's Designs in Vermont. She had read the label.

When the police had left, she had settled Zoe down for a nap and come to the woods. Colin had nodded to her before she left, a nod that said he and Martha would keep an eye on Zoe for her. Colin was probably the closest she had to a friend on this island, but still there was none of that comfortable familiarity. Last night, when he had stubbed out her cigarette and taken her hands, was the first time he had ever touched her. They did not talk easily as friends do. At times she would see him talking earnestly to Martha or laughing with her. She envied their friendship. She seldom spoke to Jeremiah either, who spent most of his time sitting at a small table in the sanctuary reading through the old books.

And then Jo had come and the silence was broken. Jo talked. At nights while the children slept, the two of them would sit cross-legged on the cots and talk and talk like school girls at a sleep over. Jo told her about her boyfriend, Steve, and about how afraid of him she was. Naomi told her about her husband, Philip, and his irregular visits. She also told Jo about growing up in Virginia, the only child of an alcoholic father and a weak mother. She told Jo that it was her mother who constantly cleaned up after her father, gathering the whiskey bottles from the house and hiding them in the garbage, calling his work with excuses of twenty-four hour flu when he was too hungover to go in.

"You must be a lot like your mother then," Jo had said.

"What do you mean?"

"You're the mother to everyone here. You make meals for everyone, for me and Colin and Jeremiah and the children. You don't have to be the big mother, you know."

"I don't mind. I like it, in fact."

But now, it seemed, Jo had lied to them and especially to her. Everything she had said, all about running away when she discovered she was pregnant, about being disowned from her large family of five brothers and two sisters, all of that was phony. According to the social worker, Jo, an only child, had grown up in foster homes and had a police record. The résumé she had presented to become the Jameses' nanny had been fabricated.

Naomi broke the end off a stick she had picked up earlier and started back to the church.

That night the wind was horrible. The power was still out, and the church dwellers took their places around the sanctuary, evenly spaced about its perimeter, no one talking. Naomi leaned against the door to the back room holding the sleeping Zoe in her arms. She was weary, but the idea of spending the night by herself in the back room was intolerable. She would be alone there without the cheery chatter of Jo who had tried to break all the unwritten rules of silence and distrust in this strange squatter's community.

DECEMBER 21, 1979

FROM THE JOURNALS OF MARTHA MACGREGOR

It is bitterly cold outside. As I sit here at my table, my breath comes out in little puffs of smoke. I have a blanket around my shoulders and another across my knees. The woodstove roars, but can barely keep up with the cold. The sky outside is dense and hovers somewhere just above the rooftops. The only thing keeping the cold at bay, keeping it from descending and smothering us like a rug, is the smoke from a hundred chimneys on the island.

Colin tells me that snow is forecast. He looks up from his reading to tell me this. He is sitting on a chair here beside the fire reading a book about boat building. (I marvel that he can still read those books after all that happened.) Down by the wharf Lenny and Jack look horridly cold and their movements are jerky as they tie up the boat. Off in the distance I see a walker. Is that Mary out there? She's braver than I am on a day like this! I'll have to tell her that next time I see her.

It is funny what I think about as I sit here. Suddenly, I am not thinking of snow and cold and the long winter ahead, but I am trying to remember how the church was decorated for Andrea's wedding. Andrea's bridesmaid was another island girl named Laura. I have no idea what has become of Laura, I should ask her people some day. Colin may know, but I dare not ask him. There are certain things that the two of us don't talk about.

What I do remember, so clearly, is that Andrea wanted everything "island" for the wedding. (She even wanted Walt to cater it! Can you imagine? I said, You mean you want greasy eggs and bacon and stale coffee for it? We both had a laugh over that one.) Still, Walt did cater it, his one and only wedding, and I remember he did a fine job. Of course, not without a lot of help from the Island Ladies Guild. Still, Andrea knew how to endear people to her, and I think Walt was pleased as punch to be such an integral part of her important day.

Here's what I remember about the church that day: Andrea didn't want what she called a decorated *wedding, as in sprays from florist shops tied neatly to the ends of the pews and wreaths at the front and flowers arranged artistically in vases and pots. Nothing that you would see in magazines, she said. So hours before the ceremony we were out there gathering baskets of flowers from the woods, the shorelines, the townsite. People even donated flowers from their own gardens. It was a wonder we didn't strip the entire island clean! We ended up with a wild agglomeration of colors and shapes, small ones, larger ones, baskets full of them. She had Walt order in one bolt of green ribbon and one bolt of white—yards and yards of it. Once we had the flowers in the church, she took out her scissors and made little bouquets of them, tying them alternately with green or white ribbon, each one different. Then she and Laura pinned them all over the church, on the edges of the pews, on the altar rail, around the doorways, on the window ledges. For all my misgivings, I have to admit that the effect was really quite startling!*

I smile when I think of this, and I look at Colin deep in his book. I want to say, Colin, remember the flowers all over the church at the wedding? Remember how the little girls in the church picked up the bouquets afterwards and put them in their hair? But I won't. I can't.

He has stood up now and is kindly offering to make tea. I don't really want tea, but I say yes. I know it will please him. He sighs as he drops loose tea into the pot. I can hear him from where I sit. Colin, I say, Does Lenny have a new boat? That doesn't look like his down there. And he says, Yes, he just brought it over from the mainland. And I say, Good, because his old one was certainly not very seaworthy anymore. I think we were all afraid of him going out and not coming back. And Colin says, Yes, it's good he was able to get a new one. Even Bill said that old junker of his was beyond repair.

That is the sort of thing we talk about on this, the shortest day of the year when snow is forecast and we sit with our tea. Not the flowers at Andrea's wedding.

NINE

TWO DAYS LATER MARGOT DOUGLAS of Margot's Designs in Woodstock, Vermont, was sitting at her sewing machine watching the television news when she heard that the police were definitely suspecting foul play in the drowning death of a girl two states away. This story had been on the news before, but Margot hadn't really paid much attention. Sometimes when she sewed, she put the TV on and just left it going through the loop of morning talk shows, game shows, and soap operas, paying attention only when something piqued her interest. Her sewing machine whirred, and the fabric took shape under her expert touch as the newscast continued. Then something made her stop, absolutely, in midstitch.

"Joanne Sypher," the reporter said, "from Mountainside, New Jersey." Margot grabbed for the remote and turned up the volume. The victim, said the newscaster, had worked as a nanny for a family of doctors in Plattsburgh, New York, and then a month ago she and the baby had disappeared. Now her body had washed up on the shore of Lambs Island where she had been hiding out in an abandoned church. The police had received a tip that she and the baby had fled there. The baby has been returned to the parents, the voice said, and the screen moved to a ponytailed young mother, Kimberly James, holding a chubby baby wrapped in a blue blanket. Beside her, with a protective arm around her shoulder was a tall, dark-haired, broody-looking man in a tan sports jacket.

Next they showed a high school graduation photo of Joanne Sypher. Margot looked at a smiling Jo, draped in her high school colors of red and blue, a bouquet of roses in her arms. Fabric fell onto Margot's lap and lay there as she thought about Jo, the girl who had lived with them, and then had left as quickly and as mysteriously as she had come.

It was a quiet, cold Thursday morning last February when Jo had walked through the door of Margot's shop, stopped, and looked around her as if she had maybe wandered into the wrong place. Margot, who was marking down some winter wools, said hello and then probably made some comment about the weather. The girl, who looked hardly older than Margot's thirteen-year-old twin daughters, stood there, the back of a mittened hand across her mouth.

"Is there something I can help you with?"

Margot half expected the girl to say that her mother needed a spool of white thread. But she sighed and said that no, she just wanted to look around some. Fine, said Margot, just let me know if you need anything.

The girl walked to the fabric books and sitting down at the chairs Margot provided, began slowly leafing through them, page by page. Half an hour later and the girl was still there.

Margot walked over. "Would you like some help picking out a pattern?" The girl quickly closed the book, but before she did, Margot saw that she had been leafing through the infant wear section.

"Nothing can help me. It's all beyond help," the girl said. Her voice was tired, dead.

Margot didn't know how to respond immediately. She probably said something like, Nothing's beyond help.

"This is."

"I bet it's not."

The girl put her face into her hands and began weeping, wiping her eyes with her mittens. Margot, still surprised, still uncertain, put her hand on the girl's shoulder. Through her sobs Margot learned that the girl had been kicked out of her home and had no money and nowhere to go.

So Margot, who tended to do things on the spur of the moment, hired her on the spot and told her she could live in the apartment above the shop. She knew Paul would hit the ceiling when she told him, but this was one girl who needed help.

Jo turned out to be a good worker, helping Margot clean and set out fabrics and wait on customers. Margot taught her how to sew, little things at first, and was surprised at how quickly she picked it up. The two would talk constantly, and Margot reflected how nice it was to have someone to pass the time with. Jo even started going to church with the family. Occasionally, Margot brought up the subject of Jo's family, but Jo would turn away. Margot didn't press. When she's ready, she's ready, thought Margot.

Then one morning Jo was gone. When she didn't show up for work, Margot went upstairs to her apartment. The door was wide open, and Jo was packed and gone. A note had been written in green ink and left on the bed. Margot had unfolded the crumpled piece of paper and read:

I'm sorry, Margot, but I had to leave. I'm sorry to have caused you any inconvenience. I'll write when I get a new address and tell you all about everything. I'm sorry about the money and the locket I took. I promise I'll pay you back when I get some. And I'll keep the locket safe, I promise. (But you'll thank me for it someday in the future.) I'll explain everything soon.
Jo

Margot was ashamed to admit it, but at the time she was more upset at the loss of the antique sterling silver locket than she was about Jo's leaving. A family heirloom, she had recently replaced the picture of her grandmother with one of her twin daughters, Sara and Pam.

After Jo left, Margot tried to contact Jo's parents. Jo had told Margot that she came from Barrington, Rhode Island. But when Margot called the only number for Sypher that the information operator had given her, the woman on the other end of the phone had never heard of Jo.

Puzzled, angry, Margot thought about calling the police. Paul asked what could the police possibly do? "She's a grown woman, free to come and go as she pleases, and that locket is probably halfway to Mexico by now. You try to help these people, and that's what you get," he had said. She didn't like his reference to "these people," and wanted to ask him about it, challenge him, but didn't. It would just lead to another fight. And she was tired of fighting.

The newscast shifted to Lambs Island and a rocky shore and a weathered looking church. "Maine State Police have few clues into this baffling death that has rocked the quiet little fishing community on Lambs Island, Maine." Margot had been to Lambs Island. Years ago, now. The twins would have been about five when the four of them had gone exploring on the back roads of Maine. For a week they had rented a condo down at Wells Beach, but then, tired of the crowds of tourists, they decided to drive north and do what Paul called "exploring," driving down roads to see where they ended up. Where they had ended up on that particular trip was Lambs Island, a picturesque little island with lobsterboats, quaint houses, an old church, a lighthouse, and breathtaking cliffs. Since there were no motels or guest cottages for rent on the island, they had driven around, had a picnic lunch, and then headed home.

And now Jo had been murdered there?

TEN

NAOMI SAT CROSS-LEGGED ON THE BACK STEPS, her wide denim skirt tucked around her knees, washing the last of the green beans, when Peter approached. Jo's death had left his hollow eyes more red-rimmed than usual.

"Do you know what Jeremiah's doing right now?" he asked.

"Studying, I would imagine."

Peter blinked at her. "But he does this all day long. And into the night."

She shook her head. "Colin says he's going through the books, categorizing them. I don't know. Listing them or something. Taking notes."

"But why does he do it?"

"I've never asked him."

Peter shifted his weight from foot to foot as she pulled more beans from the basket.

Peter said, "Can I ask you something?"

"Go ahead."

"It's about that night. Where you went with Jo. I can't stop thinking about that."

She looked up. Zoe was tearing around the graveyard, laughing, nearly tripping on the front of her dress, probably chasing an insect in flight. "I keep going over that night in my mind, too, Peter. Jo was acting really strange. She kept saying, 'Everything's going to happen now. Everything's going to happen.'"

"What did she mean by that?"

Naomi shook her head. "I have no idea."

Peter sat down on the ground, traced a stick through the dirt. He said quietly, "Do you think Jeremiah could have done it?"

"Jeremiah! You mean murder Jo? What makes y'all think Jeremiah did that?"

Peter shook his head from side to side. "Well, he's so strange, the way he just stays in there and studies. Never talks to anyone. And he wasn't here then. He came back after it was all over."

Naomi shook her head. "Whatever you think, Peter, it wasn't Jeremiah."

"But he's so strange."

"And that makes him a killer?"

"Well, I don't know, but the strange people you read about. The hermits. Those are the ones who are the killers."

"Peter, listen to me, Jeremiah didn't do it. He's the gentlest man in the world."

He was looking past her, past the church, down toward the water. "It just seems so strange to have her here and then gone. Everything's just going back to normal. It's like no one cares. The police aren't even here anymore."

"Well, that's a blessing."

He threw the stick into the grass. "No one's doing anything. No one cares."

"People care, Peter. Jo was my friend." Zoe scrambled into her arms.

"We haven't even heard if there's a funeral or not."

"I imagine her family's taking care of that."

"And now her baby will miss her. Grow up and never even know her."

"Peter, the baby wasn't hers."

"Did you ever wonder why she took it if it wasn't hers? Maybe the real parents weren't paying enough attention to it. Maybe they were hurting it in some way. Did anyone think of that? I've been trying to come up with reasons all afternoon." He rose, wiped his hands on his corduroy pants. "I don't understand this. I don't understand any of this."

"Peter…"

But he had turned from her and was walking away. She watched the back of his retreating figure, the tall body, the stoop of his shoulders. She looked at him sadly. He should be wearing blue jeans and a sports team T-shirt, not those bulky corduroy pants too short for his skinny legs underneath that old man's coat.

ELEVEN

AT SEVEN O'CLOCK IN THE MORNING a few days after the girl's death, the police were back again, waiting on the mainland side of the channel, honking and flashing their lights.

"Hold your blinking horses," Jules muttered as he made his way down the path from his cabin to the waiting ferry. He walked slowly, not hurrying. A few of his regulars were already there waiting to get across to the mainland: Grant Peterson in his pickup, Brett who walked and caught a bus on the other side, and Sally Whyte in her little Ford. But he wasn't going anywhere until John Frye showed up. He usually drove down from the townsite around 7:10, and Jules always waited for him. The police, therefore, would have to wait.

Jules had lived in the same wooden cabin on the island side of the channel for most of his fifty-eight years. The government was constantly pressuring him to live on the mainland side, and so, as a concession, he had a little apartment there but seldom used it.

When Jules first arrived on Lambs Island, he earned enough by doing odd jobs around town to buy a wooden dory with an old Briggs and Stratton inboard. Eventually, he was hired as the delivery boy, bringing the newspapers, mail, and small supplies to the island, a job he took seriously and did judiciously. Since those were the days before the ferry, he would also taxi people back and forth on occasion. He loved that boat, still had it, as a matter of fact, although it leaked some now and needed work. He always loved the sound of that engine putting across the channel, the slapping of the sea against the bottom. He loved the smell of gasoline mingled with sea water. When he wasn't delivering papers and mail then, he would explore the island shores during low tide.

When the ferry was put into service, Jules was the natural one to take on the job. He ran his ferry like he ran his dory taxi service, on an "as-needed" basis. It was supposed to run on a schedule. There was even a rain-obliterated timetable tacked up on the bulletin board outside of the ferry terminal on the mainland, but sticking to it had been abandoned long ago. He still delivered the mail, newspapers, and magazines and did a multitude of errands for the islanders.

Although they couldn't see him, Jules made an obscene gesture across the channel to the waiting police cars and then winked at the islanders. When John finally arrived, Jules powered up the ferry and took it across. On the other side Jules again took his time about loading the police cars.

He walked up to the road and grabbed the banded stack of *Bangor Daily News.* There were no magazines, he noted, and no mail yet. Glancing down he saw that the death of that girl was still front-page news, although it had been relegated to a small story on the bottom right. He wondered how Colin felt about this murder, if it reminded him of the other death at all. It does me, thought Jules.

In the pilothouse on the way back to the island, he slipped his own copy of the newspaper from the top of the stack. He'd get to it later. Jules read a lot of newspapers. He read the *Bangor Daily News* plus every one of the magazines that the island store carried: *Time, Newsweek, People, Star, The National Enquirer,* even the soap opera digests and *Ellery Queens.* Jules read everything cover to cover.

As soon as the traffic drove off and he had driven his newspapers up to Walt's store, he took his copy of the paper back to his cabin and got out his notebooks, his scrapbooks, his red-inked Bic, his yellow highlighter pen, his black Magic Marker, his glue stick, his scissors, and his roll of tape. Then he made himself a small pot of tea.

The most interesting sections were the police and court reports: who'd committed what crime, who'd been arrested and what for. He also read the obituaries and the social pages: who was visiting who, and who had married who, and who was celebrating an anniversary and which one. In his notebook he would jot down the names of the offenders, noting how many times they had been arrested and for what offenses. In another section, carefully marked with colored tabs, he would note who had recently celebrated a birthday and who had moved away. He'd note who had died and who the pall bearers were. It was of special interest to him if any of these people had island connections.

On page seven there was a half inch story about Lenny and Alexis's son, Rusty, being arrested in Bangor for impaired driving. Jules clipped that one and pasted it into a scrapbook. This was getting to be a habit with Rusty, thought Jules, this impaired driving. He clipped several other stories, including a photo of Marta and Jim Sikmore's twenty-fifth wedding anniversary. He wondered if they were related to the Sikmores on the island, the couple in the trailer with all the kids. He went through the lost and found thoroughly; people were always leaving things on the ferry—keys, hats, wallets, umbrellas. Sometimes the reward money came in handy.

That part of the paper finished, Jules made himself a second pot of tea. He was saving the front page story for last. He would savor it now, as he did his black tea every morning. He put his cup on the table and folded the paper so the entire story was laid in front of him.

Police were still investigating the suspicious death of Joanne Sypher, aged nineteen, from a place called Mountainside, New Jersey. She'd left there about a year ago eventually ending up as a nanny to a couple of doctors in Plattsburgh, New York. Everything was going wonderfully; the baby loved her, her employers loved her. And then one morning, reported Dr. Kimberly James, she and her husband came home from the medical office, and both Jo and the baby were missing. A search by police in the Plattsburgh area revealed nothing. It is still not known why Joanne and Godfrey had ended up in Maine. Jules stumbled over the name. Godfrey! Who named a baby Godfrey? He had heard that the baby's name was Curtis.

He read the article again and carefully clipped it out and pasted it into a new scrapbook he had labelled *Book of Jo*. Then he folded the paper and added it to the near ceiling high stack of papers in his cabin.

SEPTEMBER 5, 1983

FROM THE JOURNALS OF MARTHA MACGREGOR

Sometimes I worry about the old books in the church. Recently Colin and I took them down from the shelves in the back room and packed them away in trunks and boxes. Now the boxes are piled one on top of the other in the sanctuary behind the altar rail. Colin assures me they are okay there. As okay as can be. Nobody will steal them, if that's what you're thinking about, Martha, he says to me.

The books belonged to my grandfather and my great-grandfather, so I guess they would belong to me if I wanted them. I ask Colin if he wants them, he reads quite a lot, you know, and he raises his eyebrows and looks at me as if I am insane. What would I ever want with that junk, he says. But yet when we packed them, when he didn't think I was looking, he carefully, lovingly wiped away traces of mildew with a white handkerchief before he placed them in the box.

My grandfather was a scholar. That's what I'm told. I have one picture of him. In it, a stern, solemn-looking face peers out of a dark, oval frame. The photo sits here at the corner of my writing table. The picture used to frighten me when I was a child, and I would ask my mother if this is what the devil looked like. She would slap my hand when I said that and say that he was a godly man and to mind my tongue. My mother told me that he was fluent in both Greek and Hebrew and also several other languages. Colin says there are books in Latin, Hebrew, Greek, and German. I don't even know what most of the books contain. When we were packing them up I started a list, but I quickly cast it aside when the task became too daunting, and the books became so plentiful. Mostly, they are books of sermons, some Greek and Hebrew texts, various translations of the Bible, a few prayer books, some service orders, and a few hymnals and psalters.

So, I consign them to the interior of the church where they receive the full summer heat, the cold blast of a Maine winter, and the salt air which blows unceasingly across the island. I am afraid they will come to ruin, yet I have no room for them at my place. And no one else wants them. I have asked around.

TWELVE

Jo APPEARED NIGHT AFTER NIGHT in Peter's dreams. As soon as he fell asleep she would be there, tiny blue ribbon in her hair, humming while she made tea or singing to the chubby baby in her arms.

Sun-ny days, Sweeping the clo-uds away…

Twirling and dancing in the moonlight. Reciting his poetry.

And he would awaken and remember the feel of her hair against his hand, and he would hold his hand to his own face. Remembering.

On my way to where the air is sweet…

At other times he would hear her calling from below the cliffs and he would lean over the edge as far as he dared, and there she would be, grabbing hand holds, wet strings of hair matted against her cheeks, calling to him, begging him to help her, not to leave her body on the roadside with the head bent at such an odd angle. And the blood. And he would back away from the edge screaming.

He would wake up and remember that he didn't save her, that he hadn't saved her after all. *I killed someone once.*

And then his thoughts would move, he couldn't help it, to the last time, and he would again see the body prone on the dark, slick road, legs contorted back unnaturally, neck bent, crushed under the wheels of his own truck, blood snaking through the snow. And him running around to the front. Frantically running, screaming. *Get up, please be all right, oh, please be all right.* He couldn't say it enough times, but still she didn't get up, and he told them that he hadn't seen her until the very last moment when she staggered into his headlights in spike heels and a black satin party dress, her hair done up in tendrils. *I'm so sorry. Sorry. Please get up.…*

And then they had taken her body away, the police and the ambulance; cars, lots of cars, filling the dark icy streets with commotion and lights and faces and boots stomping in the snow. They led Peter, an arm on each shoulder, to the police car where he sat in the passenger seat, head in his hands weeping uncontrollably for a long, long time, lights strobing above him.

The lawyer argued that the victim was wearing dark clothing and the streets were icy. Peter was driving within the speed limit, with plenty of due care and attention given the road conditions. Because of who she was, it was kept out of the news that she was drunk at the time.

He awoke with a start and sat up, hoping he hadn't cried out. But the church was dark; it was still night. He could hear the even breathing of Jeremiah at the front. He heard Colin move on his mattress. He let out his breath and lay back down on the old mattress Colin had thrown his way earlier.

The mattress, stained and lumpy as it was, was more comfortable than the too-short bench seat of his truck. He lay on his back and stared at the pitch of the ceiling and wondered if God lived in churches that were inhabited by squatters and had For Sale signs in the front and where the only minister was a hermit who spent his time poring over old books.

A thin filament of early morning light began to filter in through the grimy stained-glass window. Peter rose quietly. The large double door to the foyer creaked when he opened it, so he did it slowly, inch by inch, until he could slip through. Outside, his Nikes crunched on the gravel. He walked toward the cliffs.

He sat on the steps of the lighthouse and watched the sun rise over the eastern ocean. He watched it ascend in pale layers of light one upon the other until the lines and layers fused into a single sky that became day. Why was he staying? He should have left by now. Jo was dead. It was time to move on. What was keeping him here? A part of him knew the answer to that. This was the first time in his long months of travel that anyone had asked him his name. The other places he had been, the coffee shops (when he had money), the rooting in dumpsters outside Wendys and McDonalds, he knew he was seen as a part of the landscape, a nameless face in the press of homeless people. Even at the men's shelters no one cared. Not really.

He didn't leave Lambs Island that day. He didn't leave the next day, nor the next. Almost a week had passed since Jo died, and still Peter was on the island, his truck still parked beside the graveyard. The police were back and forth along with the occasional reporter. He kept his face turned away from any cameras.

During that week, Naomi worked in her garden; Colin disappeared for days at a time; and Jeremiah studied the books. Occasionally Peter would watch Jeremiah kneel at the altar rail, hands covering his face, shoulders heaving. And through all of this, the police kept walking around, in and out of the church, through the cemetery, talking to people, stopping in at Walt's, asking more questions, going door to door.

For his part, Peter took advantage of Colin's original offer and began reading. Colin's books were mostly biographies of explorers; the first man to scale Mt. Everest or get to the North Pole, stories about individuals who had crossed the Atlantic or the Pacific in canoes and rafts. In his other life this was not the kind of reading material that Peter chose, but he found he was beginning to look forward each day to taking one of Colin's books to the lighthouse where he would lean up against it and be transported into a world of snow and sled dogs and provisions running low. He felt almost a kinship with these explorers and began to believe that his own trek across the northern states was of this magnitude.

When he tired of reading, he would watch the sea and imagine that he was the first person who had ever set foot on this island. Had he come across from the mainland by canoe? Or had he been shipwrecked on the eastern side of the island and had to claw his way up the cliff to safety?

This prairie boy, who had only been to the Pacific Ocean three times and had never seen the wild Atlantic, was coming to know the rhythm of the tides, the slow unchanging breaths of the sea—the one constant in a life of chaos.

During low tide Peter would venture near the cliff edge and gaze down at rocks misshapen into gargoyles and ghoulish images by the pounding of the waves. His poet's mind imagined these were sea gods captured from some underwater paradise and spewed out on the shore. Now, unable to get back, they fought against anyone who happened to venture too close at high tide. He thought about the girl Colin had mentioned, who had died down there.

Later, when he would walk back to the church, plates of tomato sandwiches would be laid out on the folding table on clean dish cloths. There was often fresh fruit and always tea. Sometimes there would be a vegetable soup or stew, the aromas welcoming him as he walked up the road. Naomi did all of this, and all of them ate her food without question. It was somehow understood in the order of things that Naomi was the caretaker, the nurturer. Sometimes he would look at her, try to catch a glimpse on her face of resentment in this role, but he saw nothing in her passive face.

Eleven days after he arrived, Peter received the first of two gifts from Jo. He was walking back to the church along the beach, taking his time, enjoying the solitude. When he came to the old scow, near where Jo's body had been found, he sat down on the rocks beside it, one arm on the edge of the boat. He was going to rise when he saw a bit of color inside the bow of the boat. He peered in more closely. Tucked up between the boards of the boat was a tiny bouquet of flowers, drooping now. A few of the flower heads fell off as he reached for them. The stems were tied together with a narrow blue ribbon. Something tugged at his memory. Jo, twirling in the cemetery, a tiny blue ribbon tying her soft hair away from her eyes. He ran the ribbon through his fingers. He tried to imagine her walking down to the beach, picking flowers as she did so, and then taking the ribbon from her hair and tying them all together. He held the tiny bouquet to his cheek and wept.

THIRTEEN

ODDLY, IT WAS PHILIP WHO FIRST INTRODUCED Naomi to gardening. He would kneel with her, plucking up handfuls of dirt, showing her how to plant bulbs root side down into the soft earth. In those days, if she did something wrong, he wouldn't laugh at her, wouldn't deride her, but would patiently take her hands in his and show her the correct way. It was her husband who nourished her love for green things, the feel of wet stems in the morning and cool, dark earth.

But now when Philip came he took no interest in the garden. He never even ventured close enough to see what she had planted there, even though she longed for him to do so. This morning as she wiped her forehead with her hand and knelt between the rows, she thought of him. Would he get home before the winter? It was getting colder now. The chill winter winds were already beginning to blow high over Lambs Island. She could hear them at night when she lay in bed holding Zoe tightly to her.

It became an obsession with her, keeping her plants alive, keeping the season of death from entering her garden. It always grieved her to watch them die, the tomato plants leggy and dark, the beans overgrown, their vines spilling onto each other, too weary to bear any more fruit. Vainly, stupidly, she was trying to keep her plants alive, patting dirt in mounds around their roots, propping up the stalks with sticks and string, covering them at night with old sheets and rags.

When she wasn't in her garden, she worked feverishly, piling up the canning, shelf after shelf of glass jars in neat rows; tomatoes, beans, peas, blueberries.

This morning, Zoe was following close behind her, crawling on the ground, tripping on her long skirt, giggling.

"Zoe, Zoe, you're getting yourself all mussed. Look at you. How's mama ever going to clean you up, you little piglet." But her voice was warm when she said these things to her daughter.

At the far end of the row, Peter was kneeling, quietly picking the last of the tomatoes. He had offered to help, and she hadn't refused.

There were times when Naomi felt she might be depriving her daughter by living the lifestyle she did with a series of strangers, mostly men, who bedded down in the front of the church. Maybe Zoe deserved more. But then she remembered other children she had seen, children who lived in the squalid inner city whose mothers were forced to beg for food and milk, children who could not play in the fresh salt air with their imaginary friends, who could not dig for crabs and star fish and clams and shells, who couldn't squat between the rows of their mamas' gardens and find earthworms. No, Zoe didn't lack for much.

Just a father who stayed.

Naomi gathered a basket of tomatoes, the last of the season, and rose to go inside. Bread had to be made. Tomatoes had to be canned. There was a lot of work to do. Idle hands are the devil's playthings, her mama used to say.

"I've got a few tomatoes here, Naomi," Peter said walking toward her, basket in hand. "But what about the plants? They look pretty sick. You want me to pull them up and put them on the compost?"

"No." Naomi wiped her forehead. "There's still a lot of life here."

Later, Naomi loaded the woodstove with logs that Colin or Jeremiah had split. She filled the canning kettle with creek water that she hauled up by bucketfuls. Standing there she briefly caught a glimpse of her reflection in the window beside the stove. She frowned. When had she developed those lines on her forehead, those squint marks at the corners of her eyes? She plucked absently at the edges of her hair while she waited for the water to boil. When had it become so gray?

The sound of footsteps made her turn. Colin was there. She hadn't seen him in days.

"Colin."

"It's hot in here." He grabbed a peach from a basket on the table.

"I have to keep it hot for the canning. You've been away."

"Working on the *Andrea C.*"

"You've been working on that boat a long time."

Their conversation was interrupted by the sound of vehicles. She glanced out the window to see a police car pull up. She sighed. Didn't they realize that no one here knew anything more than what they had said over and over a hundred times? What more did they hope to get out of them? Two officers entered the church and asked where Jeremiah and Peter were. Naomi shook her head.

"Be our guests," Colin said. "Go look for them, you will anyway. We can't stop you tromping through our private quarters."

They found Jeremiah in the sanctuary and led him through the back room of the church. Naomi watched all of this, unspeaking. She watched while they put Jeremiah into the back of the patrol car. From the window she watched them head toward Peter's truck.

FOURTEEN

LATER, MUCH LATER, PETER WOULD THINK to himself that if it wasn't for the first gift from Jo, the bouquet, he probably wouldn't have found her second gift. It was just a bit of bad luck, however, that the police happened to show up then, right at that moment.

After carrying in Naomi's tomatoes, he had decided to put Jo's bouquet in his truck. He had been carrying it around with him in the pocket of his gray coat. It needed better keeping, he thought. In his truck, under the seat where he kept his journals, he had a small styrofoam container that might be the perfect size for the flowers. When he was reaching for the container his fingers felt a piece of paper folded around something. He pulled it out and a silver necklace fell to the floor of the cab. He bent down and picked it up. A locket. He opened it and looked down into the tiny faces of two little girls. Obviously twins, they had the same light hair and blue eyes, freckles, and smile. He puzzled at this, wondering who they were and how they had found their way into his truck. His first thought was that this belonged to the person who had stolen all his clothes. Odd, then, that he hadn't come across it before. He picked up the piece of lined paper that was wrapped around the locket and read the message scrawled large and loopy in green ink:

Dear Peter,
Some terrible things are happening to me and I'm scared. I'm
coming to you because you're one of the few people on this island
I can trust. I came to the island because I needed to find Naomi,
but I think that was a mistake (except meeting you, of course). I
have done some bad things in my life, I know that, but not as
bad as everyone is saying. Please don't show this letter to anyone,
especially not Naomi. Please! She's too nice to be hurt. And

please keep the locket for me. It's very important.

You are sweet. I'll explain everything when I see you again.

Love, Jo

He stared at the letter, read it again. Then again. From the corner of his eye, he saw the cops tromping toward him. He crumpled up the paper and shoved it and the locket down into the bottom of one of the deep pockets of his big coat. One of the officers had approached him and was leaning on his elbow through the open window and looking down at him. Peter could smell coffee on his breath.

"You going somewhere?"

"No."

"We'd like you to come to the station. We want to ask you some questions."

"Questions?" His fist closed around the necklace in his pocket.

"Yes, about Jo."

"Jo?"

"Yeah, we've got some pictures to run by you, you and Jeremiah."

"Jo?" He stammered again.

"We were told that you two were quite friendly."

"I just met her. I didn't know her before I came."

The next thing he knew he was being ushered toward the police car. "Uh," he said before getting in, "you have to let me go to the bathroom first." He pointed to the outhouse on the far side of the church.

The heftier of the officers sighed and rolled his eyes. "Just make it snappy."

When Peter was safely inside the outhouse, he retrieved the letter and locket from his pocket. Frantically, he searched for a spot to hide it. He tried several places, behind the toilet paper roll? No. Underneath the bucket of stove ashes? No good. Finally, he stuffed it above the ledge at the top of the door.

Sitting in the back of the police car next to Jeremiah, he thought through his story. His name was Peter Smith and he would be from

New York City. He had driven up to Maine looking for work. One of his buddies told him there was work out here. Logging. The truck had no registration because he won it in a bar in New York City. He'd been a fool, he'd tell them that, to drive around in a truck with no registration. Too much drinking and being drunk. Too much drinking made him forget things. And he forgot a lot of things that had happened to him. But when he came to Maine he decided to make a fresh start. He would tell them that he was even attending regular AA meetings. No, he better not go that far. They'd ask him which meeting, and he'd be at a loss again. No, he'd say that he was *thinking* about attending AA, and maybe the cops could tell him where the meetings were. He thought of all these things while Jeremiah sat beside him, hands folded in his lap, staring out the window.

When they got to the police station, the officers took them into an open room. At one desk an officer was frowning at a gray-whiskered man in ragged clothes who was talking loudly and earnestly. At another, a cop in uniform was two-finger typing at a computer. At another, a woman was writing on a yellow legal pad. At another, an officer was looking through a file, and another was leaning back in his chair reading the newspaper. They took Peter to the desk where the officer sat at a file, and Jeremiah went to the woman who was writing.

The officer opened up the file and began showing Peter pictures of Jo. Did he have any knowledge that Jo was a possible kidnap suspect? He swallowed. *No.* Did he have any idea about Godfrey? *Godfrey?* Godfrey was the baby. Peter looked at them blankly wondering if they had the right person. They told him that they had been tracking her all over New England, following up on leads, one after the other. They asked him how long he had known her. They showed him pictures. He shook his head. They showed him more pictures. He shook his head again making fists inside his pockets. He didn't tell them about the locket. He didn't tell them about the twins. He didn't tell them about Jo's note. Several times he opened his mouth to do so, but clamped it shut again. *Please don't show this letter to anyone.*

They never asked him about his truck. So he never had to recite the story he had made up. They never asked him to empty his pockets. They never asked him if he had anything of Jo's.

Then they led him to the front door and told him he could go. Jeremiah was sitting on a wooden bench, a hand on each knee, waiting.

Peter said, "Are we allowed to leave now?"

"I think so. They weren't too hard on you, were they?" asked Jeremiah. He had a measured, soft way of talking, as if he thought out each sentence in full before he said it.

Peter shook his head.

"Now we just have to figure a way back."

"Won't they give us a ride?"

"That, I'm not sure of." A half-smile appeared on the older man's face. "Let me see what I can find out." Jeremiah walked to a desk where a woman with chubby arms and half-moon reading glasses on a chain around her neck was leaning into a computer.

"Is there something you want?" she asked. Her glasses fell to her chest.

"Are the two of us being escorted back to Lambs Island?"

"Not that I know of," she said. "Nobody told me anything." She looked back down at her computer.

"The police will just leave us here?"

She shrugged. "They'll take you back eventually. But let me think here a minute. If you guys need a ride back to the island right away, I saw Philip Friend over at the coffee shop just this morning."

"Do you happen to know where he is now?"

"I heard him say something about getting some work done on that truck of his. I bet you dollars to donuts he's over at Irv's right at this very moment."

"Thank you."

The streets were warm and still when Peter and Jeremiah left the police station and headed the five blocks toward Irv's. "Did you know Jo very well?" asked Peter.

Jeremiah shook his head.

Peter shrugged. "We were becoming good friends. She was so nice."

Jeremiah looked away from him when he said, "But she told lies. She made up things about people."

"Maybe she had good reason."

Jeremiah blinked and looked away. Nothing more was said until a few minutes later when they approached a T-shirted man leaning under the hood of a pickup truck.

FIFTEEN

"PHILIP," SAID JEREMIAH.

Philip stood to full height. He was a large man, broad shouldered with dark blond hair which fell forward thickly into his eyes. He brushed it back with his fingers. He had on thick horn-rimmed glasses, the old-fashioned kind, but they seemed to suit.

"Well, the good reverend, and what are you doing on this side of the channel? You never leave that place if you can help it."

Peter could see Zoe in this man's eyes and broad smile.

"You heard about the girl who died?"

"Some, yeah."

"They're questioning all of us."

Philip's eyes momentarily clouded. "I thought she drowned. Wasn't it a straightforward drowning?"

"She was strangled."

"Well, all I can say is they better not be harassing Naomi over this. And Zoe, what will this do to my daughter? A murder on the island. So they're calling it murder now?"

"Yes."

"That's not good, not a good place for them to be living. With a murderer running loose. Who was this girl who was murdered anyway?"

"She arrived a couple weeks ago," answered Jeremiah.

"Man, I've got to get Naomi and Zoe away from that place. Once and for all. This time it has to be it," said Philip.

Philip seemed to see Peter for the first time. "Don't tell me," he said with a grin. "My wife's taken you in, too."

"I'm just there for a little while. Your wife is a nice person."

"You don't have to tell me that," Philip said with a chuckle. "I know what I've been blessed with."

"We need a ride back, Philip," said Jeremiah. "You heading over any time soon?"

"Not for another hour or so. If you don't mind waiting, I'd be glad to drive you over. Got to get new plugs and points done up first. Can't be driving my family around in a truck that only works part time." He grinned and went back to the engine.

Peter walked over to a bench beside the building and sat down. It was still quite warm, and he wondered how it was that he was not sweltering in this coat. Other people were walking by in shirtsleeves, shorts, barelegged in sandals. He thought of bag ladies, then, and bums. There was one near where he lived in Edmonton. Raggy Mary, everyone called her. Even in the hottest weather she always wore everything she owned all at once: jackets, coats, wool caps, mittens with holes in them. She would push a shopping cart full of tied up plastic grocery bags, which was everything else she owned. Hanging off the cart were plastic bagfuls of empty bottles and cans. Every once in a while she would pass Peter as he stood with the others at the bus stop, young men in suits and designer coats who'd left their cars in the Park and Ride. Most everyone averted their eyes or buried them deep within the business section of the *Edmonton Journal* when she would walk past, humming tunelessly, muttering, pushing her cart.

Once, however, Peter looked up at the wrong time and saw her standing in front of him, staring at him, right into his eyes.

"Hello," she had said in her raspy voice.

He felt the color rise in his face and quickly turned away from her.

He wondered if the people who walked by now in their khaki hiking shorts looked at him that way; poor misbegotten young man, down on his luck wearing an overcoat in the summer, too-short, too-wide trousers, and hair askew and long. Needs washing. Look at that. He began to understand about the cold, too, about how Raggy Mary could wear coat upon coat, hat upon wool hat, fingerless mittens on a sweltering Edmonton day. There was something about poverty, about loss, that made one cold. Always so cold. Peter buttoned his coat up to his neck.

MAY 17, 1984

From the Journals of Martha MacGregor

Colin is leaving. He is going North, he says. The way he says it, like the word North should be capitalized. My face must show the amazement I feel because he smiles, touches my shoulder, and says he'll be fine.

I can't really blame him for wanting to leave, I suppose. With all that's happened, Andrea being only a small part of all of it. Then he tells me that when he comes back he will no longer be staying with me. I look surprised, and he says that my place is too small, and he has overstayed his welcome as it is, sleeping on my couch night after night. He needs a place of his own. I understand this. When Joe died, I moved out of the house we shared. But that was a long time ago now. No sense bringing up the past. I suppose he has worked out a place to stay, and I don't ask. I don't want to pry.

I look at Colin now, sitting across from me on the huge, soft chair, the one Joe used to sit in, and Colin's face looks like the face of an angel. Have I written that before? I'm not sure. I have thought it, though. He has very fine features, Colin does, a perfectly shaped nose, not too long, not short. No, just right, and eyes that are evenly spaced and high cheekbones. If he were a woman I would say that he looks like a Madonna with the pale morning sunlight casting fuzzy, soft shadows across his face. But since he is a man I will describe his pose as "Christlike." And then I wonder, how can a face that is so beautiful be at the same time so dark?

I ask him, What will happen to the cemetery when you're gone? It is a selfish question, I know, and it is out of my mouth before I can take it back. He looks at me and frowns and puts his hands on his knees. Colin tends the graveyard; he keeps the grass mowed, the weeds hacked down. He is the only one who does this. The place around Andrea's grave gets special attention, as well it should. Now, I suppose it will come to ruin. Like the church. Like the books.

When islanders die now they are buried on the mainland. Prayers for their souls are offered on the mainland. The funeral lunches are served on the mainland. They say it's because there's no more room in the cemetery, but that puzzles me. If you outgrow the fence can't you merely move the boundaries?

Odd, isn't it, that Andrea was the last one to be buried behind the church? I am the only one who goes to her grave now.

SIXTEEN

WHEN PHILIP ARRIVED, NAOMI WAS IN HER GARDEN. She didn't look up, but stayed on her knees between the rows of beans, pulling out small weeds, her hands nervous, her motions quick now. She hardly dared breathe, not rising to greet him, even though she knew she should. Knew she had to. A few more minutes, she thought, a few more minutes to compose myself, to think about what I should say, what I should do, how I should act.

Colin was standing at the entrance to the cemetery when he called loudly, "Phil, I see you've decided to grace us with your presence. To what do we owe this auspicious honor?"

"I'm happy to see you, too," said Philip. The big man was smiling cheerfully. He was always so cheerful. And Naomi's mind went back to the day five years ago when Philip had told her she was far too serious. "You gotta lighten up a bit."

He had been stroking her swollen belly, pregnant with Zoe. She had been telling him about her worries that he would continue his gypsy ways once they were a family, leaving and then returning at will. Was he committed to her? Committed enough to stay with her? He had surprised her by marrying her the following day in a ceremony down at the courthouse. She had worn a long white dress and pink flowers in her hair.

A week later he was gone. She was alone in the hospital when Zoe was born.

Colin was still yelling. "And just how long do you plan on staying this time? A week? Two? Maybe you won't even last a day here this time. Who's taking bets?" He looked around him. "Anyone here taking bets? We can have our own little island lottery going."

"Staying? I'm not staying at all, if it's any of your business, Mr. Workman. I'm here to pick up my family, and then we're moving on."

"I'll believe that when I see it," yelled Colin.

Naomi wiped her hands on the sides of her denim skirt and stood hesitantly, wishing with all her heart that Colin would stop. Didn't he know that he was just giving Philip another reason to leave? And he hates being called Phil. *Oh, Colin, please stop yelling,* she willed.

Zoe had run to Philip and was lifted high into his arms. Both were laughing, and Naomi was struck once again at how similar the two were, both blond-haired, smiling children. Even the same husky build. Zoe would be tall, like she was, but there was already a big-boned ruggedness about her.

Naomi walked toward Philip. He grinned when he saw her and swung her in his arms. He rubbed his face in her hair, told her how much he missed her, how crazy he was to have left, how they would be a family together. It would work out now. This time it would be different. He was tired of running. This time he was. He had a house all lined up in New Jersey along with a good steady job. And did she need any money? Did she get his last check? He couldn't bear the thought of his family living like this. He told her all of this, quietly in whispers as he held her. Her eyes were wide open, and she looked past him, over his shoulder to where Colin stood scowling, his hands in fists at his side and to where Jeremiah stood looking at her sadly. Peter, she noticed, was hurrying off to the outhouse.

When Philip let go of her he said, "I hear you've had some excitement here."

"Excitement?" She put her hand to her face.

"The drowning."

"Oh yes."

"Who was she?"

"Her name was Jo. She was here only a few weeks, a month at most."

"You two get to know each other?"

"We were friends, I guess."

They were walking, arms around each other, toward the church.

She was glad that earlier that day she had taken the time to wash her and Zoe's hair in the creek.

"What was she like?" he was asking.

"Who?"

"The girl who died."

"Nice, I guess. Dramatic. Always talking."

"Why do they think it was murder?"

"She was strangled."

"But how would they know that, if her body washed up on shore?"

"I don't think anything escapes the police these days."

"I don't like this. I don't like this at all. You and Zoe here on an island with a murderer running loose. They didn't catch the guy?"

"Not yet. They keep coming around asking questions. They're here all the time."

"That's another thing I don't like. Them harassing you."

"Philip, it's nothing."

"I still don't like it. What about the people whose baby it was?"

"The police are being pretty thorough. I'm sure they've been subjected to the same questioning we have."

Philip was wandering over to the cooking pots. "Smells good, whatever it is."

"It's sauce. Let me get some noodles. I made some yesterday."

"My wife, the little homemaker. Lambs Island's answer to Martha Stewart."

Naomi filled a saucepan with water and set it on the woodstove. Yesterday she had made these noodles, taking the entire day to knead them and roll them into thin strips which she hung to dry on chair backs, the edges of boxes, the metal ends of the cots.

As she took out plates and sliced tomatoes she looked at her husband with their daughter on his lap. It surprised her that Zoe, who saw him so infrequently, raced to him when he came. The two would be inseparable until the day he left. But he had that way with people.

He had that way with her. Why did the feel of his arms around her stir something deep inside of her, something large and weepy, a place so exposed and tender? Why did she still hope, after all this time?

"…and it comes with a fridge and an electric stove, you can get rid of that old wood burning thing…"

Naomi turned to him. "What?"

His eyes danced. He said accusingly, "You weren't listening."

"I was so."

He grinned and combed Zoe's blonde curls through his fingers. "I was talking about the house, well…apartment, really, I have lined up for us. In New Jersey. I've got a steady job there now. On the water-front."

"That's nice." She dropped handfuls of noodles into the simmering water.

"It's a good job, too. With benefits. Medical and such. I checked out the school, too. Went and met the principal. Zoe'll love it. It's just a few blocks away from the apartment. And there's a playground, too, for Zoe."

"That's nice."

"What's a playground?" asked Zoe. She was touching his glasses, pushing them up and down his nose.

"A place where you can swing on swings and go down the slide with all your friends," answered her father.

"Like Colin and Jeremiah?"

"No. Not them."

He turned to Naomi. "How soon can you be packed up?"

"Less than an hour."

Philip put Zoe down, paused, seemed to consider, then said, "Maybe we'll leave it until first thing in the morning. Give us all a good night's sleep. Never leave on a long trip without a good night's sleep. How's that spaghetti coming? My daughter and I are getting hungry here."

Naomi looked away from him, out the window to the graveyard

and said nothing. *Leave it until first thing in the morning. Give us all a good night's sleep.* She had heard those words before. Those exact words. There would be no trip. They would not be leaving in the morning.

Peter was standing at the back door, uncertainly, his long gangly figure blocking the light.

"Come for some of my wife's home cooking?" Philip asked.

"No."

"Well, come in then. What's on your mind?"

Peter cleared his throat and said, "I just wanted to know, when are you leaving?"

"Tomorrow, first thing," said Philip.

Peter looked at Naomi. "I just wanted to know if I could talk to you before you go. Privately."

"About what?" asked Philip.

He looked over at Philip. "I don't want to disturb you, but I just wanted to talk to Naomi."

Philip waved his hand. "Go on. Talk. Zoe and I won't even listen."

Naomi placed a plate of spaghetti in front of her husband and a smaller bowl in front of Zoe.

Peter began, "I just had some questions about Jo."

"What kind of questions?" asked Naomi.

Peter bit his lip. *Don't show this note to anyone...* "I guess it's nothing. I just wanted to know more about her. I'm trying to piece it all together. The stuff about her baby. Some things she told me."

Spaghetti fork in midair, Philip eyed him.

"Peter," said Naomi looking steadily at him. "She lied to us. Certain things didn't fit. I didn't notice them at the time, but now they make no sense."

"What things?"

"Little things. Like she fed her baby with a bottle."

"Yeah, so what does that prove?"

"That the baby wasn't hers, maybe? And here's another thing— when she first came she told me the baby's name was Kurt, spelled with a *K*. She clearly spelled it with a *K* and then all of a sudden it became Curtis, spelled with a *C*."

"There could be a whole lot of explanations for that."

"She lied from the very beginning. She was an actress and a good one."

Peter paused, said, "Did she ever talk to you about two little girls that she knew? Twins?"

"What are you talking about?"

"I thought maybe she would have talked to you about little girls who were twins. Maybe sisters or something. Maybe they're relatives of hers."

Naomi shook her head. "What does this have to do with anything?"

Philip looked up, "What twins?"

"Well." Peter shifted his weight, leaned against the doorjamb. "I can't really go into it. Just something she mentioned."

"She talked to you about twins?" asked Philip.

"Kind of. Sort of."

"Did you tell this to the police?"

"No. Not yet."

"Why not?" asked Naomi. She was wiping the table with a wet rag.

"It's hard to explain."

"You sure you don't want any of this?" asked Philip smiling. "You gotta admit. It smells awfully good."

"What about twins?" asked Naomi.

"If the boy doesn't want to talk about twins, don't press him. I'm sure if he feels it's important he'll go to the police, right Peter? And if he doesn't feel it's important, he won't. Is there coffee, love?"

"Maybe it's not important," said Peter. "It's probably nothing to do with anything. I just thought maybe you'd know."

He left.

SEVENTEEN

The newspapers were still talking murder in connection with Jo's death, and sitting in the periodicals section at the local library, Margot read the Maine papers with interest. There was evidence, wrote one reporter, that the victim had been strangled and the body dumped into the sea to make it look like a simple drowning. Unfortunately for the murderer, the incoming tide washed the body right back to shore again before evidence of the strangling could be washed away. An outgoing tide would have taken the body far out to sea where perhaps it never would have been found. The police were surmising that the murderer was not someone familiar with the tides. The next story gave a timeline of events leading up to Jo's death. She turns up at the James's home, she leaves taking the baby, she goes to the island, her body washes up to shore. Margot read this one carefully. *When she left my place,* thought Margot, *she must have gone directly to her nanny's job in Plattsburgh.* Margot tapped her finger on the papers, then gathered up an armful and walked toward the photocopier. She was fumbling for change when she saw the librarian motioning for her to use the office machine.

"Thanks, Dick," said Margot, walking into the office.

"There's got to be some perks to having a husband on the library board. What are you copying? Something to do with the great fashion industry out there?"

"No." She showed him the paper. "Do you remember Jo, the girl who lived with us a few months back?"

"Vaguely."

"She was killed. Over in Maine."

He adjusted his reading glasses and peered at the articles. "Really? How very strange. Most odd. Most sad. So young."

Later, in her shop with the Closed sign on the front door, Margot spread the photocopied stories out on the cutting table and went through them all again. How in the world had Jo ended up on Lambs Island?

It was late. Margot paper clipped the photocopies together and placed them in a drawer. Before heading home, she walked up the back stairs to Jo's old apartment. It was vacant. She and Paul had been advertising for a tenant, but so far there was little interest in a one room apartment with only a small microwave oven for a kitchen. Margot switched on the light. The apartment was clean now, no thanks to Jo. The day she had found Jo's note, Margot had angrily swept the place clean of papers, old lipstick tubes, cookie crumbs, moldy apple cores, candy wrappers with half-eaten chocolate bars gooily attached, and a ratty toothbrush. She had ended up filling a green garbage bag with Jo's junk to cart away to the dump.

On that day, Margot had also noticed with great annoyance that not only had Jo taken the locket and money, but she had also made off with the intricately-designed quilted silk and cotton coat Margot had made. Margot had spent almost a year on this design, refining it, perfecting it. She was extremely proud of it. It was her "signature" piece, and she had planned to take it along on all her sales trips this fall. Her mistake had been in letting Jo try it on. It had fit her perfectly.

"Jo, it looks so good on you," Margot had said. "You're so thin. Look at you. I even look at a cheese danish out of the corner of my eye and I'm up ten pounds. And I see you eating tons of that stuff, and you don't gain an ounce."

The bakery directly across the street from the shop featured designer coffee sold in urns with names such as Guatemalan Dark and Antigua Roast. They also sold pastries, muffins, and whole grains and herbal teas in bulk. Margot's personal favorite was the cheese danish, especially when they were freshly made. When Jo came down every morning, the first thing she would do would be to go across the street and bring back a cheese danish and a large coffee with double cream for Margot and a blueberry muffin and an apple juice for herself.

Two weeks after Jo left, Pam suggested that Jo hadn't left on her own, that maybe she was kidnapped. "Pammy, you watch too much TV," said her mother.

Gradually, life got back to normal. Margot hired Jane, a woman she knew from church, to help out three days a week. Jane was an expert quilter and brought a new dimension to Margot's Designs. Eventually Jane proved so indispensable that Margot offered her a partnership in the business. The two had been partners for a little over two months now.

"Mom?" Sara had seen the light in Jo's apartment and was standing in the doorway. "Are you ever coming home?"

"You walked all the way over here?"

"It's not that far. What are you doing up here?"

"Thinking about Jo is all."

"I can't believe she was killed. Are they ever going to find who did it?"

"I'm sure they will, honey. What are you doing here anyway? You're supposed to be at Heather's. Where's Pam?"

"She stayed at Aunt Heather's. We were worried about you. I can't believe all this happened."

Margot reached out and brought her daughter close to her. "There's something I didn't tell you, I didn't even tell your father. But before Jo left, she took a coat I made and also that silver locket."

Sara's eyes went wide. "The one with our pictures? Why didn't you tell Dad?"

"I don't know."

"Maybe the kidnappers took it."

"No, Jo left a note apologizing for taking the money and the locket."

"Maybe the kidnappers made her write it."

Margot sighed and ran her fingers through her daughter's hair.

"Are you going to tell the police about the note and stuff now?"

"I don't think so. There's nothing I could say that would help them. I threw away the note. I threw away all of the stuff she left. Let's go pick up Pam and go home now."

SEPTEMBER 7, 1984

FROM THE JOURNALS OF MARTHA MACGREGOR

Colin came back from the North yesterday. I ask questions, but he tells me very little. Bits and pieces I must glean from the things he says. He mentions mosquitoes and says they are the size of dragonflies. He has been to a place called Baffin Island. But when I ask him what it's like, what he did there, he just shrugs and tells me that he looked around. And I think, what on earth does that mean? For months on end he sat there and Looked Around?

He has decided not to live with me any more. He told me that before, and I was ready for that, but wait until I tell you where he has decided to stay—the church! The old church! I am practically screaming at him. How can you possibly live in that church? Have you completely lost your mind? Are you over the edge now? Is that it? He smiles, but it seems to be more like a sneer than anything pleasant. Why not, he says. It has a fairly new woodstove, there's an outhouse, and a stream not too far for fresh water. I'll bring in a cot and sleep in the back room. I'll be perfectly comfortable there, Martha. I can look after myself. I shake my head when I think about it. The church! Imagine!

A long time ago the now defunct church board enlisted a real estate firm to sell it, but I don't think they have been doing very much. I mean, who would want to buy an old church? Who could possibly be interested in that? Still, to live there? Sometimes I think maybe it's so he can be close to Andrea. That I can't fathom because he never goes to her grave anymore. I'm the only one.

EIGHTEEN

TWO WEEKS ALMOST TO THE DAY of Jo's death, the Maine state police came to the island again. Jules was the first to see them, of course, and drove his broken-down truck into the townsite to tell whoever happened to be in the coffee shop.

"Cops are here," he said quietly, dropping the stack of magazines beside the counter. "Two of them."

"So what else is new?" said Dob.

Sam was there, along with Dob and Lenny and another lobsterman named Gray. Walt was serving up his usual fare of eggs and sausage and toast.

Sam laid down his copy of the *Fishery News*. "Haven't they been here enough?"

Jules shrugged. "I don't know. I heard one of them saying that this whole thing shoulda been wrapped up by now."

"So, who came?" asked Walt. "That same idiot who's been here all along?"

"No, different ones."

"What're they coming here for?" asked Dob. "As if we know something. That girl was here what, two, three weeks at most?"

"Something like that," said Jules.

"You ask me, I think that kid had something to do with it," said Manny.

"What kid?"

"The tall, scrawny one." he said. "I think he mighta done it. He was with her, you know. I saw them together. Just by his eyes you could tell he was up to no good."

"Colin said the kid was visiting him," said Dob.

"Don't know why Colin would lie."

"He wouldn't," said Dob firmly. "He wouldn't."

"I don't know," said Jules taking a drink of coffee. "Something about him seems awful familiar to me."

"What do you mean?"

"Like I've seen him before." Jules shook his head.

"What I want to know is what do they want with us, anyhow?" said Gray. "They should be concentrating on that kid. People on the mainland."

Jules pulled a stool up to the counter, and for the next hour the group of them talked about the murder, which led to the cops, which led to the government, which led to their favorite topic of conversation—how government regulation was totally destroying the lobster industry.

By afternoon everyone on the island learned that what the police wanted this time was for all the island residents to attend a meeting that evening in the old church at seven o'clock.

Jules didn't have a lot of time that day to get to his clippings. Things were busier than usual with news people and curiosity seekers coming across the channel all day. But during a short lull, he glanced through the day's paper, noting a few items to get to later. Around six-thirty he got in his truck and drove to the church.

He was one of the first to arrive and sat halfway up. Martha, Colin, Jeremiah and Peter were seated in the first row of pews. Naomi, Philip, and Zoe sat behind them, Philip with his arm around Naomi's shoulders and Zoe on his lap. But Jules's attention was drawn once again to Peter. What was it about that face that looked so familiar? He was still puzzling over this when Dob, Sam, and Walt came in and sat down next to him. They were holding Styrofoam coffee cups with lids. Walt handed him one. "Figured you could use a cup," he said.

There was almost a festive mood about the place that night as more islanders arrived carrying flashlights and lanterns, their thermoses of tea and coffee, and their children.

At the back of the church, the two police officers stood together talking. When the island people had finally gathered, the officers moved to the front and stood in front of the altar rail. The man introduced them as Detectives Mick Wolff and Virginia MacNeil. He told them he wanted to bring them up to date on the case and to allow time for questions. He said a lot of rumors had been going around, and he wanted to clear up misconceptions they might have that the police weren't doing all they could. They knew the islanders were concerned about their safety, and they shared those concerns, he said. Detective MacNeil took over then and told them that if they remembered anything, even if it was in the middle of the night, to get right up and call them. "We're looking for even the most minutest of details," she said. "Something you may have forgotten."

"Yeah, that'll work out just fine," said Lenny grinning. "Half us over here don't even got phones. You think of that?"

"Well, write it down, then, and call us as soon as you can get to the coffee shop," said Mick.

When Detective Wolff opened it up for questions, Colin was the first on his feet. "Why are we being singled out?"

"Mr. Workman," answered Virginia, "we are not singling out the islanders as suspects. We are pursuing all avenues of investigation to solve this crime. The fact that the body washed right back up to shore leads us to believe that the murderer wasn't someone familiar with the tides and currents, therefore not an islander. What we are hoping for is information. If anyone remembers seeing anything unusual, hearing anything. These are the things we want to know."

"Then what about our safety?" Philip said. "If it isn't one of us, then what are you doing to guarantee our safety if there's a murderer running loose?"

Detective Wolff urged the islanders to keep their doors locked at all times and to take extra precautions when out at night and to report all suspicious activity. The audience snickered at this. A voice from the back said, "Yeah, and who's gonna supply us with these fancy locks. We ain't never locked our houses, and we don't intend to start."

Jules smiled and snorted with Walt and Sam.

Virginia said, "We admire your way of life here. You have little crime. Seldom do we have to even come across here. But, having said that, Detective Wolff and I are available to give you advice regarding the types of locks you might need. If we can be of any help to you, please see us after the meeting."

Jules gulped the last of his coffee, wondering if he should mention the boat he saw in the channel. But then, boats came and went all the time.

Later that night, when he was back in his cabin, Jules realized why the face of that new kid, Peter, seemed so familiar. He was clearing out a stack of old magazines piled next to his stove. Dob had been over earlier and had pronounced them a fire hazard. "You're not even going to be able to count to ten, Jules, before this whole place goes up like a tinder box. And you better not be settin' here when it happens."

So Jules was stacking up the papers when he looked down and saw it. On the back page of a movie magazine, a little box of a story on a page called, In and Around Hollywood. "Starlet Dies in Accident" was the title of the article, and underneath it a six-inch story about some up-and-coming movie star from Canada named Amanda Roos who had died when a truck swerved across the road and hit her as she was walking home from a party near Edmonton, Alberta, Canada. Amanda Roos was daughter of Henry and Roberta Roos of Edmonton, owner of Roos Films in Hollywood which had produced such blockbuster horror films as *Crib Death* and *Dark Side, Dark Side 2,* and *Dark Side 3.* Amanda had played the part of the baby-sitter in *Crib Death.* The Roos family also owned half the oil in Alberta, a beef processing plant, two of Alberta's biggest daily papers, plus many other enterprises in both the United States and Canada.

There was a picture of her there, a young woman, dark hair, a round baby face, too young for that sensual look in her eyes.

It has been speculated, the article said, that the driver of the truck, Peter Glass, had been taking drugs at the time. But there was nothing to prove that, and Peter Glass was not charged. That little photo of

Peter was the one Jules was interested in. It was a head and shoulders photo of a man in his early twenties, clean cut, short hair, smiling. But it was the eyes that made Jules stop. The eyes were the eyes of the Peter here on the island. They were hollow looking eyes, the kind that always look on the verge of being bloodshot or red-rimmed. The shaggy-haired Peter that stayed in the church bore little resemblance to the clean cut Peter Glass of this photo. Except for the eyes.

Jules walked over to Walt's and called up the *Bangor Daily News* and asked if they knew the name of the newspaper in Edmonton.

"Edmonton what? Alberta? In Canada?"

"That's the one."

"Well, I don't know."

"Can you check?"

"Do you want to hold?"

"Sure."

There was a rustling of papers and a few minutes later he was told that it was the *Edmonton Journal*. He was even given a phone number. He dug out a handful of coins and called Edmonton.

He told the woman who answered that he wanted a few back issues from the winter.

"Back issues? From what dates?"

He looked at the movie magazine article. "Just the first two weeks in January."

"Fourteen papers? I don't know. May I ask why?"

"I'm a collector."

"A collector?"

"Of local news."

"People collect local news?"

"Actually, it's for research purposes."

"Well, and where's this going, did you say?"

"Maine."

"Maine? In the U.S. of A?"

"Yeah. Maine in the U.S. of A." And he gave her his address.

NINETEEN

THE PRESENCE OF PHILIP ON THE ISLAND changed the dynamics of the church dwellers. Colin became more sullen, even more argumentative, and spent most of his time away from the church. Jeremiah was quieter, Naomi more nervous. Zoe, however, seemed happier.

It was morning, and all of them were sitting around the table in the back room, or what Peter was now calling "the kitchen."

"I don't trust the cops," said Colin filling his coffee cup. "They think one of us did it, and they're just trying to break us."

"Those guys seem nicer than the guys who came for me and Jeremiah," said Peter.

"That's just an act," Colin said, "for our benefit."

Philip laughed. "You know your trouble, Colin? You have this grand idea that the whole world's against you, that there's this big conspiracy. Let me tell you something, Colin. Nobody has anything against you because no one cares one whit about you."

Peter stared at him.

"Philip, stop," said Naomi.

"No, I'm not going to stop. I don't like the idea of him being here with you, sleeping under the same roof."

"So, you don't like it, do something about it. Get your wife into a decent house. I was living here before you both arrived."

Philip rose, moved toward Colin. Jeremiah stood between them. "Please," he said. "Don't."

"I don't like him taking advantage of my wife."

"No one takes advantage of anyone," said Jeremiah softly.

Colin walked out the door without looking back.

Philip sat back down. "What's the matter with him, that's what I'd like to know."

Peter finished his coffee in the silent tension of the kitchen, and then he left too. The morning was laced with fog, not a soupy fog, but

103

layers and pieces of mist that floated around him. The first thing Peter did every morning was to head down to the scow on the beach. He picked a tiny pale yellow flower growing near a rock and placed it gently on the bottom of the boat. He had been doing this, laying flowers inside of the boat, since he had found the bouquet there.

Then he continued eastward along the shore climbing over rocks and pebbles until he reached the path that led to the top of the cliffs. He sat down beside the lighthouse, dug his journal out of his pocket, and thought about Jo.

In his lighthouse daydreams Jo would come to him, alive, walking toward him up the wooded path, baby Curtis in her arms. She hadn't really died at all. It had been an imposter, someone who looked like Jo, a twin sister who had washed up on shore. See, I'm alive, she would tell him. Alive after all. Together they would leave in his truck and drive all the way to Florida from where they would board a boat to some warm island. He had worked out this fantasy in great detail, refining certain parts of it, eliminating others. He was writing all of this down, keeping track of it.

The wind at the lighthouse had a cool edge to it that he hadn't felt before. He leaned his back against the building and thought with longing to his ski jacket stolen down in Minneapolis. But maybe that was a good thing. Maybe someone like Raggy Mary had it. He tried to picture that. He pulled his coat collar up around his neck and reached for Jo's note and the locket he kept folded into a tiny square in the inside pocket of his flannel shirt. He took it out and read it again.

"You come here a lot."

Colin was standing behind him. Peter gasped and crumpled the paper in his fist, shoving both locket and paper into his pocket.

"Yeah, I guess."

"Why?"

"It's nice here."

"And you write, too," said Colin looking down at the spiral notebook on Peter's lap.

"Sometimes. It's something to do."

"I used to keep a journal."

"Yeah?"

"I don't anymore. Pen ran out of ink." Colin sat beside him. "This place has lots of ghosts. Don't you think?"

"Ghosts?"

"Out there." Colin pointed out past the cliffs to the murky, cold looking ocean. "See those ripples of water out there, just beyond the breakers. See the way the water doesn't flow evenly. Do you see that? Look where I'm pointing."

"Out there?"

"There's a ghost out there. Sometimes you can see it at night. If you come here at night like I do."

"Are you talking about the girl you told me about, the one who died down there?"

"The boat was called the *Andrea C.*" His blue eyes seemed translucent, like the water.

"Now her ghost is there?"

"Hers. Among others. Now Jo's."

Peter blinked at him, swallowed.

"They say," Colin continued, "that if your body washes up on shore your spirit stays and becomes part of the ocean. That's why there are tides. Tides are really spirits longing to reach solid land. Never quite making it. Coming so close. Yet being dragged out again. Over and over they keep trying. Never quite making it. Always trying." Colin's fine straight hair was blowing across his face. He looked at Peter. "You've seen her, haven't you?" he said. "Walking toward you from the water?"

"Jo?" asked Peter quietly.

"People who live inland, people who have never seen the tides, have no idea what I'm talking about. But islanders, because we live with ghosts, do."

Peter blinked at him.

"Our problem seems to be doubly compounded here because God has left this island. Most islands have churches. And the life of its residents revolves around the church. It's not that way here. We are the only island with no church. Did you know that?"

There was a long pause. Colin picked at a fraying cuff. Peter stared out to the sea. He could see them, the ripples Colin pointed at, just beginning, just starting. The tide was coming in.

"There are people," said Colin, "who are talking about you."

"People? What people?"

"People wondering if you had anything to do with the murder. You were with her a lot. But I know you had nothing to do with it. I saw your face when you looked down at her body. I know you're innocent. I know that look. No one can forget that look."

Peter rose. "People think I did it?"

"Not a lot. Some. I just wanted to warn you. Martha believes you are innocent. And she has a lot of sway with the island. I wouldn't worry too much."

SEPTEMBER 14, 1984

FROM THE JOURNALS OF MARTHA MACGREGOR

Colin is telling me that he has hired a salvage firm to bring up the Andrea C. *What a foolhardy thing, I tell him, the structure will not stand for it! You move it, you will destroy it. All you will have is a bunch of loose, water-logged boards, but he is insistent. The firm he has hired has done this sort of thing before. Many times, he tells me, with boats in much worse shape than the* Andrea C. *I ask him why on earth he wants to attempt this, and he says that he wants to bring it back to its Former Glory. Those are his words, Former Glory.*

That day, when the tide ebbed, the Andrea C. *crawled away from the rocks at the bottom of the cliff and became firmly lodged on the reef out there. The hull of the* Andrea C. *is visible during low tide, a reminder to sailors of the treacherous rocks. Colin once told me that the* Andrea C. *has been added to some navigational charts.*

Andrea would like that, I think, to be a part of a navigational chart.

TWENTY

THE TIDE WAS COMING IN, and Peter scrambled over slick, black rocks and around tide pools. But by now, he knew the path well. All he would get is a bit wet if he managed to find himself on this stretch of beach during high tide. It was not that dangerous. Not like below the cliffs. And he was well past the cliffs now. To his left was the scow and the path up to the church. But today he kept walking, thinking. People thought he had killed Jo? He frowned, stuffed his hands in his pockets.

There were no cars waiting when Peter eventually reached the ferry terminal. He stood for a while and looked down at the ferry. Maybe he should leave. Just go back, get into his truck and drive off. Pretend he never met Jo, go to some new place. But looking out over the water he knew he couldn't do that. First of all, that would only confirm their suspicions. And second, he had already run away from one death. He didn't want to do it again.

"Hello there," called Jules. He was walking rapidly toward Peter from a path from above the ferry. He was a chunky little man, built like a cinder block.

"Hello."

"You want to go across?"

"No thanks. Just out for a walk."

"Okay then." He paused, gave Peter an odd look. "I've got the tea pot on. You want to join me?"

"No thanks." Peter started walking away.

"Come on. Be my guest. Really. I've already got the tea on."

Peter followed Jules uncertainly up a beaten path to a small, rustic cabin.

"I'm having tea, but if you'd rather have coffee or even a beer, I can oblige. Now, mind, if someone wants to get across to the mainland, I'll have to run out on you."

Inside the tiny cabin high piles of newspapers and magazines were stacked against every wall: *Reader's Digests, National Geographics,* true crime magazines, movie magazines, not to mention newspapers of every stripe and description.

"Lot of newspapers," was all Peter could think to say.

"It's my hobby," said Jules pouring tea from a chipped tea pot into a mug and setting it on the table. "Here, sit down," said Jules indicating a wooden chair. "Some weather we're having."

Peter blinked at him. The weather hadn't seemed remarkable to him.

"Old man winter's on his way," said Jules. "That's the one thing you can count on in Maine."

"Yeah?"

"It'll be a long one. And an early one too. That's what they're saying."

"I'll be gone by then."

Peter felt oddly uncomfortable under Jules's stare and long glances and kept looking down at his cup of tea. He never drank tea at home.

"Where you headed then?" Jules asked.

"South."

"Yeah, too bad about Jo, huh?"

Peter looked up at him. "Yeah." Peter placed his palms around the mug of hot tea. Suddenly, he felt very cold.

Jules looked up and out the window. "Oh, wouldn't you know it. Duty calls. Just when I've got my tea."

"Someone waiting?"

"Yup. But you don't have to leave. No sense in that. You finish your tea. Then if you want, the path behind my cabin here runs right into the old cemetery; it's shorter if you want to go that way."

He watched Jules hunker down the path to the ferry. He watched while Jules motioned for the driver to come on, then he climbed up into his pilothouse and started the engine.

Peter looked around. Against the wall by the back door was a stack of scrapbooks, probably three feet high. He picked one off the top and flipped through it. Newspaper clippings were carefully pasted into it and labeled with black Magic Marker. This one seemed to be about various Maine celebrities, and the clippings came from newspapers all across the state. He put this one down and picked up another labelled, *Book of Stories*. It included entire stories clipped from true crime magazines and pasted in with glue. In the pile were scrapbooks about movie stars, one on the president and his family, each clipping carefully dated and the periodical it came from duly noted. One scrapbook labelled *Book of Lambs Island* recorded birthday celebrations, short "court news" sections, and anniversaries of Lambs Island's residents. He recognized some of the names. His hobby? By the looks of the stacks, dating back two decades or more, it would take him hours every day to keep up. On another pile he saw a scrapbook simply labeled *Book of Jo*. He reached for it and read page after page of news stories about Jo. He hadn't realized there were so many, and he was filled with a pang of sadness. One article, midway through the book told of Jo's beginnings, how she grew up in a town in New Jersey. By age thirteen she had left home and lived in a number of foster homes. She even had a police record. The reporter had quoted people who knew her. Carefully, with the edge of a kitchen knife, he removed the story from Jules's book, folded it into quarters, and placed it in his pocket. Then he shoved the scrapbook into the center of the pile.

Outside the window, he could see the ferry returning. He left by the back door and took the path to the church.

When Peter arrived back at the church, a police car was parked next to his truck. Through the opened back door, he could see the whole group of them sitting around the folding table in the back room; Detectives Mick and Virginia, plus Naomi, Philip, Colin, and Jeremiah. Martha from the town was also there.

"Join the party," said Colin as Peter stood nervously in the doorway. "We're just shooting the breeze, a bunch of good old pals just passing the time of day. Grab that chair over there and join the gabfest."

Peter did, and sat down next to Colin. He felt awkward and uncertain in the group; around Philip who tended to look through him as if he wasn't there, around Colin who seemed to make up stories to taunt people, and around Jeremiah who was too quiet, suspiciously quiet. Today Philip was carrying most of the conversation, going on about weather and New Jersey and potholed roads where he almost lost his truck on the way up here and conversations with state troopers. To Peter there seemed a forced phoniness about the man, as if he were somehow trying to impress the two officers who drank coffee and munched on slices of Naomi's brown bread. Zoe was in Philip's lap, clapping her hands in his hands. Jeremiah was leaning into the table across from Philip, his chin in his hands, the little metal glasses crooked on his nose. Naomi, sitting next to Philip, looked tired.

When conversation about Philip's driving adventures wound down, Colin piped up, "Did you know that people in social groups usually talk about one subject for an average of seven minutes before they move on to something else?"

Martha eyed him.

Colin said, "We need a new topic of conversation for the next seven minutes. I propose we talk about faithfulness in marriage." He glared at Philip. "Jeremiah, you are a man of the cloth, what would you say about keeping one's vows?" Martha put her hand on Colin's arm.

Jeremiah cleared his throat, looked down at his hands.

"What we came here for today is to find more about Jo," said Mick.

Philip was giving Colin a fixed look. "Your comments, Mr. Workman, I detect, are directed at me. How dare you judge what you know nothing about. Naomi is free to come with me anytime she wishes. She has chosen, for whatever reason, to stay here. I cannot understand her living under the same roof as the likes of you. Don't think I haven't begged my wife to accompany me."

Peter was watching Naomi through all of this, and her eyes jerked up to Philip when he said this.

"Yeah, right," mumbled Colin.

At the same time Peter said, "I thought you were going to New Jersey."

"Oh that. That fell through. At the last minute."

"Like every one of your nonexistent job offers."

"Colin," said Martha. "This isn't the time."

Colin mumbled something but looked glumly at the top of the table.

Mick turned to Jeremiah. "We understand you're a minister."

"Yes, I'm a minister."

"I can see by your—" and he motioned, "that collar you wear sometimes."

Jeremiah put his finger to his throat. "The last vestige of a long and faithful ministry." He smiled awkwardly. "If we're talking about faithfulness, I guess I wasn't faithful enough."

"You were faithful," said Colin, and Peter looked at him surprised.

"Is your name really Jeremiah?" This came from Virginia.

Jeremiah looked up at her, and Peter noticed for the first time how blue his eyes were. He was a strikingly handsome man, he thought, with those eyes and all that bushy, silver hair.

"Why wouldn't my name be Jeremiah?"

"Well, I don't know. It could be a stage name or something," she said awkwardly.

He smiled. "Actually, you're right. My name is Jeremy. When I came." He looked at Naomi. "Maybe it was Naomi's southern accent that gave me the name Jeremiah."

"Did you know Jo well?" Mick asked him.

"No," said Jeremiah. "I keep to myself a lot."

"A wise move," said Colin.

"What we need," Mick said putting his coffee mug on the table, "is help. I may as well admit that we're at a total dead end on this. We're trying to get a handle on who Jo was." Peter's hands wound around the news story in his pocket. "Certain facts are public, but we want more than that. So much of her life seems to be a mystery."

A cool breeze was coming through the open door, and Peter, who was sitting closest to it, wondered if he should close it. Naomi got up and grabbed her coat, which was hanging on a hook underneath a ratty brown thing of Colin's. She draped it over her shoulders and sat back down next to Philip. He was looking at her, the beginning of a scowl on his face.

"Can you remember any more names she may have mentioned?" Virginia was asking.

Naomi spoke for the first time. "I probably knew her better than anyone, but I've told all this to the police at least a dozen times."

Mick smiled. "We're sorry about that, that often happens in investigations such as these. But we need to hear all those answers all over again."

"You don't have to say anything, Naomi," Philip said, "not without a lawyer."

"I know, but I've got nothing to hide, and if this helps find who did this... Okay, she talked about a Jack and a Lenore and Margot. Those were the names I definitely remember. She also spoke about a boyfriend named Steve."

Mick was writing this down in a small notebook. "Jack, Lenore, Margot, do you remember what she said, specifically about each person? Could she have mentioned where these people lived?"

Naomi told him the story Jo had told her, about her rich boyfriend Steve threatening her life.

"There was no Steve," said Mick. "We've checked and double checked. Her parents are Jack and Lenore, but they lost track of her when she left home. The name Margot is a new one."

"You have to understand," Jeremiah said. "We're very private people here."

"We're discovering that," said Mick.

"We all take a vow of silence in this monastery," said Colin.

When another breeze came through the door, Naomi slipped her arms into the coat.

"Why are you wearing that?" Philip asked.

"Because I'm cold."

"Well, it looks terrible on you."

"Aren't we in a chipper mood today," Colin said.

"Mind your own business."

"The coat looks fine, Naomi. Beautiful, in fact," Martha said. "I've never seen such a beautiful combination of color and pattern. It's quilted, isn't it?"

"It is," said Naomi.

"And it certainly doesn't look terrible on you," she added.

"Yes, it does," said Philip.

"What's the matter with you?" asked Colin.

Both officers were watching the drama with interest.

"It's way too small for her," said Philip. "Can't anyone see that?"

"It used to be Jo's," said Naomi. "She gave it to me."

"Well, you shouldn't wear the clothing of the dead."

"Why not, for heaven's sake?" asked Martha.

"It's bad luck."

"Is that what this is all about?" Martha grumped. "Well, if wearing the clothing of the dead brings bad luck, then all of us are in for some pretty bad times."

"Maybe that's what happened," said Colin.

Philip mumbled something and got up to pour himself more coffee.

Virginia said, "That coat used to be Jo's?"

"Yes."

"The police were supposed to take all of her effects."

"Jo gave this to me."

"Can we have a look at it?" asked Virginia.

114

"Yeah," said Philip sitting down again and reaching for Zoe. "Maybe you should take it."

"If you're looking for clues," Naomi said, "I've already been all through it. There's nothing of hers in the pockets. And I'd really like to keep it. I have nothing to keep me warm this winter."

"I send you plenty of money, Naomi," said Philip. "Which you obviously squander on food for these lowlifes."

"Can I have a look at it?"

Naomi slipped the coat from her shoulders and handed it to Virginia who methodically went through the pockets, checking the lining, turning it inside out. "Do you know where it came from?" she asked.

"From Jo."

"No, I mean where it was manufactured. There's no label."

"Yes there is. At the neckline."

Virginia lifted up the coat and showed her a neckline with no label.

"But there was one."

"It's not here now."

Naomi looked puzzled. "But it had a label, I'm sure of it. I'm sure I even looked at it."

"You remember a label there when Jo gave you the coat?"

"I do, yes. Definitely."

"When is the last time you remember seeing a label?"

"I have no idea. It's not something that I look at every time I put it on. I really couldn't say."

"Do you remember what the label said? The store where it came from?"

"The name, I think, was something like Margot's or Margie's or maybe even Martha's Designs or Margot's Creations."

Mick was speaking now. "Could this be the Margot Jo referred to?"

"I don't know. Maybe. She didn't say much about her. Just that she was a special friend."

Mick was busy writing in his book, and Virginia was fingering the coat, examining the neckline.

"But how could a label just come off?" Naomi said. "I just don't understand."

"Give it a rest, Naomi," said Philip. "There are any number of reasons how a label could come off. You insist on hanging it beside that rag of Colin's. Perhaps when he grabbed his coat, the label ripped off. He's not the most careful person with other people's things, or hadn't you noticed?"

"No," said Virginia fingering the coat collar. "It's been cut, with scissors. Or a knife."

TWENTY-ONE

MARGOT COULDN'T SLEEP. Her digital bedside clock read 2:13 A.M. *Great,* she thought, *and me having to drive to New York in the morning, and still so much packing to do.* Driving to New York was the last thing she felt like doing at this point, especially with Jo's death. She ought to be staying with Pammy and Sara. At least until Paul got home. But the trip had been planned for a long time. She had a whole string of boutiques lined up to look at her work. Her only regret was that she didn't have the "coat of many colors," as her daughters called it.

She turned and looked at the clock again. 2:42. Maybe it was the cup of coffee she'd shared with Jane last evening. Maybe it was the cheese danish she had along with the coffee that was keeping her up. Or maybe it was the two cheese danishes. She shouldn't have eaten them at all. Hadn't she promised herself, absolutely, this time, that she was going to lose ten pounds by the time Paul got back?

Paul. The mention of his name set up a whole new chain of meandering thoughts. Maybe it was because both of them were so involved in their businesses now, but lately there hadn't been a whole lot of communication between them. Something was wrong and she couldn't name it, couldn't figure it out. 3:17. Before she had come to bed she had talked to him on a fuzzy phone connection from his California office. Things were shaping up for a really big deal, he said, and he had to stay for a few extra days, if that was okay. Fine, she had said. He was surprised to hear about Jo's death. Apparently, it hadn't made the national news.

"It occurred a while ago. I'm surprised you haven't heard."

"I've been too busy, actually, to even watch the news." He seemed anxious. "Are the girls all right with it? Do you want me to come home? Just say the word and I'll drop what I'm doing."

"No, we're okay. It just made me think of Beth is all."

"Beth? Why did it make you think of Beth?"

"I don't know. She was about the same age as Jo when she died."

"They don't seem the same at all to me. You said that Jo drowned."

"Strangled, then drowned."

"Well, you see, there's nothing similar at all. Beth was strangled but not drowned."

"Still…"

And now at 3:48 in the morning, Margot thought about Beth. Beth was a bit like Jo: inquisitive, endearing herself to Margot's family. Two years ago she and her mom showed up at church one Sunday morning. Besides being an A student, Beth was also an accomplished pianist. When she began giving piano lessons to Sara and Pammy the family got to know her and her mother, Glenna, well. Beth even worked for Paul one summer in a school co-op project in computer music.

One afternoon in late spring, Beth didn't make it home from high school. Two weeks later, her partially clad body was found in the woods outside of town. She had been strangled. For weeks Glenna stayed with Margot and Paul and was simply inconsolable. Two months later she moved back to Texas to live near her family. Occasionally Margot thought of her, wrote her or called her. But Glenna never answered her letters.

Beth's murderer was never found.

Margot hated so much thinking. She spent her days creating things with her hands, combining unusual fabrics such as raw silk and cotton, satin and denim in her creations. Not all this thinking. She got out of bed, restless, feeling that she should be doing something. Anything but lying here. She turned on the light. 3:52.

A dress that she was making for herself was hanging over the back of a bedroom chair. She picked it up and absently ran her finger across the label in the neckline. Back and forth. Margot's Designs, Woodstock, VT, was all it said. No address. No phone number. It had occurred to her from time to time that she should add her address and phone, a minibusiness card on every collar. Wearable art. That was how one reviewer described her work. Maybe she should have "Wearable Art" placed on her next batch of labels.

On the dresser beside the chair were the photocopied articles about Jo. She glanced through them again and was reminded that Jo grew up in New Jersey in a small town called Mountainside. She got out the road map. How far was that from Manhattan? *Now Margot, this is a really stupid idea,* she said to herself. Still. Maybe she could find Jo's parents. She'd tell them that despite what the papers were saying, Jo was a really great kid. Maybe they would know something about the locket. She'd play it by ear. She'd get to New York and then make a decision.

She went back to bed and finally to sleep.

TWENTY-TWO

PHILIP SEEMED DISTRACTED THIS TIME, thought Naomi as they lay together in the two single cots she always shoved together when he came. It was early morning, and Zoe was curled up and sleeping soundly between them. Philip, lying on his side and facing away from her, was asleep too. She could hear his steady breathing. Naomi watched the dawn beginning to seep into the room around the edges of the burlap which covered the windows.

Normally when Philip came he was more in tune with her and Zoe; he would talk more. He would laugh more. They would go for long walks, and he would tell her things about himself that only she would know, hard things that made her feel sorry for him, made her want to protect him.

"My mother hated me," he told her once. "She had four boys and I was the fifth child and was supposed to be a girl. She told me that."

"A mother wouldn't say such things, even if she thought them," Naomi said.

It was low tide and they were sitting close together on a flat rock at the bottom of the cliff. She was hugging her knees around her long skirt. She was here at the edge of this terrifying sea because of Philip. She had grown up near the ocean in North Carolina, but this ocean was darker, more terrifying than the golden sands of her childhood.

He took her hands. "You're shivering."

"I'm okay."

"My mother never let me forget that I was supposed to be a little girl. 'Here's my little girl,' she would tell people with that sarcastic tone she used with me. I left home as soon as I could. Maybe that's why," he let go of her hands and looked down, "I have such a problem with commitment. It's not that I don't love you. Don't ever think that."

Naomi saw tears in his sad, blue eyes, and at that moment she wanted to hold him forever, protect him from all of the people who had hated him all through his life. His outbursts, his fits of anger, it could all be explained. He needed her. In his own way, he needed her. He needed her to be there when he came.

"I know you love me," she said.

That's why his leaving always took her by surprise. How could he leave after he had shared so much of himself with her, after they had made love tenderly, gently in the grass near the creek, the soft ground lush in the summer, overhung with pine branches?

But then the next day, or the next, or maybe a week later, a new look would come into his eyes, and he would start looking not at her, but beyond her as if to some private dream. And she would know that soon he would say to her, "I have to go now, Naomi."

And she would say nothing, just turn to the pots on the wood-stove and stir the contents, stirring and stirring until she was sure that Jules had driven him off the island and he was well away. Then she would go to her place by the creek.

She looked over at him now, sleeping quietly beside her. Yesterday they had walked hand in hand to the cabin in the woods, Naomi's special place. Philip had brought a bottle of wine with him. Inside, they poured it into two glasses Naomi kept there and drank in celebration of New Jersey and new beginnings and the long and happy life ahead of them. They talked and talked then, about moving, about Zoe, about school for her, about maybe even buying a car. He told her that he loved her, he loved her so much. All of this was tearing him apart. They sat on the floor, and Naomi had held his head in her lap, stroking his hair for a long time. They would be happy together now. They would be a family. Did Philip know, even then, that the job had fallen through? He must have. There wouldn't have been time for him to go to Walt's, get a phone call, and then make it back to the meeting with the police.

Zoe turned in her sleep, and Naomi covered her with a blanket, hoping that her stirring wouldn't wake Philip. Naomi settled back down underneath the covers, turned her head away from her husband

and daughter, and stared at the black woodstove, as cold and as hard as the gravestones out back. As cold and as hard as she felt.

Carefully, as carefully as she could, she rose. She needed to be outside, away from these broody thoughts. Quietly she slipped a gray wool dress over her head and grabbed Jo's coat.

It was cold outside, but fresh and invigorating. After washing her face, she decided to head into the woods and toward her creek. Her bare feet made no noise on the wet carpet of dead weeds. She would soon have to ask Jules about finding her some boots. Her last year's boots were worn through in several places.

As she approached the path she saw Colin leaning against a tree, looking away from her. She meant to pass by him without his seeing her. But he turned and looked her way.

"You're up early," he said.

"I couldn't sleep."

"Join the club."

She knew Colin often rose before dawn. She knew he slept fitfully at best; sometimes she could hear him rising, leaving the sanctuary by the front door.

Naomi looked toward the creek. "I was just going for a walk."

"Oh. Well. Have fun."

On a whim she asked, "Would you like to come with me?"

"Sure, why not?"

They walked for several minutes without saying anything. Finally, he said, "You should have shoes on."

"I prefer being barefoot."

"It's cold, Naomi."

"I know."

"It's going to get colder."

"It always does. That's the thing about seasons, they follow one another."

"I'm serious. What're you going to do about your feet when it snows?"

"I'll get Jules to get me something."

"Good old faithful Jules. Here." He stopped, leaned against a tree and began untying his work boots. "You can wear mine for the time being."

"I couldn't."

"Why not?"

"For one thing, they'd be too big. I'd swim in them."

"So what's the other thing?"

"What other thing?"

"You said 'for one thing.'" He was busy unlacing the boots, pulling his socked feet out of them. "When a person says for one thing, that means there's another thing coming, a second point, so to speak. Don't you remember junior high and learning how to outline? You can't have a point one without a point two."

She laughed. "Okay then, the *other* thing I was going to say is, then you won't have anything on *your* feet."

"I have socks." He was kneeling there, in holey gray wool socks on the bare ground and was placing Naomi's feet into the boots.

"They're huge on me."

"They'll keep you from getting your toes frostbitten."

"I'm used to being barefoot, Colin. My feet have developed this thick skin. Look at them. I think I'm evolving into a toad or something."

"Your feet look fine to me."

They walked on the path beside the stream in silence, Naomi chunking through the brush in Colin's boots, and he walking gingerly beside her in his socks. They were walking beside the meadow now and to the right a few hundred yards was the sheltered grove which was hers and Philip's.

Colin said, "Why do you stay with him?"

She jerked her head around and looked at him sharply.

"With Philip. Why do you stay with him?" he asked.

"It's none of your business." Her hand flew to her mouth.

"He's not good enough for you."

"He's my husband. He's Zoe's father. He's a gentle, caring person if you get to know him deep down."

"You must have to dig awfully deep in Philip's case. Sewer level, I should say."

"You've no right to criticize him." She stopped and had bent down and was unlacing the boots. "You can take your boots back if you're going to speak of him like that."

"I'm sorry, Naomi. Please keep the boots on."

She rose and looked into his eyes.

"He's breaking your heart," said Colin.

"Lots of things break my heart."

"You deserve a lot better, Naomi."

"All of us do, Colin. All of us deserve better. You deserve better. Studious, prayerful Jeremiah deserves better, and so does Peter. And Jo deserved better. She deserved better than to end up strangled and dead. And you're right, I do deserve better, but we're all here, and we all have to make the best of what life dishes out. And there's not a darn thing we can do about it."

"So that's what you do, just accept it?"

"Isn't that what you're doing? I keep thinking you're too intelligent to keep coming back, winter after winter to work on that boat."

Silently, they walked. They were coming to the first of the cabins. He was laughing.

"What's so funny?" she asked.

"Feet. Feet are funny. Look at us."

"You look pretty funny, I have to admit, tiptoeing along in wet socks."

"Me, funny? You're the funny one. I was trying to come up with what you look like. I was trying to think. Now, I think I have it. Granny Clampett."

They were sitting on the wooden porch of the cabin now. This is where they were when Philip came. Neither she nor Colin had seen his approach, but he was standing perfectly still in the center of the path with Zoe in his arms. It was Zoe's call to her that made Naomi look up.

"Zoe!" she said.

"This is how my wife greets me in the morning? Off on a little jaunt with her boyfriend?"

"We were out for a walk," said Naomi.

Philip glared at Colin. "How dare you! How dare you take my wife off on your little early morning stroll!" He turned to face Naomi "And how easily you slip out of my bed and go right into the arms of this, this…!"

"Philip," protested Naomi. "Calm down, you're upsetting Zoe. I happened to be going for a walk by myself and met Colin out in the cemetery."

"How convenient of you," he said to Colin, "ambushing my wife."

"He did no such thing. I invited him. Please pipe down."

"You mind telling me how his boots found their way to your feet?"

"She was walking barefoot," said Colin rising. He stood facing Philip. "Since you can't seem to provide the necessities of life, such as shoes for your beloved, I let her borrow mine."

"You keep away from my wife!"

Zoe started to cry and squirmed in Philip's arms.

"Philip, for land's sake," said Naomi. "We just went for a walk. That's all. Come here Zoe, come to mama."

"I will take care of my daughter, thank you very much."

"And you do a fine job of it, my man," said Colin bowing slightly. "A mighty fine job."

"You keep your nose out of my business!"

"I know that in that grimy little mind of yours it's difficult to comprehend," said Colin, "that two people of the opposite gender can be merely friends, but that's how it happens to be."

"I bet that's how it is. I just bet. If I ever see you near my wife again…"

But Colin, with a brush-off wave of his hand, had turned. Naomi watched him walk away toward the church, hobbling in wet sock feet.

JULY 3, 1993

FROM THE JOURNALS OF MARTHA MACGREGOR

A man and a woman came to the island a few weeks ago and are staying in the church. Colin is gone, on his seasonal visit to the North, so he hasn't seen them. He has been going to the North every summer for ten years now. He seldom talks about it, and I have learned not to ask. Sometimes I ask him, Why don't you get married, Colin? I say that because I wonder if there is someone in the North that he sees. Then he looks at me with that cynical look of his and says, Find a nice wife and settle down and make a bunch of babies, maybe live in Bangor and get a job in a bank? No, thank you. Colin looks so unhappy. He doesn't like me telling him that. He says it's none of my business. Perhaps he's right.

I don't know what his reaction will be when he comes back to the church to see a woman and a man living there, sleeping, no doubt, on his cot and cooking food (maybe his food? Does he leave food there over the summer?).

I haven't gone over to meet them, but I have watched them. The woman is tall, very slender with thick blond hair. Quite pretty in a sad sort of way. The man is much larger. You would have to describe him as a Big Man. But not fat, no, muscular. He is blond, also, but his hair is much shorter than the way most of the islanders wear theirs, the way Colin wears his.

The couple has never come to town, but I see them sometimes walking hand in hand along the windward side of the island. Once when I was walking beside the lighthouse I looked down and saw them sitting close together on one of the flat rocks at the bottom of the cliff. It was still low tide, but I knew the tide was coming in. I could see it, those far out ripples and eddies that signify its beginning. When it starts, the flood accelerates at an alarming rate. I called to them, but they couldn't hear me. Well no wonder, with that wind! I thought about taking the path down and then calling them. I would have, too, but as I watched, they rose and hand in hand began picking their way northward along the shore.

I have never seen the woman before, I am sure of it, but there is something oddly familiar about the man, and I look at him and am puzzled. I know I have seen him before, those large shoulders, the way he moves, that long stride. I have asked Mary and Alexis if they recognize him and they shake their heads. He's pretty handsome, they say. Maybe it was in a dream I saw him, they tell me, giggling like school girls. Go on, I tell them.

All I can hope for is that the man and the woman will be gone before Colin gets back from the North. Colin can get into such rages.

TWENTY-THREE

PETER WAS DREAMING ABOUT BLAIR. They were at the West Edmonton Mall standing near the miniature golf course. There were people around, shoppers, and music and over the din he was explaining to Blair about Jo, trying to convince her that he had nothing to do with Jo's death.

Blair was wearing all black, as she did sometimes, black leggings and a long black sweater. She was running her long fingers through her short dark hair saying things like, "You killed two girls, Peter. I don't know if you can be excused from that."

Suddenly Jo was there, one of the miniature golf statue figures come to life and walking toward them, across the ripples of the mall fountain, big baby Curtis in her arms. Peter looked into her brown eyes, begged her to tell Blair that it wasn't his fault. But Jo walked past without speaking. No matter how he waved his arms and called after her, he couldn't make her see them.

He sat up suddenly on his mattress in the church and looked around him. Morning again. Early. Colin was gone. So was Jeremiah. How many mornings had he woken up here? How many more mornings would he wake up here before he left? He rose, changed quickly, and went outside where he washed his face in the bucket they kept behind the wood pile.

Since he had left Alberta he hadn't thought about Blair much. They had had a big fight before he left. He hadn't thought about his friends, about his job at the bookstore nor his apartment and the possessions he had left there.

He had said good-bye to no one. Left no notes.

During those weeks of travel, he didn't think much about his old life. It was as if he expected his old life to stay exactly the same as it was when he left. That his job might be given to another, that his apartment might be rented to another, that there was someone who might worry about him didn't enter his thinking.

The water in the bucket was ice cold. He sloshed it on his face, letting it dribble down his chin. His mother was praying for him. He didn't know how he knew that, but suddenly on this morning, splashing ice water through his hair, he could picture her, sitting on the couch by the front window, hands on her lap, praying for him.

Blair had told him once that he was very spiritual. "It's because of your poetry. You feel things other people don't." Maybe this is how he knew.

He sat down on an upended log, put his hands on his knees and thought about the night of the accident. Blair had been with him. They'd gone to a movie, one of those movies about angels. Afterward they'd walked through the cold city ending up in a coffee shop on Whyte Avenue where they talked. Blair had said, "Do you think they're all around us, like in the movie. I mean, sitting right here across from us? Looking at us? Watching over us, like in the movie?"

"I doubt it," said Peter. "I think this is all there is. But there's so much about this reality that we don't know, that we haven't explored. There's a lot of beauty and strangeness right here."

And that's when she had told him he was spiritual.

Then they had climbed into his truck and he had dropped her off where she lived with her sister and brother-in-law near the university. And he had headed home. And his life changed forever.

Can't rewind the video.

Peter walked slowly toward the graveyard. He hadn't been in here since that first morning with Jo. Idly he stopped to read some of the inscriptions. *Died while felling a tree near Witches Cove.* And on another, *Trampled by a horse at the age of five.* Some of the stones were large and square and gray, others were small, white; and still others were oblong. All of them faced away from the wind. He read: *Rosemarie Raeke, died when the flames engulfed their home. Rosemarie 1930-1954, Sadly missed, Sleep with Jesus.* And another one, *With sweet memory of Little*

Mary, now resting in Jesus' loving arms. Mary Esther Sullivan, 1923–1940.

He sat down on the *Child of the Island* one. There was a small, withered, and very old bouquet of flowers stuck up against the stone. Peter hadn't noticed this when Jo had twirled in the sunshine here and talked about being an actor. He touched the flowers, a whimsical bouquet tied together by an ancient twist of ribbon and thought of Jo's bouquet, the one he had found in the scow. The flowers fell to dust in his fingers.

"Sad isn't it?" Jeremiah was standing over him.

Peter dropped the dried flowers and gasped.

"Those flowers. Once picked in the prime of their lives. Now ash."

Peter rose, looked at the man, at the gray bush of his beard, the droop of his mouth, said nothing.

"Our lives but a flickering flame," said Jeremiah, "so short a time, barely a flicker, when you consider eternity. Yet strutting through creation striving for self-importance when we're really a lot like these flowers."

Peter regarded him warily. The man's eyes looked gentle, and his smile seemed genuine. Maybe Naomi was right. Maybe Jeremiah was too gentle to be a murderer.

"Why did you come to this island?" asked Jeremiah.

Peter cleared his throat. "I don't know. I just sort of ended up here. For a while."

"I came to this island to learn silence."

It was quiet for a moment. The only sound the early morning chatter of birds. In the distance walked Colin and Naomi down the path toward the creek.

"Those two," said Jeremiah, "are in love with each other."

Peter stared at him. "Colin and Naomi? But Naomi's married."

"Colin has a great capacity for love. But he is listening to all the noise in his soul. He needs to learn to be quiet."

Jeremiah pushed his glasses up on his nose and smiled. "You need to learn to forgive yourself, Peter. It's not your fault. Her death was not your fault."

Peter gasped, opened his mouth to say something, clamped it shut. How could this man possibly know about Amanda? No, not Amanda, Jo. He was talking about Jo, of course he was. His words came out in short stutters. "I—don't—know. I…"

"It's okay." Jeremiah put his hand on Peter's shoulder. "Let's go get some breakfast."

TWENTY-FOUR

IT CAME TO JULES IN THE NIGHT, unbidden, a threat, a night terror. The same kind of thing used to make him afraid to open his eyes in his dark bedroom when he was a boy for fear of seeing spiders crawling up and down his walls.

He sat up in his narrow cot in the small room in his wooden house beside the ferry wharf, and suddenly he knew who the murderer was. Call it intuition, but Jules knew about people. Peter! The murderer had to be Peter. Manny was right. He knew all the others. He knew quiet, serious Jeremiah; and big, buffoonish Philip; and cynical Colin; and obedient and frightened Naomi. And then Jo had come with that baby of hers and not more than three weeks later who comes along but Peter, someone who had already killed a person in Alberta. Possibly on drugs. Who's to say he didn't come all the way out here to kill that girl Jo?

He got up out of bed, lit the lantern, got the woodstove going and as he drank a cup of tea he gazed out into the darkness and looked for his *Book of Jo.* In there somewhere he was sure he'd find a connection to Canada and to Peter. He reached for his scrapbook and was momentarily surprised that it wasn't where he had left it. He knew precisely where every single scrapbook of his was at any given moment. *Book of Jo* was always the third one down in the second stack from the woodstove. As he scrabbled through his books, he became more and more certain, and when he finally did find it he was absolutely certain. Peter, who had been in his cabin just yesterday, had found this one, read through it and moved it.

A third of the way into the book he saw the blank page, the carefully cut out story. Peter! Peter had done this! He needed to warn people. And then another more horrific thought came to him. What was Peter still doing here? If he truly was the murderer, why hadn't he hightailed it out of here as soon as the deed was committed? Unless someone else was on his list.

He still hadn't received the newspapers from Edmonton. He expected them any day. But it was time to start another book. He took out a brand new scrapbook, and with his black Magic Marker wrote *Book of Peter* on the first page. The first article he pasted in was the short article from the movie magazine.

Midmorning, when he delivered a stack of newspapers to Walt's, it was all he could think about—warning the islanders. He sat down at the counter, and Walt poured him a coffee. A few people were in the store then, purchasing tins of this or that, and some of the regulars were at the counter: Dob, Manny, and Lenny.

"You look like death warmed over, Jules," Walt said.

"I know who the murderer is," he whispered.

"You do? Who?" This came from Dob.

"You were right, Manny. It had to be Peter. I've got proof. Besides, I saw him," he added.

"You saw him? When?" asked Sam, who had joined them after taking his purchases to the cash register.

"The night before it all happened," Jules said. "Saw someone rowing away from the island wearing a dark coat like the one he wears and a black watch cap with a white tassel thing at the top."

"I never saw him wear a hat like that."

"You sure about that Jules? It could've been someone from the mainland. Someone just coming across," said Walt.

"Doubt it. Let me tell you something, that kid's from Canada. I'm getting a whole bunch of newspapers from where he's from. He killed another girl there. He's probably a drug addict. You ever look at his eyes? They tell the story. He's running from the law, ended up here. That's what I think."

"How do you know all this?"

"I told you, these newspapers."

"I thought you said the papers hadn't come yet," said Sam accepting a cup of coffee.

"I read enough," said Jules. "It's all in one of those movie magazines."

"Movie magazines!"

"Yeah," said Jules. "The girl he killed before? She was some sort of movie star."

"Oh yeah?"

"Maybe he's a serial killer," said Lenny. "That's the type, you know. The quiet ones. It's always the quiet ones do things like that."

"Lenny's right," said Dob.

"So what do we do?" asked Walt. "You want to lynch the guy or what?"

"No," said Jules, thoughtfully. "I say we just treat him the way we always have, and keep our eye on him. Let him know we're onto him without telling him. We don't know who's next."

TWENTY-FIVE

IN THE MIDDLE OF THE AFTERNOON Peter received a third gift, whether from Jo or from someone else, he wasn't sure. He liked to think it was from Jo. He had lain down on his mattress in the sanctuary and felt something lumpy under his blanket. He felt for the obstruction and brought out a hat. A black woolen cap with a dirty white tassel. How did she know he needed a hat? The days were getting colder, and it was always windy where he sat beside the lighthouse. Turning up his coat collar and hunching his shoulders down into it didn't seem to be enough anymore. Could it have been Jo? He thought about the angel movie and laughed. Blair would think this was very serious, receiving a gift from a ghost. He could picture her saying, "I wouldn't laugh, Peter. They're all around us. This just proves it." He swung it by the tassel and called to Jeremiah, "Is this yours?"

Jeremiah looked up from his small table at the front and said, "What is it?"

"A hat. Not mine. Thought it might be yours." Peter walked toward him.

At the front of the sanctuary was a raised platform. Peter suspected that at one time it may have been carpeted, but now it was plain worn wood. The platform was separated from the rest of the sanctuary by a railing which ran along three sides. Drawing on childhood memories, he had a feeling that the railing may have been covered in some sort of drape. Now, Jeremiah hung his clothing and bedding over it. On the wall behind him, floor to ceiling bookshelves were crammed with old, dark books. The shelves were makeshift, constructed, it looked like, with barn boards and cinder blocks. The weight of the books had caused a few of the shelves to curve downward in the center. Jeremiah sat at the table surrounded by several candles, unlit now because it was day. On his table were a few thick books and a notebook. This was

Jeremiah's domain. Peter had never ventured up here before.

"This," said Peter holding out the hat. "Is this yours? It was under my blanket."

Jeremiah put down his pen, took the hat, turned it inside out and over, and handed it back. "No, I haven't seen it before."

"Someone left it on my bed."

"Do you need a hat?"

"I do. Yes."

"Then take it as a gift from God."

Angels again. Peter grinned. He checked with Colin and Philip, but they also said it wasn't theirs. When he showed it to Naomi, she looked at it for a long time, running her hands over it, tracing the tassel through her slender fingers, but in the end said she couldn't be sure, but she didn't think she'd ever seen it before.

So he took to wearing the hat all the time, wearing it when he went to the lighthouse with his journal or one of Colin's adventure books; wearing it on his long walks around the perimeter of the island and when he sat out in the cemetery on one of the tombstones, watching the water in the distance.

TWENTY-SIX

ONE OF THE THINGS NAOMI FOUND most difficult about the winter was keeping herself and her daughter clean when the creek froze over. She or Colin or Jeremiah kept a part of it pickaxed open for as long as they could, but sometimes it froze in thick layers. Then they would be forced to carry their drinking water in barrels on sleds over the snowy path from the townsite. Taking a bath in the winter meant heating up precious water on the woodstove. She suspected that Colin and Jeremiah showered at Martha's, and sometimes she did too.

As well, washing clothes was difficult in winter. In the summer she washed hers and Zoe's in the stream and hung them to dry on lines beside the cemetery. In the winter she had to heat kettles of water, and then hang up their wet things on lines strung up around the sanctuary. Sometimes it took many days for things to dry.

Laundry was what she was doing on a bright fall morning, lugging her and Philip's and Zoe's clothing down to the stream. The water would be cold on her hands now, but at least the creek wasn't frozen.

Across the flat rock she always used, she lay a pair of oil-stained jeans of Philip's that she had drenched in the creek. She began scrubbing them with soap and a brush. The knees were especially grubby. When she reached into the pockets, she brought out a little piece of cloth. She placed it in her palm and stared at it. It surprised her more than frightened her. She was holding in her hand the missing label from her coat. Margot's Designs, Woodstock, VT. How on earth did this end up in Philip's pocket? She looked at it, shrugged, then shoved it within the deep pockets of her denim skirt. She'd ask him later.

Philip was away from the island today. He had taken Zoe for a quick trip to run errands on the mainland for truck parts, he told her.

"Hi."

She turned and looked up into the face of Colin.

"Hello," she said.

He knelt beside her. "Let me help." Before she could protest, he was squeezing suds through a sundress of Zoe's.

"You're good at that," she said.

"Tricks I've learned in the north."

He shoved his hair back behind his ears with a soapy hand and continued. They knelt together for half an hour, scrubbing, rinsing, scrubbing, rinsing. It felt odd to Naomi to have him there. "When we're finished here," he said, "why don't you come with me to the *Andrea C.* You haven't seen her in a while."

"I'd like that."

There was silence for the next few minutes while they washed and scrubbed beside the stream.

"It must be nearly finished," she said.

"The laundry?" he asked.

"No," she laughed. "Your boat."

"Long way from that, I'm afraid."

For as long as she had known him he had been refurbishing and refitting an old lobster boat which had been brought up from the bottom of the bay. The only other time she had seen it was before Zoe was born. At that time it was a faded hulk of a thing, boards bleached and rotting as it sat high and lofty in a cradle down at Bill's boatyard. Along the stern she made out the name *Andrea C.*

"Who's Andrea C.?" she had asked.

Colin hadn't answered her.

He squeezed water from a couple of dishrags and looked at her. "Do you have to check in with His Highness first?"

She didn't look at him. "If you mean Philip, he's on the mainland."

"He's gone? You're sure he's coming back?"

"He has Zoe with him." What she didn't say was that as much as he professed to love his daughter, he would never take her. Just as he wouldn't take Naomi. All he would have to do is say once, "Come with me," and she would be packed. She continued, "You're not being fair to him. He's really a good and gentle person."

"So you keep saying."

She rose, placed the wrung out pieces of clothing in her basket, and said, "Okay, I'll come to see the *Andrea C.* as long as the subject of Philip is out of bounds."

"Fine with me."

After they hung the laundry on the line, they walked together on the path to the townsite. It was cool within the shelter of the branches and several times, Naomi wished she had remembered her coat.

Past the townsite they headed down the path that led to Bill's boatbuilding operation. Bill was a quiet fellow, almost a hermit, but was somewhat of a legend on the Maine coast. He had been written up several times in *WoodenBoat* and *Maine Boats and Harbors.* Whenever this happened, Walt cut out the articles and tacked them up on the bulletin board down at the coffee shop.

The path ahead opened up to a couple of very large barnlike structures. Ahead of them boats sat on cradles in various stages of construction. Naomi followed Colin into the building at the far end of the yard.

The first thing she noticed when Colin flicked on the lights was the immenseness of the *Andrea C.'s* hull. It loomed at her like a gigantic barge, the bottom of a huge whale. Then she noticed the shine. No longer a collection of splintered boards, the hull gleamed and shone a lustrous green, so shiny she thought maybe she could see her reflection in it. The top half of the hull was painted a high gloss white. Above the hull was the pilothouse, which stood tall and square near the front of the boat, leaving a lot of open space in the cockpit area. The pilothouse was of highly varnished natural wood. Along one side of the hull was the name *Andrea C.* Along the other were the words *Lambs Island, Maine.*

"It's beautiful," she said. She placed her hand near the hull, then moved it away.

"It's okay," he said. "You can touch it."

"It looked wet, that's all. It's so shiny."

She watched as he caressed the side of the hull. "This boat has a history."

"You told me some about it once, the last time I saw it, about it being sunk and then brought up."

"Then Bill and I got the basic design, got pictures, the original plans, and decided to rebuild her."

"It's so beautiful."

"You want to go up inside?"

She followed him up a paint-spattered ladder that leaned against the side of the boat near the stern.

The deck was tongue and groove of some pale wood. It gleamed like the rest of the boat. Ahead of the deck area was the pilothouse which provided access to the cabin. The door stood open, and she followed him inside. Along one side was a small sink and next to it a two-burner stove with what looked like an oven underneath. She wondered if it worked. And everywhere cabinets and shelves, exquisite in their workmanship. Below, she peered into a sleeping quarters, although now she saw it was devoid of a mattress. She did, however, see a few of Colin's clothes strewn about, plus cans of what looked like paint and rags. It had a clean smell of new wood and varnish.

"Is this where you sleep?" she asked.

"Yes."

"You should take your mattress from the church with you. Wouldn't that be more comfortable?"

He looked at her, an expression of horror on his face. "I would never take such a grubby thing onto this boat."

"I can see your point. This is so beautiful."

He smiled, a broad smile, showing lots of even teeth. She seldom saw him smile.

"Would you take this out for actual lobstering?" she asked.

"No. I don't know. I wouldn't."

"It looks almost finished. What else do you need to do?"

"Lots." But he didn't explain.

They sat inside the cabin where he took out a bag of Oreos from a cupboard and offered it to her. She took one. He made tea on the little stove, and they talked. At one point she found herself fingering the little label that she had put in her pocket. She brought it out and laid it on her lap.

"What's that?" he asked.

"The famous missing label from Jo's coat."

"Where was it?"

"Philip's pocket."

He stared at her. "What was it doing in Philip's pocket?"

"I don't know. I'm going to ask him when I see him."

"Can I look at it?"

"Here." She gave it to him.

"Can I keep it?"

"I don't care."

"You're not wearing your wedding ring."

"You're observant."

"You always wear your wedding ring."

"I thought we weren't going to talk about Philip."

"I'm not talking about Philip, I'm talking about your wedding ring. The ring you never take off. Ever."

"I take if off when I knead bread. And the last time I made bread I took it off, and then when I went to put it back on, it wasn't there. I know it's in the room somewhere, I just haven't had a long stretch of time to look for it."

"I'll help you look later." He looked at her a moment, then said, "Naomi, if you ever need anyone to talk to, I'm right here, staying at the boat now. You can come any time."

She looked away from him, not understanding what he was offering, piqued that he would think she needed someone to talk to. "Thank you for the offer. I'll keep it in mind."

Later, when she told Philip about the label, he shrugged and said he must have picked it up off the floor. But when he asked her for it, he blew up when she said she had lost it, that she had probably dropped it down by the creek or something. She feared his wrath if she told him she had given it to Colin.

That evening, before it got dark, she could see him, combing the sides of the creek, bending down, scrabbling in the dirt with his hands.

APRIL 13, 1994

FROM THE JOURNALS OF MARTHA MACGREGOR

The woman Naomi, and the man who comes now and then to stay with her—she has told me his name is Philip—are putting a garden in behind the church. It's on a stretch of land located a little to the left of the cemetery. It's where we used to have Sunday school picnics back when I was a girl. A long time ago now.

I was walking around the island, I do that sometimes, when I saw them, the two of them, Naomi in her straw hat and a pair of baggy work pants, and Philip, shirtless and muscular. Both had shovels and were turning over little clods of earth. I wonder about the quality of the soil back there, and thought to myself, They're going to encounter nothing but rocks. Also, the winds are strong here, and tender plants need to be protected. I walked over to them and when I told this to the man he nodded and said that he'd thought all about that and that was all taken care of. The next day he came driving a pickup onto the island loaded with fresh topsoil. I really don't know where he got it. Topsoil is expensive, and I know those two don't have two nickels to rub together. He told me he has a friend with a farm who gave it to him. Well, that would explain it. During the course of the week he brought over two more pickup loads of topsoil and some manure, as well. He is also planning on building a small wind break. That will help. I admire those two, there aren't two people on the face of this earth who work harder than those two, I think. Especially Naomi.

Colin is away for the summer again, and it's just as well. I sometimes wonder how the three of them get along living in the church like they do.

TWENTY-SEVEN

WHEN MARGOT PHONED HOME THAT NIGHT from her motel she spoke to Sara and Pammy and both were full of questions about New York, and wouldn't it be neat if they could go with her sometime? She told them yes, she would love it if they could go with her sometime. She'd plan her next trip when they didn't have school.

Next she phoned Jane who brought her up to date on business and said that everything was running smoothly except she did receive one strange phone call.

"Strange phone call?" asked Margot.

"Really strange. Odd ball, if you want my opinion. First of all this man who refuses to give his name, he asks if he could please speak with you, and when I said you were away on business, right away he wants to know where you are and could I give him the phone number where you could be reached. He said it was an emergency."

"What sort of emergency?"

"I asked him that. He wouldn't say. Just that he *had* to speak to you."

"Did you get his name?"

"Nope. Wouldn't give it. He kept asking for the name of your hotel, that it really was an emergency and then he said that surely, if I was your business partner, I would know of a number where you could be reached. Well, I wasn't about to give him your cellular, not with the way he was acting. Not with that voice and all."

"Voice?"

"It had sort of a—I don't know how to describe it—a whispery quality. Like he was in range of other people hearing and he didn't want anyone else to know he was making the call. Well, finally, after a whole lot of talking, I finally get him to tell me the nature of his business, and he says it has to do with the murder of the girl who was found on that island in Maine. He asked if you knew her. Well, I wasn't about to say that she worked for you. So I kept my voice calm and said I would be in contact with you and was there a message I could give you?"

"What did he say?"

"He had a question. He wants to know…here it is, does the name Philip Friend mean anything to you?"

"Who?"

"That's what I said."

"He called and wanted to know if the name Philip Friend meant anything to me? And that it had something to do with Jo?"

"Yep. That's it."

"I never heard of Philip Friend. Have you?"

"Never, and I told him as much."

"Did you call the police?"

"No. Should I?"

"I don't know."

"As soon as I got off the phone with him, I dialed that number, you know, the one that's supposed to give you the last number that called your number, but they said the number was unavailable."

"Jane, when I talk to Paul tonight I'll ask him if he knows someone named Philip—what was the last name again?"

"Friend."

"Friend, okay."

When she hung up, Margot sat for several seconds, the phone cradled in her lap. And then she decided that tomorrow morning, first thing, she would drive into New Jersey and talk to Jo's parents. She would offer sympathy, tell them that Jo had worked for her. And she'd ask them if they knew Philip Friend.

Figuring it to be midafternoon on the west coast, she called. When she asked to speak to Paul the receptionist said no one by that name worked there.

"He doesn't work there. He's there in meetings. A course or something."

147

"Let me have another look then. What company is he with?"

"East Coast Group Computers. From Vermont."

"Hmm. Looking at the sheet here, East Coast Group isn't due in until next month. I have it right here in front of me."

Margot was growing impatient. "He's there now," she said.

"No, I'm afraid not. I could have him paged, but that might take a couple of minutes. Do you want to hold?"

"No thanks."

"I give up!" said Margot out loud when she hung up. She tried his cellular. He answered on the second ring. "Paul, some receptionist there gave me the runaround. Said East Coast wasn't there until next month."

"What? What a bunch of incompetents. Of course I'm here, love. There's no mistaking that. Wish I wasn't at times. These long meetings. I feel totally coffeed out, let me tell you. What number did you call, by the way?"

When she told him he chuckled. "You'll have to forgive me. I gave you the wrong number. Now I'm the incompetent. She's right. We don't go there until next month. I have so many of these blasted numbers and places and corporations to visit. Let me see, unbelievable. I don't have the correct number in my Palm Pilot. But, you know you can always reach me on my cellular. That's a given."

"I was just trying to save money."

"I know, love, and I appreciate it, but from now on call me on my cellular. You know you can always reach me that way."

"I wanted to ask you something. I got a call…actually, Jane did. Some guy wanted to know if the name Philip Friend meant anything to me. Do you know a Philip Friend? He said it was in connection with Jo's death."

There was silence.

"Paul, are you there?"

"I'm here. Bad connection. You were saying?"

When she told him again, he said, "Philip Friend?"

"Yes."

"I have no idea who that is, do you?"

"No, I never heard of him either."

"Is he connected with the computer industry or the fabric business?"

"I have no idea." Margot nervously looked around her motel room. "Should Jane call the police about this?"

"She hasn't already?"

"Not that I know of."

"Hmm, did the mysterious caller leave a name?"

"No."

"Well, if he or she calls back, try to get his name, okay?"

"Okay."

When she hung up, and when she settled down into the motel double bed and pulled the faded maroon bedspread over her, something nagged at her. She wasn't sure if it had to do with the mysterious caller or with Paul.

TWENTY-EIGHT

JEREMIAH SAID IT WASN'T MY FAULT and that I should quit blaming myself. I wonder if he would say that if he knew about Amanda.

Peter was writing those words in his journal while he sat on his mattress, his back against the outside wall of the church. It was cold and damp inside the building and Peter had lain his coat on his outstretched legs. Outside, the wind wailed and rain fell unrelenting in sheets. He could hear it hitting the sides of the old building, oddly, a comforting sound. In front of Peter the pews spread out like a maze. Through it he could glimpse Colin's area; his books lined against the wall. But his bedding gone. Colin had been away for many days. At the front of the church Jeremiah was hunched over his table, candles flickering.

Peter wondered where he'd be now if nothing had happened to Jo, if he could rewind the video, start over from that point. Both running, maybe they would have left the island together. Maybe both of them would have jobs and new names by now. He wrote her name, Jo, on top of the page. And he thought of her face. But then her face was suddenly replaced by the face of Blair. He heard her accusing voice on that afternoon when they'd had their last fight. "Peter, you didn't do anything wrong! Why can't you get that through your thick head?"

"But look what they're saying about me."

"You didn't do anything wrong!"

"Look at the articles in the paper."

"Yeah, and who owns the papers, the Roos people. She was drunk."

"Yeah, but no one believes me."

"The police do, and that's all that matters. Hold your head up! I'm sick of being with you if all you ever do is mope around."

"Fine then, leave."

And she did. He watched her retreating figure in the park that day, walking away from him, tall, lean body bending slightly forward into the wind. He never saw her again after that.

If the province of Alberta had a royal family, it was the Roos family. If they had a princess it was Amanda. The day after the accident, when he was still in shock, he received the first of the phone calls. His mother had driven up from Red Deer and was sitting with him in his apartment when the phone rang. It was from someone representing the Roos family who said a bit too merrily, too chattily, "It would do no one any good if it were made known that she had been drinking. We have a story worked out that will keep good the name of Roos, and also ensure that your sentence is minimal…" *Minimal?* Peter stared at the phone. He had said, "I'm planning on telling the truth." But the truth wasn't what this family wanted. The calls became more frequent, more threatening. "The Roos family employs a lot of people in this province. If this comes out, think what will happen."

The media cast Amanda as an innocent victim, pointing to Peter's age; some speculated that drugs were a factor. And then the editorials came out against drunk driving, driving under the influence of drugs, and the whole thing became a major topic on radio talk shows. When Peter talked to the police about the phone calls and the articles he was reading, they assured him that his blood alcohol level was zero, and that he showed no evidence that he had taken any drugs, and by the look of the braking patterns, he was in the clear, not speeding, and his good driving record would stand up. They told him not to worry.

In the end, that is exactly what happened. His license wasn't revoked and he would have no police record. That wasn't enough, however, to stop the nightmares. He had to leave.

A horrifying thought took hold of him then. Had Roos's men followed him here? Had they murdered Jo as a kind of warning? Kill everyone that is important to Peter?

The thought filled him with terror.

TWENTY-NINE

MARGOT WAS STANDING IN LINE at the convenience store with her large coffee and cellophane-wrapped blueberry muffin looking at the rack of magazines next to the counter when the lead story in a woman's magazine caught her attention. "Is Your Husband Having an Affair? How to Know for Sure." She picked it up and paid for it along with her purchases. Then she asked the girl behind the counter if she had a phone book. The girl pointed toward a phone booth.

Balancing her purchases, Margot found the number for Jack Sypher and jotted down the address on the back of the magazine.

The Sypher home was one in a block of well-kept two-story homes which faced a tree-lined street. The words "old money" came to mind as she drove down the street looking for 221. The Sypher home stood out as the only dark wood building on a street of white houses. The front yard was full of windblown leaves. Neighbors on either side were raking theirs into large piles, but the leaves in the Sypher yard were inches deep. The house looked quiet. Desolate might be a more descriptive word, she thought.

There didn't seem to be any sort of bell, so Margot rapped on the wooden door. The house was badly in need of paint. Leaves had even scattered themselves into piles on the front porch. No one answered, and Margot was about to turn away, when she saw a movement behind the front curtain. She waited. Her knock was finally answered by a small woman with a worried look. She opened the door a crack and asked, "Are you a reporter?"

Margot assured her that she was not, and said she was most sorry to intrude, but that she just wanted to convey her heartfelt sympathy.

The woman stared at her. "What?"

"Jo. Joanne. Your daughter? You're Mrs. Sypher?"

The woman nodded slowly. "You sure you're not a reporter?"

"No. Absolutely not. I'm a dress designer. Jo worked for me."

"Are you with the police?" The woman continued to look at her warily, her large eyes opened wide.

"No."

"What do you want then?"

"Just to convey my sympathy."

Several times the woman turned around nervously, and Margot looked past her to the interior of the house. It looked dark and lifeless and cold.

Margot extended her hand. "My name is Margot Douglas and Jo worked for me last year. I was so sorry when I heard what happened. I was in the area and decided to drop by. I'm sorry to intrude. Jo was a special person. A good friend to my two daughters. I just wanted to tell you that. I thought you should know."

From inside she could hear the sound of movement. Then Jo's mother said, "Please, you have to leave now." Then she paused. "Do you want to talk about Jo? I'd like to hear about my daughter. Can we meet somewhere? There's a coffee shop down at the corner in Westfield. I can be there in fifteen minutes. It's called Coffee Au Lait. Please go now." As the woman closed the door, Margot heard a booming voice, "Is someone there, Peach?"

Westfield wasn't a huge town, and Margot easily found Coffee Au Lait. Even though she had just had a coffee at the convenience store, she ordered a regular dark with double cream and sat down to wait at a small round table near the back, away from the window. She had an idea that Jo's mother might appreciate that. She draped her cape over the back of the chair beside her and dug out the magazine she had bought.

Is Your Husband Having an Affair? She didn't even want to consider it. Still, she had bought the magazine, and she was reading the article, even now. But the whole thing was crazy. Didn't he come faithfully to church with her every Sunday? But why was what she was reading ringing so true? For a long time now there had been an undefinable distance between Margot and Paul; there was a part of him she couldn't penetrate. Occasionally she would ask him about it, and he would look up from his computer or his paper or the book he was reading and say, "Things couldn't be better." But she wondered.

She supported him in his work, always accompanied him to the required dinners, wine and cheeses, Christmas parties, and get-togethers. And she had seen the way Paul looked at the women there, at the casual ways they would touch him, a hand on his arm, a look in his eyes. None of this escaped her.

"It's just part of the job," he would tell her later. "It's called schmoozing. It means nothing."

But Margot wondered.

She also wasn't unaware that a lot of the men her husband's age had already left their wives for women half their age. A part of her began to wonder if this were inevitable, her very handsome husband leaving her for some younger, more beautiful, thinner woman.

There were also times of late when she would come upon him in his study to find him laughing in an intimate sort of way on his cellular. He would hang up immediately when she entered and scowl at her.

She finished reading the article, then went back and began going through it, more slowly this time, jotting down the name of the author who had also written a bestselling book on the subject.

"Hello."

Margot looked up at a woman, Jo's mother, standing there.

"I'm sorry I'm late," she said, unzipping her windbreaker. Underneath she wore an orange T-shirt and navy sweat pants. Her hair looked uncombed, although that could have been the wind. "I told Jack I was going for a walk. He's been so upset lately. We've had so many news people and the police. It's all so…" She looked away from Margot and bit her lower lip, a gesture that reminded her of Jo. "You said you knew Jo?"

"She worked for me. I was so sorry, stunned, actually, to hear what happened."

"My name is Lenore. Did I tell you that?"

"I don't remember. Would you like a coffee?"

"Okay, but if Jack walks in and sees me here, he'll kill me. I'm not supposed to be out. I had to beg him to just let me go for a walk."

"What do you take in it?"

"Nothing."

When Margot returned with the coffee, she placed it in front of Lenore and sat across from her. "I know you must have heard lots of strange things about Jo in the papers, but I thought someone should come and tell you what a special person she was. She worked for me in my shop and really was a friend to my daughters. She was a good worker and a good friend."

"It's nice of you to say that."

"I have a question. Do you know anyone named Philip Friend?"

"No. Was he one of Jo's friends?"

"I'm not sure. His name came up recently in connection with Jo, so I was just wondering."

Lenore shook her head.

"I also have another question."

Margot fiddled with the plastic coffee lid, breaking pieces of it off in her fingers. "I'm looking for a silver locket that Jo borrowed before she, uh, died. Have you seen such a thing?"

"No. But I haven't seen Joanne in a long time. Have you been to that island, the island where she died?"

"Not recently. Once, long ago, on vacation."

"Why would she go there?"

"I don't know. The papers don't say why, just that she went."

Lenore was rapidly shaking her head, dabbing at the corners of her eyes with a napkin. She hadn't touched her coffee. "I just don't understand it."

"It's hard, I know."

Lenore leaned across the table. "I haven't seen Joanne, you know, since she was fourteen."

"You haven't?"

"She ran away then. Or they took her. She lived not more than ten miles from here, and she never even came to visit her own mother. My own child and she never stopped by. There was a wall between us. I blame Jack for that."

"Jack is your husband?"

"Yes, Joanne was my only child. I couldn't have any more babies after her. But they wouldn't let me see her. Not once. Even Jack agreed with them." Lenore was becoming more wild-eyed, her voice louder. Already several patrons were looking in their direction.

"Lenore," said Margot gently, "I didn't know. I'm sorry. That must have been hard."

"I should have been a better mother. I tried my best. But they took her anyway. Jack made them come. I blame him. It was those Frye people."

"Frye people?"

"Her foster people. Troy and Brenda. She stayed with them. They never let me see her."

"I'm sorry."

"I'm trying to be strong now. I don't want to go back to the hospital."

In Lenore's eyes, Margot saw the same sadness, the same vulnerability that had made her say to Jo that first time, "Why don't you stay here?"

Lenore was still talking. "But why would she steal a baby?"

"I don't know."

"That's something I'll never understand. Why she would steal that baby."

Lenore rose and her chair tumbled behind her. "I have to go. If Jack sees me in here, he'll kill me. He threatened the both of us, Joanne and me, on more than one occasion. Did I tell you that?"

"No."

"He's not a nice man. That's why Joanne left, because he threatened her. It wasn't because of me. That's why I blame him."

She zipped up her jacket and ran from the place. Margot righted the chair and the young man behind the counter said, "She's kind of strange, that one."

"Did you know Jo?" she asked.

He shrugged. "A little. We went to different high schools. I went to Westfield. Sure heard about her, though."

"With the murder and all I'll bet."

"Even before that. She was always getting in trouble. When I heard what happened to her, I wasn't even surprised."

OCTOBER 16, 1995

FROM THE JOURNALS OF MARTHA MACGREGOR

Naomi has come back with a tiny baby. She is alone this time. I visit with her now and then and always feel a sadness when I walk home after seeing her. Her husband, Philip, is a logger, and must be away in the bush for long stretches, sometimes months at a time. The first time I visited Naomi it was just after Colin had returned from the North. I wanted to go and introduce myself to this woman whom I had seen off and on. I felt it was only right. Colin wasn't there when I went. Now, I don't know what transpired, and I never asked him, but when I got there, Colin had moved his sleeping quarters into the sanctuary leaving his cot for Naomi. I was proud of Colin for that. I know Colin can be sensitive and thoughtful.

There are two cots in the kitchen now. One belongs to Colin, and I don't know where the other one came from. Possibly from Philip.

Today when I visited, Naomi was nursing her baby. Such a tiny little thing. But healthy looking, for sure! I have to admit I am surprised she is still here. I guess I assumed that once the baby was born, she and her husband would be moving into a proper house. But there they are, still in the church. Today I told her that surely there are better accommodations in town. I personally know of several places available and if she wanted I could look into them further for her. And did she know that the winters get awfully cold on this side of the island, what with the wind and all, and that now she has a tiny baby to think about? She just smiled and said she will stay here, that she will be fine here, that she is used to the bush. I used to work in a logging camp, she told me. You! She smiled and said, Yes, I was a cook there, that's how I met my husband. That's why I'm used to it. I would like to stay here if that's all right, that way my husband will know where to find us. Well, what could I say? Of course she can stay there.

But I wonder why they must live in an old church. The only thing I can come up with is that they are as poor as church mice and don't want to accept charity. If that's the case, you have to admire them for it. They are certainly hardworking! When I was there, she served me coffee, and I also noticed she was making bread pudding with leftover bread and had ingredients out to make noodles. That woman is always doing something.

I brought over a few things, though. Some more blankets, especially for that baby of hers. Maybe I can help out that way.

THIRTY

WHEN JULES RECEIVED THE BUNDLE OF PAPERS bearing the postmark of Edmonton, Alberta, Canada, he cleared off a space on the top of his table with the side of his hand and laid down all the papers on top of each other, in order by date. And there it was, the lead story on the front section of the very first paper he looked at.

> *Amanda Roos Dead in Fatal Accident. Nineteen-year-old Amanda Roos, daughter of Henry and Roberta Roos, one of the most prominent families in Alberta, is dead following a traffic accident late last evening on Stony Plain Road.*

Jules read that she had been attending a party and was waiting along the side of the road for a ride, when a truck, driven by twenty-year-old Peter Glass, also of Edmonton, ran into her. There was a grainy picture of an ambulance, police cars, and the road at night. Amanda was a University of Alberta student, Jules read, and hoping to pursue a career in drama. Already she had been in a number of minor roles in some major motion pictures.

Jules read all of the accounts very carefully, including the editorials and letters to the editor. He read about the inquest and noted that Peter Glass was in the clear. There was no evidence of drug or alcohol use. Yet, the newspapers seemed definitely on the side of Amanda, with a number of editorials coming out against drunk drivers and hinting that Peter may have been on drugs, and that the police had failed to test for these.

In a paper dated a month later, in a story that wasn't more than two inches square, Jules read that Peter Glass was no longer living in Edmonton and that his whereabouts were unknown. His mother in Red Deer had contacted the police and was pressing them to declare him a missing person. She told reporters that Peter had been despondent and depressed following the accident, and she was worried about him. But so far no one knew where he was, and it looked as if the police were only making a halfhearted effort to find him.

Jules took out his *Book of Peter*. He got to work on the scrapbook, pasting all the articles in order. The Peter here on the island, disguised now with all that long hair and those scruffy clothes, was really Peter Glass, murderer. And this only confirmed in Jules's mind that Peter had murdered Jo. The other day Dob had said to him in a low voice, "I saw Peter the other day. He was walking through town, and sure as I'm standing here in front of you, he was wearing a hat, just like the one you described."

"He was?"

"Yeah, Jules. It was just like you said. With a white tassel."

"You'd think he'd have the smarts enough to at least cut the tassel off."

"Yeah, but he didn't know you saw him, did he?"

"You're right about that."

THIRTY-ONE

MARGOT LOOKED UP THE NAME TROY FRYE in the phone book at the same convenience store she had been in earlier. The young man behind the counter told her the address was up in the Berkeley Heights area. Following the directions he gave her, she crossed Route 22 and headed through a somewhat winding road to Berkeley Heights. A few minutes later she was driving up the paved driveway of a large gray, fairly new bilevel home.

She was met at the door by a man in a T-shirt which said, Just Do It. The shirt seemed about two sizes too small for his ample belly.

"Are you Troy Frye?"

"Was the last time I looked." His voice was deep and merry and he chuckled when he talked. Margot had an idea he would be a good mall Santa.

"You're going to think I'm strange," said Margot, "just barging in here. My name is Margot Douglas. I'm here about Jo Sypher. Did she live with you?"

The merry eyes narrowed. "You're a reporter."

"No," said Margot, "I'm not a reporter, at least I wasn't the last time I looked…"

"What can I help you with then?"

"Jo used to work for me. I was just over at her parent's place, and I talked with her mother, Lenore. I just wanted to express my sympathy to her. And then I thought of coming up here."

"Jo used to work for you?"

"Yes, I have a business in Vermont. She showed up one day. I felt sorry for her, and I hired her."

He chuckled again. "That sounds like Jo."

"When she left me she took a very valuable silver locket. Have you seen anything like that around?"

He laughed, a loud guffaw that shook his belly. "That also sounds like Jo. Why don't you come in?"

He opened the door wide, and she followed him up the steps through a cluttered living room and on into an equally cluttered kitchen. The place smelled vaguely of cats and looked definitely lived in. He motioned her to sit at a large table which bore the grimy marks of meals eaten and not totally wiped cleaned. While she was sitting there, a small black-and-white kitten jumped onto the table and meowed its way to where Troy was sitting. He laughed, reached for it, and held it in his meaty hands. The kitchen was cluttered with boxes of cereal, empty milk cartons, and a bundle of newspapers which looked like they were headed for the recycler. The table contained piles of children's games, magazines, coloring books, and crayons. The refrigerator was papered with children's art work and school notices.

"We haven't seen Jo in quite a while, so I really can't help you much with the locket. But I'm not surprised she took it."

"You're not?"

"We had problems with her from day one. We have a lot of kids here. We're good at what we do. But Jo was different."

"How so?"

He shook his head. "Well, I shouldn't say that, not really. You met Lenore, you said?"

"Yes."

"Well, the apple doesn't fall far from the tree as far as that family is concerned. Jo's main problem was stealing. That's why I said I'm not surprised she took your locket. She stole things every place she lived, always saying she'd pay it back."

Margot shrugged. "I guess stealing that baby was the last straw, though."

Troy looked at her. The large features of his face immobile. "She had a good reason for stealing that baby, or what she would call a good reason."

"What kind of good reason?"

"That baby was hers."

Margot leaned back in her chair. A small black kitten scooted into the kitchen. Troy picked him up, held both of them in his hands now. The effect was gentling.

"Hers?" Margot said.

"She gave it up for adoption. Those whatchamacallit people must have adopted it, and Jo stole it back."

"How do you know this?"

"Doesn't take a brain surgeon."

"Do you know this for a fact? Or are you just guessing?"

He put the kittens down. They mewed around his ankles. "I know it for a fact."

"How? I thought you hadn't seen her in a while."

"We saw her a year ago and she was definitely pregnant, as pregnant as they come. The wife and I helped her adopt it out. It was supposed to be a closed adoption. That's what Jo wanted. So, I don't know how she found out where that baby was. But Jo, one thing she was, was resourceful."

Margot leaned forward. "Why would someone want to kill her?"

Troy rubbed his massive hands over his face. "The police asked me that, too. And I'll tell you what I told them. I have no idea." He raised his hand. "And I'm sorry. I don't know where your necklace is. So, you came all the way down here for nothing."

"It wasn't for nothing. I had business in New York."

"I was going to say you could have phoned. Saved yourself a lot of trouble. I could have told you we didn't have your necklace. Just curious, when did she work for you?"

"Just before she went to the James's."

He chuckled and looked at her. "We had her, the wife and I, for three years. I can't tell you how many times she ran away when she was here. But let me tell you something, she would have rather been here than at that place of hers. We always treated her right."

"That place of hers, you mean her home, right? Lenore told me her husband threatened both Jo and her on a regular basis. Are the police looking at her father as a suspect?"

"I'm sure they are. But Lenore, like Jo, lies. I wouldn't put a lot of stock into what she says. In actual fact, she's a nut case. The reason we got Jo was because of her mother being a nut case and her father being a total control freak. You put that combination together, it's a recipe for disaster. Lenore couldn't accept that Jo got pregnant out of wedlock, as she so delicately put it."

"The police know about it being her baby?"

"Of course." He rose, poured milk in a small dish. No sooner had he set it down than an armful of cats were meowing around it. "They know all about that. That's not news to them."

"I never read that in the paper."

"I think the James's wanted it kept out. That would be my guess."

"Does the name Philip Friend mean anything to you? Did Jo ever mention that name?"

The man shook his head. He picked up a small kitten and stroked it in his lap until it purred. "Who is he, the father of the baby?"

JANUARY 25, 1996

FROM THE JOURNALS OF MARTHA MACGREGOR

I am sitting here, looking down at the cove and trying to remember when it was that we put that partition in, the one that separates the sanctuary from the back of the church. It was after Andrea's wedding, that I know for sure, but it was also before her death. I remember the decorating we did for that wedding and I recall clearly that the sanctuary extended the full length of the building then. Since there was no study of any kind, the minister kept his books in tall bookshelves at the front left of the church, near the woodstove. It made sort of a cozy alcove then, with his bookshelves and a small desk. An odd arrangement, but it worked for us.

The parsonage or manse as we called it, was not located next to the building as is so often the case, but was a house in the townsite. Manny lives in that house now. I think there was some wisdom in not building a house on the windy side. I can't imagine the wife of any minister bearing that winter wind. No, a house in the town was so much better.

But that's not what I want to write about. I sat down to write about the partition. We decided that we needed a place where we could meet for church suppers and hold small meetings. So we had two choices: build a small addition or partition the existing sanctuary. We chose the latter. Jake was in charge of getting the supplies from the mainland. For a while there was a regular parade of trucks bringing drywall, nails, and lumber. We also invested in a new woodstove, which the church badly needed.

I can't remember now why the work stopped. I think it was that fewer and fewer people began showing for the work parties. Those few sheets of drywall and a door are all that we completed. So that the workmen would have a place to eat their lunches, we borrowed the folding table and chairs from a community center on the mainland. They have never been returned. It would be strange to return them now, after all these years, don't you think? I'm sure the community hall—I can't even remember which one loaned them to us—doesn't even remember that we borrowed them. Naomi and Colin eat from that table now. And Philip when he comes. Naomi kneads her bread on that table, and folds the baby's laundry on that table. No, it would not be right to take those things away now.

THIRTY-TWO

IT WAS STILL RAINING. Jeremiah was at his table, and Peter was lying on his stomach on his mattress reading one of Colin's books. This one was about a boy who had singlehandedly sailed a small sailboat around the world. He was younger than Peter when he started out. That's what I should do, thought Peter, sail around the world. Maybe I could start my new life there.

"Ready for a break?"

Peter looked up. Jeremiah was talking to him across the tops of the empty pews.

"What?"

"Well, I am," said Jeremiah. "Sometimes I think my brain will get totally muzzed by all of this."

"Muzzed?"

"See, it's happening already." He took off his glasses and rubbed his eyes and smoothed his hair away from his forehead. "I'm losing the Queen's English. Using words like *muzzed.*"

Peter inserted a small chip of wood as a bookmark, closed the paperback and placed it beside him.

Jeremiah got up and walked toward Peter, down the steps of the platform. "Sometimes I don't know why I'm doing this, going through all those old tomes. Don't know if any of these writers have any more answers than I do."

He had plopped down on the pew closest to Peter.

"I used to think that life had to be fair," Jeremiah said. "Now I read of lives, hundreds of them up there," he indicated the books, "where life was anything but."

"What are you reading?"

"Biographies today, going through them. Of missionaries and monks and martyrs. All ghosts now. All of them. There's a wealth of

169

information in those old books. Old translations of the Bible, Greek texts, Hebrew. I studied Greek and Hebrew in seminary. I don't know who they belong to, but a part of me believes that God brought me here. I'm writing down thoughts. I'm trying to figure out who God is. Who God *really* is. That make any sense to you?"

"A little. Do you believe in fate? That things happen for a reason, and we just have to find that reason out? And that the reason, whatever it is, is always for our good?"

Jeremiah pushed his glasses up on his nose. "I used to believe that. But I used to substitute the word God, for fate. I believed that God had a wonderful plan for each one of us. I used to have all the answers. But they were all simple answers. Simple answers to hard questions." He paused. "I know God. Yet my life is spent in searching for Him."

"Would God forgive you if you did something really bad?"

Jeremiah looked up. "Oh absolutely." He said it without question, and the quickness of his reply surprised Peter.

Peter bit his lip. "If you thought you knew who killed Jo, what would you do?"

"Probably I'd go to the police, but in our case we don't have to. They come to us with regularity. Why? Do you know who killed Jo?"

"I'm not totally sure, but I think it might be someone from my past."

"*Your* past?"

Peter nodded.

"Someone who knew you and Jo?"

"They may have killed Jo as a warning. To me."

Jeremiah leaned into the back of the pew, legs spread out in front of him.

Peter continued, "It may be a warning to me. I came all this distance because I thought I could escape them. But they may have followed me here. They may try for me next." Peter told him about the accident and the threats, and finally leaving, not telling a soul, not even his mother. Just leaving.

"So now you think this Roos family is after you?"

"Yes."

"You're afraid these people might be on the island?"

"If they killed Jo, maybe they'll kill me next."

From the back room they could hear Philip shouting and Naomi crying.

"The unfairness of life," said Jeremiah looking toward the closed door. "You are innocent and are being chased across the country. I am innocent and I am being chased across the country. Naomi is innocent and she cries. If I have learned anything it's that life is mostly not fair. We have this innate belief, learned somewhere in childhood, perhaps, that all of life should be fair. But it's not. But we work toward fairness. All our lives we work toward fairness. But it never happens."

Peter felt a drop of something wet hit him on the face. He looked up. A small pool of water had collected along the joints of the roof and was dripping on his mattress.

"It leaks sometimes," said Jeremiah. "You learn to live with it. I'll get you a bucket, but you may want to move your mattress down a bit. It's cold and damp in here, but the stove heats up this place pretty well in the winter as long as we keep the door open. And I should get out there and chop some wood. Earn my keep around this place."

"I'll help."

"You'll need gloves," said Jeremiah, rising. "I've got an extra pair."

MARCH 17, 1996

FROM THE JOURNALS OF MARTHA MACGREGOR

I am trying to persuade Colin to do something about fixing the church. It is really going to ruin, I tell him, rack and ruin. The roof leaks in places, and the broken window was repaired with boards that had been stored underneath Dob's porch for who knows how long. They were rotten and logged with sea water, yet these were the boards that were nailed up there. I tell Colin there was a time on this island when people gave of their very best to the church. If a call came out for wood for repair, or fabric for draping, people took their hard-earned money and bought highest quality fabric and the best grade of lumber. Now, it seems just any old thing will do. When I tell Colin this he just looks at me and says, Well, times have changed.

I remember the day that window broke. A group of boys from the mainland decided to come over and see what trouble they could make. They thought that throwing rocks at the church was great fun. Naomi and Zoe were in there alone at the time. I know Naomi was frightened even though she told me later that she and Zoe were fine. Jules is much more watchful now of who comes and goes on the ferry.

Now, it's the roof that is giving the problems. It leaks, but Colin won't lift a finger to fix it. The old church is falling down around him, and he does not care. I'm being too hard on him, I know. And maybe I shouldn't be. If I were the one to have lived his life, would I be doing things any differently? Maybe not.

THIRTY-THREE

NAOMI KNEW WHERE TO FIND HIM. She was pulling a wagon with a small cardboard box balanced on the front. In it was a jar of hot soup, a thermos of coffee, and a loaf of dark bread with homemade preserves. Zoe sat in the back, her arms around the box, chattering as she was pulled along the pathway by her mother.

It was the day after the rain, the day after Philip had thrown his things hastily into his beat up duffle bag, looking at her sadly, telling her that he truly loved her, he honestly did, and how it grieved him to leave them again. But he had to get down to New Jersey, had to find out what happened with the job. He also had to cancel the apartment down there. He had made a down payment on a washer and dryer which he also had to cancel. He had to do those things in person. That's why he had to leave.

She had cried. She had begged him to take her with him, calling after him, desperate, not caring that the rain was drenching her, drenching them both. She had grabbed for him and had held onto his jacket. And then he had turned and looked at her sadly. Were those tears on his face or just the rain? Then he did an odd thing. Out there in the rain, both standing in the mud, he put his arms around her and held her tightly until she stopped shaking. Then he stroked her hair, which hung in wet hanks down her back. "I have to leave now, Naomi. You have to let me go," he said. "But no matter what happens, I've always loved you. I will always remember you."

And then he had pulled away from her. She watched him climb into his truck. She watched him drive away, the tires making ruts in the mud. He did not look back. She stood for a long time in the rain, shivering, until she fell, kneeling in the mud, calling after him, until Jeremiah came out and put his arm around her and gently led her back inside. He had added a log to the woodstove, and it was warm.

He placed a thick towel around her shoulders, dried her long hair with another one. He dried off her arms, set her mud-spattered feet in a basin of warm water and sponged them clean. He gave her tea and sat with her while she stared out at the rain, hugging the teddy bear Philip had brought for Zoe, staring at the place where Philip's truck had been. All night Jeremiah sat with her until the dawn rose clear and bright and the rain was gone.

In the morning she told Jeremiah she would be all right now. That it usually took her just one night to be all right again. He said, "I know. But each time he leaves, Naomi, a little bit more of you dies."

Naomi had looked at him and remembered a time, not all that long ago, when it was Jeremiah who needed the comfort, and Naomi had been the one to make the tea.

"Mama, Mama, look!" Zoe was pointing at a little squirrel which ran across the path in front of them.

"Look at him! Yes. Isn't he pretty, Zoe?"

The path to Colin's boathouse was rutted with mud, and Naomi had to pull the wagon to the side of the path, straining and shoving.

She got no answer when she knocked at the large door to the boathouse, and she thought that maybe he wasn't here at all. She knocked again. When she received no answer, she opened the door and pulled the wagon inside.

"Colin," she called. Dim light filtered through the grimy windows, and shadows of boat parts, an engine block, parts of oars, and paint cans appeared as spectral ghosts. It was deathly still in the building and also very cold.

"Unca Colin," Zoe called loudly. "Unca Colin, where are you?"

"Shh," said Naomi. "Uncle Colin might be sleeping."

"I'm not." He was standing in the back of his boat and peered down at them from above. "What are you here for? What do you want?"

"I brought you some food."

"Is Philip gone now? Is that why you came?"

Naomi looked up at him. His hair was askew, wild, unwashed, and uncombed. Over a pair of mud-encrusted jeans, he wore a dirty, misshapen gray sweater which hung longer in the front than the back. "Philip's gone, right?"

"He left last night."

"And so now that Philip's gone you think you can come to me. Good old buddy, Colin." He wavered, lunged, and then righted himself, hanging onto the side of his boat.

"Colin, be careful. Are you okay?" she called.

"Never better."

"I just came to see if you were all right."

"And now that His Highness is gone, you can do that."

"The last time I was here, you said that anytime I needed to talk to you, I could come to see you. You said that."

"I must have been nuts. The salt water does that. Gets in your brain, makes it so you can't think. Rusts it out."

Zoe was running around, exclaiming at all the various pieces of machinery, the cans of paint.

"Get her out of here. It's unsafe for kids around here," he called, leaning dangerously over the edge of the boat pointing at the child. Naomi could see that he was holding a bottle of something in his other hand.

"Are you drunk, Colin?"

"Me? Drunk?" He staggered backward, fell onto the cabin floor with a thud and out of Naomi's sight.

"I brought coffee. I'll bring it up."

"I hate coffee," he yelled from above.

"Zoe, come on." She rounded up her daughter, placed her firmly back in the wagon, covered up the food and hot coffee, squinting away the tears as she did so.

Just as she was about to walk through the door, he called, "Wait." His voice was so desperate, so beseeching that it made her stop. "Come up."

She carried Zoe up the ladder to the cabin first. Then she went down and brought up the food. Zoe was sitting on one of the berths when she returned. Colin took the coffee that she poured and drank two full cups before anyone, including Zoe, said anything. Then he wiped his mouth. "I'll come back to the church now. Now that Philip's gone."

Naomi was sitting on a wooden crate. Colin sat on a folding chair. Naomi could see where he had slept; a few blankets were hastily thrown against the wall. And a few bottles leaned against the wall, empty. A couple of paperback books.

"I'll come back now…"

"That's good. It's cold here."

"It's cold all over the world."

"Why do you hate him?"

"Who, Phil? I did some checking on him, Naomi."

"What do you mean, checking?"

"I have a friend in Bangor who used to be a cop. He's an expert in finding people; that's his specialty." He was talking more coherently now. "I told him about Philip. I told him, 'There's this guy, Philip Friend, he visits his pretty wife a couple times a year, then he leaves, makes her life miserable. Besides the fact that she spends her life waiting for the creep.' Well, Chris runs the name Philip Friend through the magic machine and you know what he finds?"

Naomi held her breath.

"Nothing. A big fat zero. Philip Friend, my lady, is an upstanding member of the driving public. He's got a valid State of Maine driver's license. No previous record, not so much as a traffic ticket."

"I could have told you that," said Naomi.

"Except my friend Chris calls me back. There's one thing that gets my friend Chris a little concerned. At first he doesn't notice it, he says. Phil Friend's got no Social Security number. Zippo. Nothing. Now in these here United States one needs a Social Security number to get a job."

"But he sends me money."

"That's what I tell my friend." Colin was leaning forward, his hands on his knees, staring at her. He blinked several times. "I says to him, I say, 'this wonderful husband, he sends his good wife the princely sum of fifty dollars a week, so where does he get that money if he doesn't have a job?'"

"He works for cash. Odd jobs," said Naomi.

"Even for odd jobs people need Social Security numbers. It's sort of the law. And so, of course, without a Social Security number our friend Philip Friend has never filed an income tax return in his entire life. Curiouser and curiouser." Colin was shaking his head.

Naomi stared at him.

"I say to my friend, I say, 'Chris, how is it that someone never files an income tax thingy in his entire life and gets away with it? Isn't that something that all upstanding members of our great U.S. of A. are required to do on a more or less regular basis?' And my friend says that he's turned his name and driver's license over to the police. The ball's in their court, now. 'It could be something simple,' that's what my friend says to me. Just a clerical error, something like that. Sometimes this happens, and then it turns out that he did file taxes, maybe just he uses his middle name or initial or something. A clerical error."

"That's probably what it was."

"I also called that Margot's Designs in Vermont, the place where you got your coat."

"Why?"

"I wanted to see why Phil got so crazy about that coat."

"He gets like that sometimes. Little things set him off." A picture of Philip scrabbling in the dirt beside the creek came to her then, looking for the label. She pushed it from her mind.

"I talked to some lady who works at the shop, one of the owners. She says she's never heard of Philip Friend. This Margot person was away, but I asked her to please ask Margot if the name Philip Friend meant anything to her. I called her back yesterday, and lo and behold,

Margot Douglas has never heard of Philip Friend either."

"Why are you doing all this?" Naomi asked.

"Because I don't trust the gentleman. Never have. Never will."

"Philip and I understand each other. He's not a settled sort of person. I am, and that makes our marriage difficult."

"Marriage? You call what you and Philly have a marriage? I was married once, and what you have, my dear, is not a marriage. I don't care what you say about how wonderful your Phil is, you don't just leave a wife and daughter for months at a time and then come home expecting to be welcomed with open arms. Which you apparently do. Every time."

She looked at him. "You were married?"

"Did I say that?" He looked past her then, at the remnants of the bread and preserves on the counter, at Zoe, sitting quietly on the floor, playing with the fringe on Colin's blanket. "Forget I said it. It's ancient history."

"I never knew you were married."

"I said it was ancient history. Thanks for the coffee. And this bread is up to its usual standards, I must say."

"Thank you."

"Now, I think I'll just gather my belongings together and get them to the church. I see you still aren't wearing your wedding ring."

Naomi rubbed her ring finger. "I can't find it anywhere. I've been over the place a hundred times."

"It'll show up. Your feet are muddy, by the way. If you're not going to talk to Jules about getting you some boots, then I will."

THIRTY-FOUR

PHILIP LEFT. JULES KNEW IT WAS FOR GOOD when the man kept his eyes averted on the ferry. Normally Philip chatted on the way over, laughing and joking, arms slapping Jules across the back as if they were old friends. Philip had done this a few days ago when he, with Zoe buckled into the passenger seat, had driven cheerfully onto the ferry. After he had ferried him across, Jules scribbled a quick note, "Getting the mail, back at 2," and tacked it onto the terminal building. Then staying at a discreet distance, he had tailed Philip to a phone booth where, holding Zoe in his arms, Philip made a call. Jules sat on a bench behind the booth facing away from Philip. He bent forward and threw bread crumbs to the pigeons while he strained to hear, "Yes, I'll be back soon, just…a few details here…Yeah…Great…looking forward to it."

Next Jules followed him to the post office where he mailed a small package wrapped in plain brown paper. He couldn't read the address from where he stood behind the door. Then, Philip drove past a bank machine where he withdrew a stack of bills. From where Jules stood, it looked like a lot. Then they went to an outdoor ice-cream stand where Philip bought two ice-cream cones. When Philip headed back down the ferry road, Jules took a shortcut through the brush and got there ahead of him.

A few things struck Jules as odd. First, Philip could have given Jules the package to mail. Everyone else on the island did that. Second, he could have used the pay phone on the island. That's also what everyone else did. Third, Naomi said Philip was checking on that job in New Jersey. Well, it sure didn't sound like that from where he sat. And fourth, why did Philip have to take out all that money? Was it for Naomi? And where did he get all that money in the first place?

Jules squinted his eyes as he piloted the ferry across the channel. Something, too, was odd about Philip's demeanor that day on the mainland. The way he looked over his shoulder several times before making his phone call, in line at the post office. Jules began to get the idea that Zoe was brought along for show while Philip went about his nefarious business. Was Philip working for Peter? Were they in cahoots?

Later, as Jules sat in his cabin working on his *Book of Philip,* Colin rapped on his window and then walked in.

"Jules."

"Hello, Colin." Jules closed his scrapbooks. "You need something? You need to go across?"

"Naomi needs boots."

"Yeah?"

"She's barefoot."

"Yeah, so why doesn't Philip buy her some? He's got the money. Lots of it. Tons of it."

"The guy's a bum. She says you sometimes get her boots from the mainland." Colin counted out some bills and handed them to Jules. "Here, you know her size, right? Get her some boots next time you head into town."

"Will do."

Colin was sidling up to the table looking with great interest at the *Book of Philip.* "What's this?"

"Part of my collection."

"You have books on everyone, don't you?" He had already picked up the *Book of Philip* and was flipping through it. "There's not much here."

"I know."

"Mostly stuff you've written yourself." Colin looked up. "You followed him? You actually followed him? Like a detective?"

"I guess, yeah."

"Why?"

Jules shrugged. "I didn't have much in his book. I needed to figure him out."

"Why do you need to figure him out?"

Jules shrugged again. "It's what I like to do."

"You follow everyone?" Colin stared at him.

"Nope." Jules took the scrapbook and placed it on the pile. "I just happened to be in town and there he was."

Colin sat down and placed his hands palms down on the table and regarded Jules. "You got scrapbooks like this on everyone around here?"

"Everyone," said Jules proudly. "Philip, you, Jo. I also collect stories, all kinds of things. It's my hobby. Here." He reached for a scrapbook. "These are my favorite crime stories of all time."

But Colin didn't even glance at them. He said quietly, "Do you have one on...Andrea?"

"Somewhere I do, yeah."

"Can I have it?"

"Why?"

"I'd like it, that's all."

"What would you do with it if I gave it to you?"

Colin looked him square in the face. "I would burn it. I would burn the entire thing without reading it. That's what I would do if I had it."

"Then, Colin, I can't let you have it."

Colin got up and walked out the door.

After he left, Jules dug in the layers of scrapbooks until he found the *Book of Andrea* and began leafing through it page by page.

THIRTY-FIVE

MARGOT SAT ON HER MOTEL BED leaning against the headboard, knees up, sketch pad on her lap. In front of her CNN, the volume muted, flickered its images into the room. She looked at her watch and picked up the phone. Paul didn't answer his cellular. She did a quick calculation, five in the evening in California. Maybe he was enjoying predinner drinks in some hotel. With Miss Computer Bimbo in a skinny black dress. She shut her eyes.

She called Jane then and found out that things were going well. The Christmas rush hadn't started yet, but the fall sewing classes were well underway, including the new quilting one that Jane was giving. A few customers were wondering when Margot was coming back.

"Mrs. Penney wants you to make her a new coat for winter. I said I'd check with you regarding your time. She wants a cape sort of affair, the kind you wear."

One part of Margot listened and said, yes, yes, fine, while another part wondered where Paul was.

"Oh, and that mysterious caller called back. So I told him you've never heard of Philip Friend."

"You didn't get his name this time, did you?" asked Margot.

"Still wouldn't give it."

"Jane, if you have time, could you start looking through all our files, people on the mailing lists, suppliers, what have you, and see if you can find the name Philip Friend? That's if you get to a place where it's not too busy."

"Dream on."

"I met Jo's mother and foster father."

"You what? You went down there?"

"Yep."

"What are they like?"

Margot told her. "I'm still trying to find that locket, you know. I'm thinking, crazy as it is, of driving up to Plattsburgh."

"What's in Plattsburgh?"

"That's where the Jameses live, the place Jo went after she stayed with me."

"You're actually going to drive all the way over there? Margot, you're insane."

"I know."

Next she called her sister and spoke with her daughters. Sara asked when she was coming home.

"Soon," said Margot. "I hope you're behaving for Aunt Heather."

"We are. We're helping with the baby. She told us we can come and stay any time."

They talked about school, about homework, about friends and permission slips and school trips. Finally, Margot said, "I want to ask you a question, and I want you to think very hard when I ask it. Have you ever heard of anyone named Philip Friend?"

"Who's he?"

"You've never heard of him? He's not a teacher or anything at your school?"

"Nope. Am I supposed to or something?"

"No."

She asked the same thing of Pammy, who, like her sister, had never heard of him either. Then Margot asked to speak to Heather.

Heather was Margot's younger sister, seven years younger, and had a new baby. Her twins often spent time there, especially if Paul was away and Margot was working late. Heather, too, had never heard of Philip Friend.

"Who is he, an old boyfriend?"

"I'm serious about this, Heather. Have you ever heard that name before?"

"No, I haven't. Why do you ask? And what's with the solemn tone of voice?"

184

"While I was away some mysterious person called Jane and wanted to know if I knew Philip Friend. And then I got to thinking—something about the name is so familiar, I just can't put my finger on it. I know I've heard of him, but I can't place it."

Heather started humming the *Twilight Zone* theme.

"Heather, I'm serious."

"You want me to get Jared to look into it?" Heather's husband was on the local police force.

"You're making fun of me. And yes, I would like Jared to look into it. That would be exactly what I want."

"Does Paul know this Philip person?"

"Paul's never heard of him either. Will you ask Jared?"

"Here, ask him yourself."

Margot explained the entire thing to her brother-in-law all over again. While she talked she could picture Jared rolling his eyes and giving looks to Heather. Margot persisted, nonetheless. Finally, he said he'd run the name through a few of their channels. "And by the way," Jared concluded, "when you're talking to Paul, tell him that all of us miss him at men's Bible study."

"Oh, he'll be back in a couple of days. He wouldn't miss it."

Jared was silent. Then he said, "Margot, Paul hasn't come since before spring."

"What?" Margot stared at the muted CNN. A picture of the White House. Someone talking. A press conference.

"Not before February. I think it was then he quit coming."

"He always goes to work so early anyway, I was just assuming that he was going to that morning Bible study. But he's been awfully busy. I guess we just don't keep tabs on each other."

"Yeah well, you tell him we miss him. All of us do. We've been praying for him."

"Thanks, Jared. I will."

She hung up and stared at the television. On her bedside table was the book she had just bought by the author of the magazine article on adultery. So far she hadn't even cracked the cover. It couldn't be true, she thought, yet she kept coming up against these little lies. She tried to think back. Both of them got up every morning at six-thirty. He showered first, then it was her turn. By the time she got out of the shower, he was usually gone. No breakfast at home, no coffee. He'd grab something on the way, he always said. Then she would wake the girls up and the day would begin. But on Fridays, the day of the early morning men's Bible study, he rose at six and was out the door before she even got up. *Don't want to miss the Bible study*, he always said.

She sat on the bed hugging her knees and rocking back and forth. They were so far away from each other all the time, emotionally, spiritually, physically. *Sex and intimacy are the glue that keeps a marriage together.* That's what the article had said. Six months, she thought. That wasn't normal, was it? *Too tired*, he would always say. Yet he never seemed tired. He would take his daughters out to Dairy Queen while she stayed at home. *Too busy*, he would also say, *too much on my mind.* Yeah? What's her name?

He came to church with her, he always did that, but she had the feeling that he came only because of her. It was Margot, not Paul, who said grace with the girls every morning at breakfast. It was Margot, not Paul, who tucked them in every night with a prayer and had done so since they were toddlers.

She lay back and stared at the ceiling, hugging the faded maroon bedspread to her face, keeping it near her wet eyes until she fell asleep. She woke, suddenly frightened. She sat up and pressed cold fingers to her cheeks. This was not like her. She was the practical one, the one that took charge. The successful one. Then why was she feeling such fear?

Frantically she reached for the light on the bedside table. What had she been dreaming? What had made her so afraid? The name Philip Friend kept invading her mind. Someone was in danger. Was it Paul?

Paul answered his cellular on the first ring. She could hear the sounds of traffic in the distance.

"Paul," she said, trying to keep her voice even. "I just woke up so afraid. I needed to hear that you're all right."

"I'm fine. Just got out of a meeting. Can you believe the marathon meetings they're putting us through? I'm in a cab now, heading back to the hotel. Gotta get some shut-eye."

"I woke up afraid." It sounded silly, she knew it did.

"Bad dream?"

"I guess so."

"Are the girls okay?"

She ran her hand through her short hair. "Uh, yes. Fine. I'm not home from New York yet."

"I thought you'd be home by now."

"I took a detour. Went down and paid a sympathy call to Jo's mother in New Jersey."

"What did you do that for?"

"I don't know. I was in the neighborhood. Maybe meeting Jo's mother and the fatigue and driving's giving me these crazy thoughts."

"That's probably it."

"It's just that I got to thinking about Philip Friend. And I had a bad dream, and I think it had to do with that man."

"What man?"

"Philip Friend. I just told you."

"You met him? You know him? I thought you said you didn't know who he was."

"I keep thinking about him."

"Sounds like you're overtired. I wish you would've waited until I got home. We could've gone to New York together. I hate the thought of you facing all that traffic on your—Hey watch out, buddy! Where'd you learn to drive, preschool?—Sorry, hon, some idiot nearly ran me off the road here. The traffic's insane this time of night."

Later, when Margot was drifting off to sleep, something played at the corner of her mind, some little detail missed, something wrong with this picture....

It wasn't until the following morning as she sat in the motel cafe, sipping coffee and tearing apart a blueberry muffin, that she figured out what. She was thinking about this and gazing out of the window watching a cab drive by when she knew. She frowned, twisting her wedding ring, not even noticing the middle-aged waitress who had sat down across from her, her pink uniform strained across her ample bust.

"You okay there?"

"What?" Margot looked up. "Oh yeah, just jim dandy."

"You want more coffee?"

"Yes, please." But the waitress made no move to get up.

"Man troubles?"

Margot looked at her

"That book." The waitress whose name tag read Erma, pointed to the book Margot had bought and intended to read over breakfast. "I read that one too. Saw her on a talk show. *Oprah* I think. She's good."

"I think my husband's having an affair," said Margot suddenly.

"Let me tell you something. No man is worth that kind of grief. You take my advice, you walk out on him before he walks out on you. You look like a smart woman. You want sugar with that coffee?"

"No, I take it just with cream."

"That's how I should take it. Sugar puts on the pounds. Me, I like three sugars. But let me tell you what I done. My man stepped out on me one time too many so I dumped all his clothes on the front lawn and changed the locks on all the doors. I saw that on a movie once. It worked."

Margot smiled.

"You shoulda seen him, knocking on the front door, screaming and swearing at me. I called the cops on him too."

Erma looked toward the kitchen. "Gotta go. Boss is giving me the eye. But I want you to think about what I said...no man is worth that much grief."

"Thanks."

"By the way, that's a nice cape thing you're wearing. Where'd you get it?"

"I made it. I'm a dress designer."

"There, smart lady like you, you tell that bum of yours to shape up or ship out. They should get you to make us some new uniforms. Look at these things they make us wear. One spill of coffee you got to wash it." Erma put her hand on Margot's shoulder. "You're gonna make it. I got a feeling about you. Now, I'll get you that sugar."

"I don't want sugar..." But Erma had already bustled away.

FEBRUARY 21, 1997

FROM THE JOURNALS OF MARTHA MACGREGOR

There is another person living in the church now. Naomi tells me his name is Jeremiah; he is a minister, and he spends his days reading through the old books that Colin and I packed in boxes years ago. Well, I am glad, at least, that someone is getting use out of them. He was there when I visited Naomi today. He has been here for about two weeks, but this was the first time I'd seen him.

Jeremiah has seen a lot of trouble, Naomi said as she fixed tea. Through the window I watched him chopping wood. Chopping wood is good, I told her. It's good for the body, good for the soul. As I age, patterns become important to me. The tides and the season, the rhythm of wood being chopped. It's almost meditative, I told her. She smiled and nodded. We both have done our share of wood chopping.

Jeremiah is a tad taller than Colin, and where Colin's hair is fine and straight, like feathers, this man's is thick, bushy, and curls around his ears. His hair is completely gray, as gray as mine, and his beard is woolly, though not as gray as his hair. He was wearing a flannel shirt today and looked like a logger, and I asked Naomi how she knows that he is a minister. Because he told me, she said. She spread peach jam on bread and said that when he came he didn't speak. Not for three days. She found him standing in the graveyard, unable to move, unable to speak. Just standing there, she said, looking around him wildly, staring at her with tears trembling down his face. When she told me that, I thought of the story in the Bible about the Man in the Tombs. Didn't that make you nervous? I asked. A strange man in the cemetery, glaring at you. She shook her head. He wasn't glaring, she said. He was in pain.

When she walked over to him, he lunged at her. I was stunned when she told me this! Weren't you frightened then, Naomi? But she still shook her head and looked at me with that sad, wistful look of hers, like a Madonna. She said that when he grabbed her, she used all her strength and held onto him tightly and walked him to this room. She helped him lie down, and he lay on that cot over there, the one Zoe usually sleeps on. She washed his face and hair and covered him with a blanket. Sometimes he would get up and wander around outside, but he said nothing, not one word for three days. She talked to him, and she and Zoe read to him from Colin's books. On the third day he told her he was a minister.

After he chopped the wood today he came inside, helped himself to tea, and sat with us. He is one of those rare individuals who listens more than he speaks. But I have a feeling this isn't something innate, but a thing learned through much trouble.

THIRTY-SIX

Because she arrived in Plattsburgh in the middle of the day, Margot decided to drive to the medical clinic where the James couple worked. She found the address of the clinic in a gas station phone book, and then realizing that she had no idea where the address was, she had to wait in line to ask for directions. She stood behind a portly man who, in addition to purchasing gas, also bought two large bags of chips, two cappuccinos, four candy bars, and a quart of chocolate milk. He counted out change in his pawlike fingers and wasn't satisfied until he had dug in his pockets for the exact change.

When it was her turn, she bought a pack of gum and asked for directions to the clinic.

"You don't want to go there," the fellow behind the counter said. "It's not in the best of neighborhoods."

"I've got to go there."

"Well, all I can say is, lock your car."

"I will."

The West Country Walk-In Medical Clinic was located in a neighborhood of run-down tenement buildings where old men sat on stoops in their undershirts, where children played stick ball in the street, and where drugs and prostitution were dispensed on the corner. Margot made sure her doors were locked as she drove around and around the block looking for a place to park. She ended up driving several blocks out of her way before she saw the sign with the big finger pointing to Clinic Parking Only.

Inside, the waiting room was overfilled with pregnant mothers, babies, toys on the floor, and old people hunched in their seats, eyes forward, staring at nothing. In a corner of the room a small television was tuned to a soap opera. Posters on the walls announced the next sessions of prenatal or stop smoking classes, urged patients to practice safe sex and say no to drugs. Margot announced her presence at the desk and said she didn't have an appointment, but would Dr. Kimberly James be able to see her for just a minute or two? It wasn't a medical matter, but was a personal matter having to do with a mutual friend. She also said that had she known how busy the place was, she would have phoned ahead.

The girl behind the counter, a dark-haired, dark-skinned girl with smooth skin was strikingly beautiful. She brushed a stray hair away from her face, smiled widely and said, "This is nothing. You should see it some days!"

Margot found the only available seat, between a nursing mother and a skinny man who kept sneezing. Margot found a two-year-old *Woman's Day* and began leafing through it.

Forty-five minutes later her name was called, and Margot was ushered into a tiny examination room. A few minutes later a young pretty woman in a white smock opened the door. Margot recognized Kimberly James from the pictures she'd seen on the news. Her medium length blond hair was tied back in a ponytail; she wore glasses, and had a stethoscope sticking out of her pocket.

"Lucia told me this was a personal rather than a medical matter?"

"Yes, I'm sorry to be bothering you like this, especially with the people waiting out there, but I've driven all the way up from New Jersey today to talk to you about Joanne Sypher."

Her eyes narrowed, the smile faded. "All the way up from New Jersey. I don't believe the lengths you reporters will go to! Randy and I have had our absolute fill of reporters and police and anyone else who may come along. We're just too busy to answer any more of your questions. We have our son back with us, and we just want to move on and be a family."

"I'm not a reporter. I'm not a cop. I'm not a private detective. I'm not a writer of true crime books. I'm a dress designer from Vermont. Jo worked for me for a couple of months last year. I was in New York City on business and decided to drive over to see her parents. Jo took with her a valuable piece of jewelry of mine when she left, and I would dearly like to find it."

"Did you go to the police about that?"

"No, not yet."

"Well, I should think that would be the place to start." Her pony-tail bobbed as she talked.

"Oh, I know you're right. I just thought there may be a chance she left it with you."

Kimberly moved toward the door and leaned against an antidrug poster. She said, "I've got a box of Jo's stuff. The police've already been through it. Randy thinks I'm crazy for not trashing it a long time ago. I don't remember a locket being there, but if you want to come over later I could let you have a look."

"Thank you."

"So she stole from you too?"

Margot nodded.

"Join the club. She took money and all kinds of things, not to mention our son. Randy and I thought Jo was the best thing to come into our lives. I mean, Randy and I both work here, and we aren't exactly your Hollywood plastic surgeons. We barely make a living. There was no way we could afford a nanny. When Jo came along, said she just wanted the experience, that she'd just work for room and board, we agreed." Her voice lowered. "We had no idea that Jo was the biological mother, and I'm sure you know that if you've talked to her parents or her foster parents."

"I'm so sorry. This whole ordeal must've been terrible for you."

"It was. Still is."

"What time should I come and look at that stuff?"

Kimberly looked at her watch, a large man's watch that she wore on her left wrist. "Theoretically the clinic closes at five-thirty, but we're seldom able to get out of here before six-thirty. Why don't you come over, say around seven-thirty?"

Margot got directions to the house and left, pleased that her car was still in one piece when she got to it.

THIRTY-SEVEN

PETER AND JEREMIAH WERE SITTING SIDE BY SIDE at Walt's lunch counter. Jeremiah was drinking his coffee, but Peter, who had asked for iced tea, had left it untouched. Instead, he kept twisting the tassel of his hat which lay in his lap. A number of regulars were sitting at the counter. Martha was there, along with Dob, the man he had met with Colin. A few others rounded out the lunch counter, and even more were in the store, filling their baskets with cans of soup, coffee, and boxes of cereal. The coffee shop talk seemed centered around a tanker from Newfoundland which was taking on water out in the Atlantic. The search and rescue from Portland had recently been dispatched, someone said, but the seas out there were high, what with the hurricane that just went through.

And then someone else said that wouldn't it be something if the murderer had escaped to this tanker, only to have it go down? That would be justice, someone else said. A woman who was digging out bills to pay for her purchases at the counter said, That's stupid, how would he get out there? A man in a torn yellow slicker said he could have stolen an old fishing boat or something and gone out there. In these seas? said another. He would have to be insane. Someone else argued that a guy who could kill someone and not get caught could do just about anything. Others said that no boats were missing, were they? And then they went through the list of known boats, and no, no one knew of any missing boats. If someone had stolen a boat, it would have been noticed. Then Martha said she wasn't altogether happy with the way the police had conducted the investigation in the first place. They were here just a short time, and then they left. Asked questions. Kept them all in the dark. Still keeping them all in the dark, as far as she was concerned. Walt poured her more coffee, slopped some on the table. A man Peter didn't recognize said that the killer was probably long gone by now, and that if he were the killer, he sure as heck wouldn't be sticking around. Walt said he was sure the murderer was still on the island. Hiding out. A few nodded their heads.

Walt cracked an egg on the grill and stared intently at Peter. "The police may not have found the killer, but island justice is something else. Sam here'll tell you just how protective we are of each other's traps. You tell him, Sam. We may not have known Jo very well, she may have been from away, but I'll tell you one thing—we would rather have ten strangers from away than one murderer walking around free."

He was still staring straight at Peter, who was nervously stirring spoonfuls of sugar into his glass.

Jeremiah, who had been quiet during the exchange, leaned forward now and said, "There's something Peter and I want to know. Have any of you seen any strangers through here lately?"

"What kind of strangers?" asked the yellow-slickered man.

"Men in suits. One of them may have been bald," said Peter.

"Peter and I think we know who killed Jo," said Jeremiah. "Or rather Peter does."

"I'll just bet he does." This was said by Dob.

"And if you would all try to remember if you saw some strangers through here," added Jeremiah.

Martha turned to Jeremiah. "What are you saying? That you think you know who killed Jo?"

"It's only an idea," said Peter.

"A theory," added Jeremiah.

The men looked at Peter, then looked at each other and shook their heads and said, no they hadn't seen anyone strange on the island. A lady who was paying for Cheerios and baby food said it was only her opinion, but everyone who lived on the island should have to take a lie detector test. Lenny said he heard that they didn't work all that well and that true criminals could get their minds to think about other things and that innocent people, because they were so nervous could sometimes get the machines to say that they were guilty. That was a fact; he read it some place. And Martha said, And how would everyone on the island like their dirty laundry hung out for all to see? She could think of a few things to ask every one of them sitting around the counter here. Think about that for a minute.

"But we need to only ask one question," Walt said, "only one question. Did you kill that girl. It's as simple as that."

Peter was still twisting the tassel of his hat when Mary rushed in with the news that Jules's cabin was on fire.

They left then, all of them running, including Walt, who turned the stove off and placed the CLOSED sign on the door. Rushing westward they smelled smoke, saw smoke, and every once in a while a lick of flame above the tree tops. They forgot about their previous conversation, and three and four abreast on the narrow path, they made their way toward Jules's cabin.

"Is Jules all right?" someone asked.

"We're pretty sure," another replied. "The ferry's on the other side. Someone said he's up in town."

"He may not even know about it yet."

"Place went up like a tinderbox. One minute it was standing there, and the next, flames were shooting out the windows."

"Well, no wonder. You know what he keeps there—them stacks of papers. Sky high."

"It's a wonder we didn't lose this place sooner."

"I told him the last time I seen him, I told him he was settin' on a disaster."

"You know him. Stubborn as an old coot, there's no mistaking."

"Don't know why he didn't clean out that place once in a while."

As they neared the ferry terminal, the smell of fire grew hotter, more pungent in their nostrils. The air was dense with heat and noise. It seemed the entire town was there with shovels and buckets and opinions.

Jules's cabin was completely consumed. Occasionally, a fire blown newspaper would fly up like a misguided paper airplane and land on the ground. Someone handed Peter a shovel and he got to work helping to dig a trench in the soft pine needles and earth around the cabin. Others were filling it with buckets of water. The noise was deafening.

"Good thing we had that rain," someone yelled.

"Yeah, but she's still pretty dry out there. And the wind, that's not going to help us one bit."

He looked up briefly and across the channel could see a waiting tanker with two firefighters in full dress, frantically waving. But there stood the ferry. And Jules up in town.

The islanders ignored the ferry and the truck and did their own thing. Down at the ferry loading ramp, those with trucks filled barrel after barrel with water, and then drove them up to the fire and filled the trenches with sea water. The salt burned on Peter's skin where it was red and hot from the flames. He kept digging, barely looking up.

Somewhere along the way, although Peter had no knowledge of how long any of them had been there, Jules came back. The tanker arrived and doused the rest of the cabin, which was now a black mass of charred and smoking shapes.

Peter saw Jules sitting on a log outside of his home. He was still sitting there when the majority of islanders, dirty and spent, drove or walked home. He was still there when Peter and Jeremiah, filthy, muscles aching, faces black with soot and smoke, bodies drenched with sea water, took off down the path toward the church.

THIRTY-EIGHT

Margot spent the rest of the afternoon wandering around the shops and side streets. She found several boutiques of the kind that carried the style of clothing she designed, and she showed them her pocket photo album of her designs that she always carried, talked to a few managers, and left a few business cards. The time was not completely wasted. At five-thirty she walked into a big bookstore and bought a book on fashion through the ages that she saw on a sale table in the front and sat reading it in the coffee shop until seven-fifteen.

Kimberly and Randolph James lived in a comfortable looking ranch home on a corner lot in a neighborhood of other homes that looked just like it. She was met at the door by Kimberly who had changed from her smock and skirt to a pair of jeans and a pink sweatshirt.

"Come in," she said opening the door. "Just so long as you promise that you didn't lie about not being a reporter."

"I promise."

"For a while they were camping out with their vans right in our driveway. It was so upsetting, especially to Randy."

"I'm not a reporter."

"Good. I have to tell you that Randy was kind of upset with me for inviting you. I should've checked with him first. This has been harder on him than it has been on me." She lowered her voice. "Because of the police."

Kimberly took Margot's cape, hung it on a wooden coat tree beside the door, and invited her into the front room. The room looked clean but oddly barren, as if its occupants had just moved in and were waiting for their furniture to arrive. A few small throw rugs were scattered on the pale hardwood floors. The only places to sit were a small loveseat and an armchair. Both looked new. There was no television, stereo, and no artwork on the walls. In one corner was a baby swing, a blanket, and a few colorful toys in a plastic laundry basket.

"Come in. You might as well have a seat. I'll go get that box."

"This is a very nice house. Have you lived here long?" Margot asked.

"About five years. Ever since we moved back from Africa and took on the practice."

"Africa?"

"My husband and I worked for a year at a refugee camp in Africa. The pay was nonexistent, but the rewards were tremendous. When we came home, neither one of us could see ourselves fitting into the lifestyle of the doctors for the rich and famous, so we came to work in the inner city." She smiled. "The pay's still nonexistent, but the rewards, while I wouldn't say they are tremendous, I would say they're there. It gets tiring though." Kimberly's brow furrowed. "And three times this month alone we've been broken into. People looking for drugs. They all get locked in the safe at night, but we still get broken into."

"You must be very dedicated."

Kimberly stood by the door, one long arm on the doorjamb. "Someone's got to do it."

A tall, slender dark-haired man emerged from the back of the house and levelled his eyes at Margot. A more disparate couple, Margot had never seen. Kimberly with her bouncy blond cheerleader looks and this man who looked as though he could fit the description of every villain in every movie.

"So, you're the one who wants to look through Jo's things?" he said.

"Margot, this is my husband, Randy. Randy, this is Margot Douglas."

"Nice to meet you," Margot said.

"So, she stole from you too? I understand you're looking for a necklace."

"That's right."

Kimberly turned to her husband. "How's Godfrey?"

"Sleeping like a baby. I just put him down." He turned back to Margot. "What did Jo do for you? Was she your nanny too?"

"No. I own a fabric shop. She cleaned up, waited on customers. She was very good. People liked her."

Kimberly jumped up. "I forgot! Let me get that box."

Kimberly gone, Randy sat down in the armchair. There was a faintly bemused expression on his face. "Have a seat," he said motioning to the loveseat.

Margot sat down, arranging the folds of her dress around her.

Nothing was said until Kimberly returned with a cardboard box, which she plunked down in front of Margot. Margot began lifting up the various items that Jo had left behind. Something seemed so familiar about them, and once again Margot felt a pang for the dead girl. In it were a spiral bound notebook with blank pages, two T-shirts, a pair of earrings and other assorted pieces of jewelry, some photographs, more clothing, but no locket. And no coat, either.

"No, it doesn't seem to be here," she said.

"You wasted your time," said Randy. "Kim could have told you it wasn't in the box."

"Well, I couldn't be sure, Randy," said his wife. "And I had to be sure."

"I'm also looking for a coat," Margot said. "It's in shades of blue with a sunburst pattern on the back."

Kim looked up. "I've seen that coat. Jo used to wear it all the time. It was quite beautiful. I commented on it once, and she said a special friend had made it for her."

Margot sighed. "Not exactly true. I made it, but not for her. That's another thing she stole. It was part of my fall collection that I take around to stores. It happened to fit, so she took it, I guess."

Randy leaned forward, his arms resting on the chair, a dark lock of hair fell onto his forehead. "So Jo stole a coat and a necklace from you, but you can be thankful that she didn't steal your son."

"That must have been terrible for you."

Kimberly smoothed her hair behind her ears. "This is all so upsetting. What will Godfrey think when he's older, if he happens to come across all these horrible newspaper stories? None of this should have happened."

"It was a closed adoption," Randy said. "We were led to believe that the mother wanted absolutely nothing to do with the baby, and that she wouldn't come looking for him. We had that guarantee. Had it in writing. And so when Jo showed up looking for work we had no idea she was the baby's mother. It never even entered our minds."

Margot looked at them sadly.

"The police were absolutely sure I killed her, that I left all my patients in the waiting room and drove all the way over to Maine and killed her. I drive all the way to Maine, strangle Jo, leave her in the ocean, and then drive back without Godfrey. I mean, if Godfrey was the reason I drove over there to kill her, I wouldn't have left him in the care of some incompetent social worker. I tried to tell that to the police."

"Stop it, Randy!" said Kim. "Don't say those things!"

"I'm so sorry," said Margot. "I'm sorry that any of this happened." She rose, then paused. "I wanted to ask you one more thing before I go. Do either of you know anyone by the name of Philip Friend?"

Kim screwed up her eyes. "I don't know...the name's familiar. Wait a minute, I heard Jo speak of him. I remember that name. Do you remember that name, Randy? I'm sure Jo spoke of him."

Margot sat back down. "In what way? What did she say?"

"Let me think, something about trying to find him." She took a rubber band that was around her wrist and smoothed her hair back into a ponytail. "I'm sure of it. Yes, Philip Friend. I know that name."

Randy turned to Margot. "Who is Philip Friend?"

She shook her head. "I have no idea. I had a mysterious caller ask my business partner if we knew Philip Friend. I asked my husband, but Paul hadn't heard of him either. I thought for a long time that it had to be someone in his computer company."

Randy eyed her. "Is your husband by any chance Paul Douglas of East Coast Group Computers?"

"Yes," said Margot surprised. "You know him?"

"He installed our office software."

Margot stared at them. "What an absolutely amazing coincidence!"

"Not really," said Randy, "considering he's probably installed all the Medicaid-Medicare claims processing software in the entire northeast."

"He comes in every so often to service it," said Kimberly. "We're such luddites, we're constantly crashing it. But Paul's such a pro. One phone call and he's right here. A nice guy, too," said Kim "So helpful. Spends a lot of extra time with Lucia."

"I'm sure he does," said Margot evenly.

Later, in her hotel room, she dialed Paul's cellular and he surprised her by telling her that he had just gotten in and was wondering where she and the girls were.

"The girls are up at Heather's and Jared's."

"When will you be home?"

"Tomorrow."

"How was New York?"

"Fine."

"Great."

"You remember the people, the Jameses in New York, the ones whose baby Jo stole?"

"That whole thing still on your mind?"

"I got to thinking about them. Seems something's familiar about them. You ever run into the Jameses? In Plattsburgh, New York? Receptionist by the name of Lucia? Name ring a bell?"

"Nothing. Sorry. Wait a minute. Let me think. No, false alarm. They're doctors? I may have run into them with the business, but no, can't even be sure of that."

MARCH 1, 1998

FROM THE JOURNALS OF MARTHA MACGREGOR

There is a darkness in Colin now, an indefinable smudgy blackness around the edges of his soul. I try to talk to him about it, about the deep unhappiness I sense there, but he refuses to talk. He changes the subject. Martha, he says, I was thinking of repairing that back porch of yours. Do you want me to get started? So I sigh and say, Sure.

We used to be so close. All those weeks and months after Andrea died and he stayed at my place and slept on my couch, and we would talk far into the night about Andrea and Joe and grief and suffering and what it means. If anything.

I haven't gone down to see the Andrea C. in quite a while, but I think his depression has something to do with his boat. This sounds strange as I write it, because that boat has consumed him for such a very long time, has given him such joy in the past. About a month ago Bill told me the Andrea C. is nearly done. It's a beauty, too, he said shaking his head. A real beauty. Well, he's been working on it long enough.

Normally, it would take even an expert boat builder only a matter of a couple of years at most to restore a boat, but Colin has spent more than a decade on the Andrea C. Perhaps he is realizing that the end of this project is in sight. Perhaps Colin is reluctant to say good-bye to Andrea or the boat. Or here's another idea; maybe he's thinking that now that the boat is complete it will have to be launched. Have to be sailed. Maybe a part of him is reluctant for this to happen. I know that doesn't make sense, but that's what I think.

THIRTY-NINE

Jules was still sitting on the log when the firefighters came with their notebooks and asked him question after question. Where was his woodstove in relation to the stacks of paper? What about his lantern fuel? How about an electrical short? Why did he keep all that paper? How close was it all to the woodstove? When was the last time he cleaned the chimney?

He sat there watching them tromp through the rubble that was his house and was still sitting there when they came and told him the fire was most likely started when the stacks of paper closest to his stove overheated and ignited. Jules sat there when he met the replacement ferryman who came over from Bar Harbor. It will only be a day or two until you are on your feet again. That's what they told him.

No one even mentioned, no one even came close to what Jules knew was the truth. He knew that the fire was deliberately set. And he knew who did it. He had seen Colin turn the color of ash when he told him yesterday he had a scrapbook of articles about Andrea, that he still had them after all these years. *I would burn it. I would burn the entire thing without reading it.* His exact words.

Yesterday, after Colin left, Jules had dug out the thick *Book of Andrea* from the bottom of the stack beside the back door. He knew exactly where it was after all these years. The book began not with Andrea but with an announcement of her wedding engagement. There it was, submitted to the paper no doubt by Martha, who was very proud of her daughter. The edges of the paper crumbled in his fingers.

It was just an announcement; no pictures on this one. *Drs. Jonathan and Dierdre Workman along with Martha MacGregor are pleased to announce the engagement of their children Colin Charles Workman and Andrea Claudine MacGregor. April 13, 1971.*

Jules read the announcement again. He knew the story really began way before his first scrapbook entry, way before he even began keeping scrapbooks. Jules was just a young man himself then, only older than Colin by about ten years. That would have made Jules around eighteen when Colin first started coming over with his family. There was no ferry service then, so Jules had the job of ferrying the entire family over in his dory, all four of them, every summer. A few days later, their small trailer would arrive by barge. And there they would stay all summer, every summer, Colin, his sister, Sarah, and their parents.

Colin's parents were some sort of botanists, both professors at the university. Apparently the island had some unique vegetation that kept the professors coming back each summer. If he shut his eyes, Jules could still see them, the way they looked in their knee-length khaki shorts, hiking boots, wool socks, and safari hats, walking through the woods, notebooks in their hands, cameras around their necks. They always reminded Jules of some missionaries in the jungles of some African country, rather than university professors in Maine. They were careful to replace the flora and fauna exactly the way they found it, and they carried their garbage out. They didn't even burn much wood. This at a time when island residents burned every scrap of garbage they generated. The laws are stricter now, Jules thought.

The professors tried to coax the islanders to harness the power of the stream or the wind on the point or even the sun, but that kind of thing never caught on. Later, after they stopped coming, the two Drs. Workman were some of the biggest lobbyists for the preservation of the Maine coastline. Jules had saved some of those clippings. Essays and editorials written by the Workmans were pasted in the back of the *Book of Andrea* although they didn't really fit.

Right from the beginning, Colin was different. His interests didn't lie in the island's vegetation. While his parents and sister were busy wandering around the interior collecting data for their books and articles, Colin hung out down by the wharf and talked to the fishermen. His interest, it soon became apparent, was not in the lobsters or the fish caught, but in the boats themselves: how they were made, why that particular design over others, why that particular wood. When he was a teenager he spent most of his time down at Bill's. Sometimes at low tide, Jules would steer his dory over to Bill's and wander up to see what Colin and Bill were up to. Jules remembered being quite impressed with young Colin's work.

"Well, what do you think?" said Bill. "This lad shows promise, doesn't he."

Eventually this skill led to summer jobs for Colin: repairing hulls and decks and refinishing cabins. While the islanders merely tolerated the elder Workmans, never quite trusting them or the ideas they brought with them, Colin became one of them.

It was only a matter of time before the young Colin would notice Martha's raven-haired daughter, Andrea. Andrea had lived all of her life on the island and knew every inch of it, knew the tides and their currents as well as she knew her own name. By the time she was sixteen she had her own lobster traps and her own boat, which Colin helped to refinish. Her boat was originally a lobster boat circa 1920. Colin, with Bill's help, restored it to perfection and renamed it the *Andrea C.* despite Bill's protests that it retain its original name, *The Lucky Lady.*

"It's bad luck to change a boat's name," he said.

But Colin scoffed. "That's just an old wives tale and a stupid one at that. It's going to be called the *Andrea C.*"

No one could tell Colin anything in those days. You still can't, thought Jules.

Colin presented it to Andrea, and their friendship and romance grew.

For years Andrea and that boat were inseparable. She took chances with the sea, priding herself that she could make it through any storm, through any riptide. She took chances even seasoned lobstermen avoided. She seemed to revel in the rain, the wind, the waves washing over the bow. If Jules shut his eyes he could still see her, the way she looked standing there at the wheel, dark hair blown straight back, making her way expertly between the traps through the storms. She would arrive drenched but happy.

Jules turned a page in the scrapbook. Their wedding picture. There was an openness about Andrea's face, the ready laugh, her head thrown back. There was Colin with his long hair—the style of the day—and Andrea with her very long, straight dark hair underneath a halo of flowers, both of them descending the steps of the island church in the sunshine. That was back when the church was part of the life of the islanders, when islanders came for weddings, for baptisms, for funerals, for morning services and evening prayers, for Christmas Eve candlelight services, and Easter services. They also came for community meetings and school plays and summer stock theater. The bells rang back then. And often.

There were various other clippings grouped together on the next page, announcements of Jonathan Workman being awarded some prize at the University of Maine, of Dierdre Workman being acknowledged by the University Women for her work in the environment, of their daughter Sarah's fellowship to study anthropology in New Guinea. Jules wondered where she was now. Wiry little Sarah who traipsed behind her parents, as serious as they.

On another page was a picture of Colin, a smiling youthful-looking Colin accepting a position teaching boat building at the community college on the mainland. He had also started his own boat building venture and was working on a refined design for lobster boats, which he did when time allowed. Andrea kept her lobster traps and worked along with her husband. And every year for five summers they came back to the island, where Colin worked with Bill, and Andrea plied the bays for lobsters in the *Andrea C.*

It was getting chilly in the cabin. Jules got up, added more wood to the fire and turned the next page. It was so ironic that Andrea, who was never afraid of the sea, lost her final battle with it.

They said she was trying to free a caught lobster trap that had been pulled around to the bottom of the cliff, when the tide caught her. She thought she could race it. That's what they said at the inquest—that she could get in, get her trap, and then get back to the bay before the tide rushed in. She had done it before. She would have done it this time too were it not for a nor'easter which came up just at the wrong time. She was unprepared for it, and the boat jammed in against the rocks at the bottom of the cliff. All this while Colin and Martha looked down from above. The Coast Guard had to wait until low tide to free her body.

Jules turned another page. At about this same time, Colin was accused of rerouting some thirteen thousand dollars from the college budget into his own boat building business, which was flagging. At the least it was conflict of interest, at the worst it was embezzlement. It wasn't true, at least no one on the island believed it, but with Andrea's death, the fight had left him. Instead of staying and fighting, he declared bankruptcy and disappeared for two years.

So long ago. So many lives ago.

Jules had shut the scrapbook, placed it on the top of the pile, and headed off to bed.

FORTY

DURING THE FIRE NAOMI AND COLIN stayed at the church. Naomi was there because of Zoe. She didn't know why Colin didn't go out to help. When she asked him he said, "They have enough bodies out there without my help."

He had been reading from the selected works of Edgar Allan Poe when they rushed over frantically shouting "Fire!" He ignored them, barely looked at them when they stood in the entry of the church. When they left he leaned the back of his chair against the wall and continued his reading. Naomi went back to cleaning the stove, sifting the ashes into the bucket. She was really looking for her lost ring. If Colin knew what she was doing, he said nothing.

At one point he looked up from his book and said, "I've moved my things back into the church."

"You'll be warmer here."

"Is there enough wood?"

"I think so. Jeremiah and Peter got a lot chopped the other day."

"Maybe I should go out and chop some more." He gazed out into the gathering dusk.

She looked at him. He had washed his hair since the last time she had seen him, and it shimmered like silk ribbons in the light of the lantern. Hers needed washing again. So did Zoe's. Tomorrow she'd have to heat a tub on the stove. It would be back to that now.

"I hate it when winter drags on and on," she said.

"Yes." He got up. "I'll go chop some wood."

When he left, she placed another blanket on her sleeping daughter and gently stroked her face. Outside, Colin was chopping. She could hear him, the rhythmic sound of the axe, the wood being split, falling in mounds around his feet. She stared around the little room that was her home. The folding tables, the chairs, the two cots. The burlap at the windows nailed up irregularly in the corners, her canning in neat rows against one wall, the plastic bag of Zoe's clothing. The jackets hung on nails beside the entrance.

The day before Philip had driven off the island, he had come to Naomi wanting to know if she had found her ring yet. She didn't even want to face him. "No," she said quietly looking down at the floorboards.

"Naomi." He had looked near rage. "How can you be so careless with things?"

Maybe it was this that caused him to leave. Her carelessness. Maybe it was the dirtiness of the place. She tried to keep it clean, she honestly did, but with muddy boots and such, it was an impossible task. And her mind wound back to another picture: Philip, wearing a pair of thick, yellow rubber gloves, and washing. He had all the dishes down from the cupboard and was washing them in hot, sudsy water. When she asked what he was doing he said, "I come here, find my daughter not properly taken care of, plus every glass and dish in the cupboard crawling with germs, what else am I to do?" He also proceeded to wash down the walls, the doors, the windows, and the floor.

Maybe if she had been more careful, maybe if she had worked harder, made things nicer, kept Zoe cleaner, kept the dishes cleaner, made more homemade noodles, made more spaghetti sauce and bread, kept the floor swept and mopped, maybe then Philip would have stayed.

She walked over to the jackets and placed her hands in the pockets. She had done it a hundred times in the past few days, but she did it again, got down on her knees and reached under the woodstove. Her ring wasn't there. Of course it wasn't there. She had already looked there. She had already been through all of the pockets in every coat that hung there. Already, she had examined every piece of lining and had shaken them out on the floor. She had already looked through all of the packages of food, the bags of clothing, the bedding.

The only place she hadn't been was the sanctuary. She carried the lantern into that dark room. For a long while she stood at the front of the sanctuary. Three blanket mounds were set out; Jeremiah's at the front behind the railing, Peter's half way down the center on the right, and Colin's at the far back left. She went there. She didn't want to admit it, but a part of her thought that Colin may have taken it. She knew he had a deep hatred for her husband. What other reason could there be to check up on him?

She was running her hands over the tops of Colin's books. Then she moved the row of books away from the wall a few inches and ran her fingers behind them. No ring. Colin taking the ring made perfect sense. What better way to get Philip to leave than to take his wife's ring? Maybe he had done it just for that reason. She felt under his bedding, checked in the pockets of his shirts, and felt in and around the plastic bags of his clothing. No ring. In the corner at the left of his books, she saw a small wooden match box wedged into a crack in the wall. She pulled it out. When she opened it there was her ring! Colin had taken it! By the dim light of the lantern, however, she saw not one, but two rings. When she picked them up she realized hers was not one of them. They were gold.

"What are you doing?"

She looked up, startled. Colin stood above her, glaring down at her. Immediately she closed the box, attempted to shove it back into place. "I…I…"

He reached down and snatched the box away from her. "What were you doing in here?"

"Nothing." She wiped her hair away from her face, swallowed and stood up. "I'm sorry. I was looking for something, I was—"

Naomi had never seen him so angry. His eyes were screwed tight and his mouth set in a thin line. Tears threatened at his eyes, and he blinked them rapidly. "Why did you do this?" he demanded. "Why did you come here?"

"I don't know, Colin. I'm sorry. I truly am. I was…I was looking for my ring."

"Your ring. You were looking for your ring in my things."

"I'm sorry." She was rubbing her palms together.

"And you thought I would take that little worthless scrap of metal! That I would care enough about that worthless scrap of metal to steal. Oh, Naomi," his voice took on a softer tone. "Naomi, you are so deluded, so very, very deluded."

FORTY-ONE

THE COLD SALT WATER STUNG PETER'S HANDS, his head, his face as he cupped handfuls of it and poured it over his head. It was night, the fire had been quelled, and Peter and Jeremiah were down past the church at the water's edge washing the soot and smoke smell from their faces by the moonlight. Peter's hands were raw, and his muscles ached. His eyes stung, and he blinked them rapidly, wishing for a freshwater shower. Maybe tomorrow he would head over to Martha's for one. His jacket was covered with soot and lay beside him on a rock. He had shaken it out numerous times, and each time more ash fell to the ground. Yet, while every muscle in Peter's body felt exhausted and spent, Jeremiah seemed invigorated by the encounter with the fire and chatted while they drenched their heads with sea water.

"You ever been near a fire like that before?" Jeremiah asked, eyes bright.

"No. And I hope that's the last."

"Something, though, about fighting the forces of nature, wouldn't you say?"

Peter looked at him. "I guess."

"To fight the forces of nature and win, now that's another thing altogether."

"But we didn't win. The cabin burned to the ground."

"Precisely. But there's a certain energy that comes from at least trying. Staying and fighting, no matter what the odds."

Colin was chopping wood in the darkness when they arrived at the church. He barely looked up when they passed. Naomi was in the kitchen sweeping ashes from the floor. Neither she nor Colin spoke to them or asked about the fire. In the sanctuary, Jeremiah changed into a pair of jeans and went outside to hang his wool pants over the For Sale sign at the front. Wool was the worst, he said, for holding in the

215

smell of smoke. Peter hung his jacket on a nail outside the front door of the church.

He lay down on his mattress and, still smelling the stench of smoke in his nostrils, he dreamed of Jo and Jules and the fire. Jules was crying to him from the fire. And then it wasn't Jules, but Jo. He tried to save her, he tried to race right into the fire, but he couldn't. He couldn't breathe. He kept smelling smoke. Or he would arrive and his bucket would be empty. Or his feet were lead and he couldn't get there in time. She stayed, just inches beyond his reach, inches beyond help, calling for him.

Something woke him, and Peter lay in the darkness. He turned, lay on his side, and through the maze of pew legs he saw Colin sitting on his blankets, his back against the wall. Beside him, a small candle glowed. The light gave him a ghostly look. He was holding something in both hands. A small box. He kept it in his hands, not looking at it, just cradling it, eyes closed, head against the wall, entranced, as if he were meditating.

AUGUST 31, 1998

FROM THE JOURNALS OF MARTHA MACGREGOR

The church has opened its doors to another stray. That's how I think of it now, the church that we closed is now taking in people who need a place to stay. First there was Colin, then Naomi (and to a certain extent, her husband, Philip), then Jeremiah, and now a nineteen-year-old girl named Jo.

Naomi came across the pathway with Zoe on her wagon this morning, and we sat on the breakwater and she told me about Jo. Jo has brought her baby with her, Naomi said. Another baby! I am astonished. But we are fine, said Naomi laughing, and it's nice to have someone to talk to. And the children love each other; you should see Zoe with Kurt; he is such a dear. She tries feeding him with a little spoon, then wipes his face with a cloth. It's so cute.

At the mention of Kurt's name, Zoe's eyes brighten and she says, Kurt is my new baby friend. Naomi said, You need to come over for a visit, Martha. Jo is such a nice girl, and her baby is such a dear. I said I would, and does the baby need anything? And how will you manage? Two babies over the winter. We will be fine, Naomi assured me. I have managed with Zoe all these years; it's really not so bad. It's warm, and we have plenty of food and water. I never have to chop even a stick of firewood. Colin and Jeremiah take care of all of that.

Naomi's eyes were bright, and I saw a difference in her. It's good for you to have a friend, I said. I am thinking of Colin when I said this. His moods and his darkness. She needs to be with laughing people like Zoe and Jo and this baby Kurt.

FORTY-TWO

I WILL ALWAYS REMEMBER YOU. Why had Philip said those words to her? Those exact words? He could have said, *Until next time. I love you and I'll come back for you. I'll be back. I'll be back for you and Zoe. I promise. Next time will be different.* All of those things he had said on other occasions when he left. But he had never said, *I will always remember you.*

Naomi would wonder at the significance of those words when she stirred her sauces and soups, when she pulled out the last of the garden plants and smoothed over the earth against the coming winter, when she brought in armloads of firewood to stack neatly beside the stove. She would think about those words as she lay in her narrow cot at night, Zoe tucked into the crook of her arm, both of them covered with a gray wool blanket.

And now it was Saturday afternoon, and Naomi was thinking of those words as she pulled out the ingredients to make a batch of bread. Outside, Colin was chopping wood again, the rhythm a familiar song.

I will always remember you.

I will remember you. Will you remember me?

I will not forget you.

She listened to the chopping and tried very hard not to think about the fact that she hadn't received her usual Friday money from Philip. Every Friday afternoon for the past four years Jules had driven to the church with an envelope containing fifty dollars. Every Friday without fail. Friday at precisely noon, fifty dollars was deposited to her account. Jules, who had her ATM card, would withdraw it and bring it to her in one of the deposit envelopes they kept beside the bank machines. That pattern had not altered in all these years.

Until yesterday.

I will always remember you.

Earlier that morning, she had gone to see Jules. Naomi hadn't been down that path since the fire. For several minutes she stared at the charred remains, black and sodden with water.

"Hey, Naomi." Jules was walking up toward her from the ferry.

"Jules, I'm so sorry about your place. How awful."

"Yeah, well. Don't mind about the place going. It was just a place to hang my hat. Thing I can't replace is my scrapbooks. Gone. Finished. Years of work."

"That's too bad. "

"If you came to get your money, there wasn't any."

She stared at him. "There wasn't?"

"I was over yesterday right after lunch and the ATM machine said you had a zero balance in your account. I tried later. Still nothing. So I went in and checked with the tellers and such, and it turns out Philip hadn't made his deposit yet. I went over this morning, still nothing. But the bank's closed until Monday, so I have to wait until then to check. I'm thinking he couldn't get to a Western Union or a bank, maybe, to make that transfer. That's what I'm thinking. He could be working out in the bush somewheres, with that job in Jersey fallen through and all. There'll probably be something there on Monday. I wouldn't worry. I'll keep checking for you."

Naomi was folding and unfolding her hands. "I hate to trouble you with this. Especially now."

"Walt'll let you go on credit for a while."

"I don't like to do that."

"Everyone does, Naomi. You're the only one pays cash on this whole island."

"I know, but…"

"Phillip'll come through. He always does, right?"

"Maybe something happened to him."

"I wouldn't worry none about Philip. That fellow can get out of any jam there is."

Naomi looked around her. "Oh Jules, I'm so sorry for going on and on about Philip. Especially when you've got nowhere to live. Where are you staying now? There's room in the church."

Jules pointed toward the ferry. "Up there."

"On the ferry?"

"There's room. The pilothouse is dry and warm. Besides, then I'm right there if someone needs to go across." He chuckled.

"But you wouldn't have any place to heat anything or make tea."

"I got me an alcohol stove, and yesterday Sam brought me over a lobster, and Martha brought me over some beans and bread. I go over to Walt's if I want coffee. He's always got it on. I'm surviving."

"I'm going to make bread later. I'll bring you some tomorrow morning first thing. And some jam to go with it."

"Well, I can't refuse that, now can I?"

And so she had come home with no money. And there was very little in the jar behind the stove. She needed boots, and Zoe needed a winter coat. She knew Philip did his best.

She set the yeast to rising in a little glass mug on the shelf above the stove. Then she dumped the measured amount of flour into her large wooden bowl. The brown flour felt cool and good on her fingers, like garden earth. Keep busy, she told herself. It was something she learned from her mama. When life gets you down, bake something. Cook something. When her father came home in one of his rages, her mama would go to the kitchen in their little southern home and try out a new recipe.

Naomi pulled out the board Colin had given to her. It was a smooth, square piece of oak—a cabinet top that was cut wrong, he told her—but it made the perfect kneading board. Colin was always doing things like that: chopping wood, bringing over bread boards, fixing the canning shelves, entirely rebuilding the outhouse door, adding a little, old-fashioned half moon at the top. She sighed. Now he passed by her without saying a word.

She placed the board on top of the metal folding table. The yeast ready, she added it to the bowl along with the honey, oil, salt, and water. She began mixing, then squeezing, adding more of this and that until the dough felt just right in her fingers.

The worse thing you can do in a time of crisis, said her mama, is to sit on your hands. That's the time to be up and doing; idle hands and all. When Naomi was little, she would climb up on the stool and watch her mama mix cakes, brownies, pies, and bread and rolls of all kinds and shapes and sizes. Her mama even got so proficient that she baked things for a restaurant. Naomi was never allowed to touch her restaurant things, not even a lick. The home things she could try.

That law, however, didn't apply to her father, who seemed to delight in destroying her mama's creations. He would slice into pieces of cake that were destined for restaurants, take one bite and declare them too salty, too sweet, too lumpy, too hard, too soft. "What you need is a cooking lesson," he would tell her. Many times her mama would be up until two or three in the morning making a new cake to replace the one her father had ruined. Naomi's mother took to hiding the restaurant baking in Naomi's room, way up in her closet in an empty place she had cleared out. Naomi hated when her mama did this. She was afraid her father would come into her bedroom at night and tear through her dresser drawers, looking for the hidden food. Most of her early nightmares centered around food in her bedroom. Cakes and cookies that would melt and expand and explode to fill her whole room, suffocating her with their doughy smell. Then Naomi would wake up in the hot room with the covers twisted around her head.

The chopping had stopped. Naomi looked out the window. Colin was talking to Jeremiah who was pouring gasoline from a small red can into Colin's chainsaw.

In the graveyard, Zoe was on Peter's shoulders, and she was clapping her hands, coaxing him to run faster, faster.

She turned back to her work. She sprinkled flour on the board and began kneading. Back and forth, back and forth rhythmically in pattern. Like the song of the axe and the chainsaw.

I will always remember you.

The chainsaw stilled. Outside she saw Colin lay down his axe, look toward the road, nod to Jeremiah. Next, Naomi saw a stranger get out of a small blue car. Colin and Jeremiah and the man who wore jeans and a sweatshirt talked for quite a while. Several times they looked toward the church where Naomi stood at the window. She began to feel uneasy.

A few minutes later the three of them came in the back room. Jeremiah spoke first. "Naomi, do you have any idea where Philip is?" The tone of his voice made Naomi feel cold.

"What?"

"This is serious. Do you have any idea where he is?"

"No. I…" She put a floury hand to her cheek, stared at him, at the grim expressions on all three of their faces. Outside, Zoe and Peter laughed.

"Did something happen to him?" she asked.

"This is the friend I was telling you about. Chris," said Colin. "He used to be a cop. He told me the police are looking for Philip."

"Why?"

"He's wanted for questioning in connection with the murder of Joanne Sypher," said Chris. "Some evidence was found linking her to him."

She stared at the stranger. "Linking Jo to Philip? But he didn't know her. He told me that. And she didn't know him."

"Not according to the evidence the police have."

"What evidence?"

"They found his truck abandoned…" said Colin.

"His truck was abandoned! He could be in trouble! Is anyone out looking for him?"

"Yes, everyone is looking for him," said Chris. "Every cop in the state."

Naomi commanded her hands to remain still at her side. But they would not. She needed to knead bread. Or slice carrots. Or peel potatoes. She wiped her floury hands on a rag and walked toward the window, looked away from them, outside where Peter and Zoe scampered around the graveyard.

"Where did they find his truck?" she asked.

"On a gravel road near Moosehead Lake," said Chris.

She turned back. "See. That proves it. His truck broke down. He's out there lost somewhere."

"The tank was half full," said Chris. "And the engine started first crank."

"The police will be coming back here, Naomi," said Colin. "They'll be asking all sorts of questions. And their attention will be focused on you because you're his wife. They'll think you're hiding him."

"They ran the license plate through," said Chris, "and discovered that the address Philip Friend used was phony. No such address. No such street even exists in this entire world."

"What does that mean?" Naomi smoothed her hair back, fiddled with the large barrette, but her fingers were shaking, the clasp wouldn't hold. Jeremiah combed her hair through his fingers and closed it in the clasp for her.

"You said something about evidence linking him to Jo. What are you talking about?" she asked.

"Show her the note," said Colin.

Chris reached into his jeans pocket and pulled out a folded piece of paper and handed it to her. "This is just a photocopy. The police have the real one. It was written in green ink, if that means anything."

Naomi opened it up and read:

*I know who you are, Philip Friend, and I know what you've
done and your threats mean nothing to me. I know what kind of
a husband you are, and I will tell. Don't think I won't. Jo*

For several seconds Naomi said nothing, just read and reread, as if many readings would alter the note's contents.

"Where did you get this?" She could not control her voice, and it came out high pitched and too loud.

"The police found it in his truck. They were lucky to find it. Philip had wiped the entire thing clean—no registration, no license, nothing—and then shoved down between the seats we found this note, obviously missed by Philip."

Naomi sat down, the note still in her hand. She looked at the fat ball of dough on the board.

"When was the last time you saw him?" asked Chris, sitting down across from her.

She didn't look at him. "Why should I tell you?"

"Because he's a friend of mine," said Colin, "and he wants to help you."

"Listen to him," said Jeremiah.

Naomi looked up and out of the window.

"When did Philip leave?" asked Chris.

"About a week ago."

"And you've had no correspondence with him since then?"

She thought about the missing money. "No. None."

"He didn't say where he was going?"

"He never does."

"Did he leave anything here? Any clothes?"

Naomi shook her head.

"Naomi, do you have any papers that might have Philip's address on them?" said Chris. "We're grasping at straws here."

"Not really. Well, just our marriage license. But I don't remember if that has an address or not."

Chris's face brightened. "You have that here?"

Naomi rose. "I keep my important papers in a wooden box under my bed." She bent down, brought out a wooden box with a lid. "I've got Zoe's birth certificate in here too, and some insurance policies," she said opening the lid. "But I don't know what address is on it…" She looked down, unable to speak. She showed them the empty box. "I don't understand."

"You kept those papers in this box?" asked Chris.

She was on her knees, crawling underneath the bed, frantically looking through Zoe's box of clothes, her own things. "They're gone," she kept saying. "I don't understand. They were always right here. Always."

Jeremiah took her arm, led her to a chair, sat her down.

"When was the last time you looked in that box?"

"A month ago, maybe. Just before Philip came the last time."

"What exactly was in that box?" he asked.

"My marriage license, Zoe's birth certificate, and an insurance policy."

"An insurance policy?" asked Chris.

"Philip had a life insurance policy for me, so that if he died, Zoe and I would get some money."

"Not the other way around?" asked Colin.

She looked at him. "I don't know."

Chris said, "You can replace marriage licenses and birth certificates just by calling up the department of records. All that stuff is on file. Same with insurance policies."

"I don't have a phone," said Naomi.

"Still no problem. I can do that." Chris had an easy way about him, thought Naomi, and a kind face. "It might be better, though, if someone went in person. In case there are any problems. I'll add that to my list of things to do here." He pulled out a small notebook from the back pocket of his jeans.

"I could go," said Jeremiah. "I don't mind doing that. That would free you to do other work. Maybe Peter would lend me his truck. I'm sure he wouldn't mind."

"Maybe you two could go together," added Colin.

Naomi sat down and stared at the lump of dough on the board while they decided that Jeremiah and maybe Peter, they'd have to ask him, would drive down to the department of records in Augusta and get those papers. If Naomi could remember the name of the insurance company, they would check that out, too. They could leave that afternoon, the sooner the better.

When the three men left by the back door and went out to the graveyard to talk to Peter, Naomi went back to the kneading. She moved and slapped and flung the dough on the board until her arms ached from the effort and the dough was a perfect ball, without a ripple, smooth and flawless. Then she set it to rise in the bowl above her stove with a cloth on the top. Keep busy, her mama said. There would be supper to make, for all of them, even Chris now, no doubt. And then the dough would need to be punched down later, and then came second rising in the bread pans. And then the baking. By evening the place would be filled with the warm, yeasty, welcoming aroma of baking bread. Tomorrow she would take a package of food down to Jules. As she promised.

I will always remember you.

FORTY-THREE

WINTER WOULD SOON BE HERE. Jules could feel it. It would start slowly, like it did every year, just a hint now and then of coolness at night. But soon it would come like a flood tide over the land, merciless, chilling, cold. And the wind would blow like a gale through the channel, and Jules would have to shovel and salt the deck of the ferry after every trip. He would have to plow out the ferry terminal on both sides after every trip and the only thing people talked about would be the weather.

He was sitting on the floor of his pilothouse. He had slept fitfully since he moved here, hearing every whisper of the wind, every creaking of the ferry. It was night, and he knew that sleep would not find him quickly. He lit a candle and placed it on the floor beside him. He looked up and out of the window. He found a half-eaten Mars bar and chewed on it, while he thought about the fire. He had been quick to blame Colin. But Jules had known Colin for a long time. He knew the man could do a lot of things, but burning an islander's home was different. Colin was like Jules, very protective of the islanders. No, Jules had been wrong. It couldn't have been Colin. He thought next of Peter. Had Peter set his cabin on fire? What would be his motive? There was something else bothering him about Peter. He had watched him chopping wood. They were not the same movements of the figure he had seen in the boat so many weeks ago. No, the person in the boat was not Peter. Despite the hat. First thing tomorrow he'd head down to the coffee shop and tell them he'd been wrong. Peter was not the murderer. Colin was not the arsonist.

On the seat were two days of the *Bangor Daily News* and a whole slew of magazines he hadn't looked at yet. Did he really want to start doing up scrapbooks all over again? He sighed and pulled down the most recent newspaper and laid it on his lap. Old habits die hard, he reflected. It wouldn't be long before he was in town, buying scrap-books, scissors, tape, felt pens, and glue. Starting all over again. It was inevitable.

When the light from one candle became too dim, he lit another. There were the usual wars and people saying this and that, and govern-ment passing this or that bill. In the second section he read a curious story. The police were searching for a man whose truck was abandoned out on the road to Moosehead Lake. The man was identified as Philip Friend, address unknown, but most recently of Lambs Island, Maine. Jules read it over again. Then he carefully folded the paper this way and that, and tore the story out of the paper evenly. If his *Book of Philip* hadn't burned, this would go into it. He read it once more, flat-tening it out on top of Martha's quilt.

Jules stood up and looked out his pilothouse window into the darkness. Philip Friend, he thought. The one scrapbook that was prac-tically empty. He sat back down again and took another bite of the candy bar. He heard a sound outside, or thought he did. He rose, looked out, but saw nothing. That mutt of Walt's, most likely. He sat down. He was reading through the day's "Special Supplement"; boring stuff for the most part. Who's Who in New England business. He read every word, nonetheless. Old habits die hard.

He yawned and threw the candy wrapper into a little plastic garbage bag he had hung on a knob. He heard the noise again. There was definitely something there. And those were footsteps, not animal sounds. Maybe someone wanted to go across. At this time of night? He stood up, rubbed his eyes, yet saw nothing. No headlights in the blackness.

He opened the door. "Yeah?" he called.

No answer.

He closed the door, shrugged, and went back to his "Special Supplement." On page four of the twenty-page supplement he stared down at a grainy image. And suddenly he knew. Suddenly all of it made sense.

At that moment, the door of his pilothouse opened and a figure stepped inside. Jules wasn't at all surprised to see who stood there.

"It was you," said Jules. "I just figured that out. I figured it out this very minute."

FORTY-FOUR

IT WAS MORNING IN AUGUSTA, MAINE. Peter and Jeremiah had spent the previous night sleeping in the truck at a highway rest stop underneath a sign that read No Overnight Parking. The park was equipped with restrooms and clean water. Cold water, but water just the same. So they took their chances and stayed. Peter had stretched out in the cab and Jeremiah slept in back underneath a pile of blankets.

Back out on I-95, Jeremiah said, "Look at that building over there. That barn, do you see it? I stayed in there on my way to Lambs Island. I sneaked in and stayed there. No one knew I was there. In the evenings I would sneak out and walk to the nearest convenience store and buy what I needed. Then at night I'd go back there and sleep in the hay. Me and the animals. I wasn't altogether human then."

Peter looked at him.

"Hey, watch your driving," said Jeremiah. "You want me to take over?"

"That's okay. I was just surprised you stayed in a barn."

"I was running too. I killed someone too. You're not the only one."

"You killed someone?" Peter's eyes were wide.

"Not a someone. Not exactly. Well, a marriage. And a family. And a whole church. You can call that killing, I suppose."

Peter didn't say anything, just kept the truck on the highway, his eyes on the road.

"You and I have a lot in common," Jeremiah said. "Both running, but both innocent. Forgiven by God, but unforgiven all the same."

"Back at the church you said that God would forgive you no matter what you did."

"God will. Yes, I guess I said that. God will. But people won't. And unfortunately our world isn't populated by little gods but by human beings. Those are the ones we have to deal with every day." Jeremiah turned to him. "Peter, do you know who I am?"

"You're Jeremiah. That's all I know."

"My real name is Jeremy Stephenson. Doctor Jeremy S. Stephenson. Jeremy Saul Stephenson. I have written books—major works, they were called—on church planting in North America. The books I wrote also had study guides and came out on audio and video tapes. People came from all over the country just to see how we operated. And people who couldn't come to the church would buy the videos to show in their evening services. I went to one of the most prestigious seminaries in the United States."

Peter stared at him.

"You have no idea what I'm talking about, do you?"

He shook his head.

Jeremiah sighed. "Perhaps all the churches in the country should be for sale. Then maybe we could start all over again. Start from the bottom up. Start from scratch."

Peter watched the highway ahead of him. There was very little traffic but the sun was blinding. He said, "I used to go to church when I was a kid. My mother still does."

Jeremiah smiled. "Isn't that what everyone says, 'I used to go to church, my mother still does.' I have gone from being Dr. Jeremy S. Stephenson, sought after speaker and host of a syndicated radio program and award-winning author, to Jeremiah, the melancholy prophet. Now, I chop wood and study old books in a church that's falling down." He paused and pushed up his glasses on his nose. "There's a leak over the platform. That was me getting up and trying to find a bucket to catch the drips. Hope I didn't wake you."

"You didn't," Peter said.

"And is it better for you now that you moved your mattress farther near the back?"

"Yeah, I haven't noticed any drips."

"Good. There's the sign for Augusta up there. Exit 31."

"I see it."

Jeremiah smoothed back his hair. He wore it in a pony tail today which brushed the back of his neck. He said, "I don't look anything like I did back then. My hair's long and gray and I have a beard. Back then I was so clean cut. I don't look anything like the picture on the back of my books. You'd never recognize me from them. It's easier here to grow a beard. I see you've discovered that too."

Peter nodded.

"If they'd known it was me in that soup kitchen…" Jeremiah chuckled. "Funny thing about hair going gray, I'm not that old, really. They say a serious stress can turn hair gray. There's a story about a dark-haired man who descended into an ocean whirlpool. He survived, but when he came out, his hair was completely white. Every strand. That's from *A Descent into the Maelstrom* by Edgar Allan Poe. The complete works of Poe are in the church."

They were travelling down the exit road that led into Augusta. In the distance on a hill to the left they saw a church spire. "Chris says you just stay on this road," said Jeremiah looking down at the handwritten directions.

Up ahead was the green dome of the capitol building. The Department of Human Services would be across the street. "This looks like it," said Peter, pulling into the small lot beside it.

They made their way to the entrance and Peter caught a glimpse of their reflection in the glass doors. They looked like loggers from the north. He hoped they would be able to get the things Naomi needed.

Right inside a double set of glass doors, they saw the sign for births, deaths, marriages, and divorces. They made their request to a small woman with short straight brown hair. She asked them to fill out forms.

Jeremiah said, "This is kind of urgent. Isn't there any way you could check for us without having to go through all the formalities. Actually, we're just looking for a couple of addresses."

She looked up at him through her owl-like glasses. "Let me see here," she said, turning to her computer.

"What we need is a marriage license—just a copy would be great. For Philip and Naomi Friend." Jeremiah looked at the piece of paper Naomi had given him. "Maiden name Forrest, Naomi Forrest. And here's the date they were married." He showed her the slip of paper.

"I don't know if I can do that without authorization. Are you a family member?"

"Yes," said Jeremiah.

Peter looked at him.

"Please, miss. This is so urgent."

Something in his eyes must have reached her because she sighed, turned, and punched some commands into the computer. A few moments later she said, "They're not registered."

"What does that mean?"

"It means there's no record of that marriage. It would help if you had a copy of the marriage license."

"But that's why we're here in the first place. If we had the marriage license we wouldn't need to be here."

She shook her head. "I'm sorry. I don't have it here on our records."

"Okay then, how about a birth certificate for a little girl born four years ago." Jeremiah handed her the paper, which included Zoe's pertinent information.

Again she punched a few commands. "Sorry," she said turning to them. "There is no such person as this Zoe Friend."

"She's a little girl, about four," said Peter. "She lives on Lambs Island."

The tiny woman was punching in new commands. "There's a Zoe Forrest here, is that the girl? Born the same date in the same place. We've got a mother's name as Naomi Forrest. No mention of a father."

"How can there be no mention of a father?" asked Peter.

She stared at the computer, eyes puzzled together. "It's unusual, but not totally uncommon."

"No addresses?" asked Jeremiah.

"None."

"And no father?"

"No."

"Can you print that out for us?" asked Jeremiah. He looked at her. "This is so important. You've no idea."

They paid the fee and left with a printout in their pocket, a promise that the real birth certificate would be mailed, and a promise that she would try to locate the marriage license.

Next they went to the insurance company, where a thin, middle-aged man told them they had no policies with the name of Philip Friend or Naomi Friend or Zoe Friend or Zoe Forrest or Naomi Forrest or any combination of the above.

"It would help if we had the policy number," he said.

"That's the whole thing," said Jeremiah. "The policies were lost and we have no records of them."

"It's really important to keep those numbers in a safe place, jot down the numbers in another place, keep them separate from the policies. It keeps this very thing from happening," he said. "Are you sure it was with this company?"

"Fairly sure."

By midafternoon they had checked at five other insurance companies with the same result. Nobody named Friend. Nobody named Forrest. They grabbed a fast-food lunch and decided to head back north to Lambs Island. Jeremiah drove.

"Do you know where I got these?" said Jeremiah fiddling with his glasses.

Peter looked up. "Got what?

"At a soup kitchen." One hand was on the wheel and the other tapped the frames of his crooked glasses. "It happened in prison. My own glasses, well, I won't go into what happened to them, but suffice it to say they got stepped on and I needed a new pair. A few weeks after I got out I went to a soup kitchen to volunteer. Well, that, and to get something to eat." He grabbed his paper cup of coffee from the dashboard and took a sip. "No one recognized me there. My looks had completely changed by then. There were these glasses sitting there in the lost and found. I'd seen them there before. I asked who they belonged to, and they told me they had been there for months. Well, the guy they belonged to had eyes amazingly close to my own. They told me to take them. So I took them and here they are. A little bent though. I should get new ones. You don't have to wear glasses?"

Peter told him he never had and hoped he never would.

Jeremiah said a lot of things then, as the two of them travelled north on I-95 toward Bangor. He spoke of how your life can change in the matter of a few minutes, how one day everything is just fine, just the way it always had been, steady and on track, getting up and going to work, and how all of a sudden it can turn completely around. Peter told him he knew all about that one. Peter talked about rewinding the video, to which Jeremiah grunted and said, "You only get one chance, one go-around. We're actors on this great stage called life, and we don't even get a dress rehearsal. We only get one chance to get it right. Doesn't quite seem fair, does it?"

Peter nodded, smiled, took a sip of his Coke.

Jeremiah told him then that he was accused of sexual molestation. He sounded out every syllable of that word, making it sound like a disease.

Peter bit on the edge of his Coke cup and said, "What happened?"

"I didn't do it, of course, if that's what you're thinking, Peter."

"I wasn't."

"It really doesn't matter anyway. I've come to think that maybe I should've raped her after all, because I was tried and convicted as if I had."

Peter stared at him, his hand around his cup.

"No." He shook his head. "Scratch that. That was unkind. I don't wish I'd raped her." He paused. "I lost everything—my church, my ministry, my family, my children. All except my mother, who, bless her heart, believed me to the end. But she died a few years ago. Even Pauline left me."

"Your wife?"

He nodded. His eyes screwed up. And for a moment Peter wondered if the older man was going to cry. "Pauline is a nurse. She quit her job to raise the boys. She felt very strongly about that. You have to admire her for that. Like Naomi, spending so much time with Zoe, reading to her, teaching her numbers and the alphabet."

Jeremiah told him that a fifteen-year-old girl in his church had accused him of raping her. "She happened to be the daughter of one of my board members. So it got to be her word against mine. And in those kinds of things the poor victimized female is always listened to above the rich, handsome preacher." He paused and smiled at Peter. "I used to be handsome. I worked out, watched my weight, kept my brown hair short and respectable." He ran a hand through his hair. "I did everything right. I guess I was a little bit stuck on myself, so maybe pride was my sin. But not rape. I didn't commit rape. I did not."

Peter said that he believed him. It seemed awfully important to Jeremiah that Peter believe him.

"Thing is, the girl never backed down. I went to see her alone, just to find out why she was lying. That's all I wanted to ask her, 'Why are you doing this to me? Why are you lying?' That, my friend, was a mistake. A Big Mistake. I should've taken someone with me. I know that now. I was just so confused at the time." He sighed and paused, both hands gripping the wheel, stared straight ahead. "Because she went screaming to her father and said that I had come on to her. Again." He paused, his upper lip quivered, his eyes blinked rapidly.

"You don't have to tell me this," Peter said.

"I thought maybe they were going to cast me into the dungeon where I wouldn't get out until I could interpret dreams."

Peter looked at him uncomprehending and finished his Coke.

"The case was thrown out because it couldn't be proved that I raped her. As in, she hadn't gone to the hospital after the so-called rape, and so they couldn't match any DNA or whatever they do. My lawyer argued that there was no physical evidence that she had been raped. I thought that would be the end of it. But where there's smoke, there's fire, you know, that's what everyone said. I was defrocked and dethroned and de-familied just the same."

"There was nothing you could do?"

"The tabloids had a field day. They love it when the mighty fall. You sure you never heard of me?"

Peter looked long and hard at him, at the thick gray hair tied back, the blue eyes behind the funny little glasses, the beard, the gentle smile, but no, he did not know who Dr. Jeremy S. Stephenson was. "Maybe I was too young when it happened," he offered.

Jeremiah didn't say anything for a long time, just stared straight ahead at the road whipping underneath the truck.

"Why don't you call your wife?" It was a stupid thing to say. Peter realized that at the time, but said it anyway.

Jeremiah looked over at Peter, said quietly, "I wouldn't know what to say now, it's been so long."

"You could tell her that you really didn't do it, that the girl was lying and that you'd like to see her."

"I told her all that. Over and over. She didn't believe me then, why would she now? He looked back to the road. After a while he said, "I miss my kids. I miss them terribly."

Peter looked out of the window, realizing that now he knew what Jeremiah thought about when he sat at his table, the candle flickering, his sad eyes staring straight ahead into the darkness.

SEPTEMBER 28, 1998

FROM THE JOURNALS OF MARTHA MACGREGOR

Sometimes when I am in the church, it almost seems a living thing to me; an organic thing, breathing, swelling, like the tide, ebbing and flowing.

Naomi told me today that yet another person has come to live in the church, a young man named Peter. He arrived just today. I haven't met him yet. He is frightened, sick and very thin, she said. When she described him I am reminded of Jeremiah who was so lost at first. This young man has driven here in a truck from New York. She hasn't asked him where he's from or why he came. No one asks questions of each other over there. It's not their way.

When she told me all of this, I thought, of all the places that someone could come, he ends up here? Coincidence? Surely not. No, the church is a living, breathing entity. I told this to Colin the other day and he laughed so hard I thought he was going to split a side. Oh, Martha, you have such ideas!

But I ask you, don't you think it could be true?

FORTY-FIVE

PAUL WAS IN HIS STUDY WITH HIS AFRICAN VIOLETS when Margot found him. He didn't hear her approach. His back was to her, and he was whistling. She watched him pinch off the dead blossoms, add fertilizer to the pots. She looked at his rows of violets on the window sill, their soft, fuzzy leaves, like the ears of teddy bears. She stood there watching him, looking around, and suddenly something seemed wrong with the place. She had been in here many times, yet today she noticed it for the first time; things were too precise here, too perfect: the bound books arranged by height on the dark wood shelves, the marble pen stand with the two pens jutting out at just the right angle, the uncluttered desk. No framed pictures of her or the girls sat on his desk. There was a starkness about the room. Aside from the African violets there seemed to be no personal touches.

Something must have alerted him to her presence because he turned and faced her.

"You shaved your beard." It was the first thing she could think of to say.

"How long have you been standing there?"

She shrugged.

"I waited for you," he said. "I waited all day for you."

"Well, I'm here now." Margot thought of the book. She had read it entirely through last night.

"I wish you could have come to LA with me."

Margot turned her head away from him. "I don't think so," she said quietly.

"What's the matter, Margot?"

She frowned and put a hand to her forehead.

He moved toward her. "What's wrong? Something's wrong." He put his arms around her and she smelled earth, the tangy aroma of

240

growing things. "Tell me what's the matter. I've missed you so much."

Margot shrugged out of his arms and backed away. "I know what's going on, Paul." Her voice was shaking. "I know exactly what's going on. I know everything."

"You do?" He looked surprised and then said, "Margot, love, you'll have to enlighten me. Going on with what?"

"Paul, I know all about what's going on."

"Please tell me what you're talking about, Margot."

"All your little lies. I know it all, Paul, don't act so innocent."

He looked at her. To Margot it looked as if he were weighing something in his mind. "Don't deny anything, please," she said. "I couldn't bear it. I know you were in California with your...your mistress. I know you haven't been going to those Bible studies."

"You think I'm seeing another woman?"

She nodded.

He looked down at the floor and was quiet for a long time. Without looking up at her he finally said, "How did you find out?"

Margot stared at him. Not this, she thought. Anything but this. She expected, hoped, that he would deny it, prove her wrong, but here he was *admitting* it! And so easily, without a fight. The book said he would deny it. That's what happens, the author wrote. Finally Margot whispered, "Who is she?"

He slumped into his leather couch, bent his head in his hands. His shoulders heaved under his blue designer sweater. Margot stared at him, unable to move. When he finally lifted his head, his eyes were wet. "I never wanted to hurt you, Margot. That was never my intention. I'm sorry. Yes, I have been seeing someone else. But it's all over. I've come home. I wanted to tell you that. That's why I waited here all day for you. I wanted so much for you to come yesterday. Can you ever, in your heart of hearts, forgive me?"

Margot turned and walked out of the room.

That night in bed, after Margot had picked up the girls, after Paul had regaled all of them with tales of LA, and the movie stars he had seen, and the wonderful weather out there, Margot felt numb. She had put up a good front through all of this. That night after the girls were in bed he told her that first thing in the morning he was going to call their minister and get counselling for both of them.

"This whole thing can be put behind us, Margot. I love you and I want to make things right." He also told her he was going back to the Bible study. He wanted to make a brand-new start. He said it was over with that other woman and that he was making a clean break with the past.

Lying on her side of the bed, she gazed through the darkness to the far wall. Paul reached for her then, pulled her close under the blanket, covering her neck with kisses. Sorry, so sorry, he kept saying. Never wanted to hurt you. Never will again.

As if that would make everything all right. As if things could ever get back to normal.

She wrenched herself from him and fled from the bedroom. She locked herself in the bathroom and took a wet washcloth and rubbed her neck until it was raw. She kept rubbing at her neck and sobbing. She stared at her reflection in the mirror. The person who looked out at her was overweight, frumpy, with blotchy skin and streaks of gray in her mussed up hair. No wonder her husband sought other women.

It seemed to her now, in her memory, that when Paul had looked up at her from the leather couch in his office, he had not been crying, but laughing.

FORTY-SIX

THE MORNING SKY WAS PAINTED OVER WITH SUNLIGHT. But to Naomi it seemed too bright, too garish, as if the sun were somehow trying to make up for the darkness gnawing at the edges of her. She closed the burlap curtains against it, but sharp shafts of light found their way in around the sides of the makeshift curtains. She pulled on jeans and a sweater. Zoe was sitting on a chair and chattering, asking about Unca Peter, and when was he coming back? I don't know, Naomi told her. But mama, when's daddy coming back? I don't know, said Naomi spooning coffee into the dented metal percolator. But I want him to come back; he promised, right, mama? Not this time, little one, not this time. She placed the coffee pot near the front of the stove where it was hottest.

A few moments later Colin stood there in his baggy sweater and jeans.

"Coffee's almost ready," she said. "Was it warm enough in the sanctuary last night, Colin?" Ever since he had come upon her going through his things, she had been shy around him, solicitous, wanting to make up for it. They didn't talk about it.

"Plenty. Yeah."

"You could've come and opened the door."

He looked at her. "The police'll be here soon, Naomi."

"You told me."

"You better be prepared for some hard questions."

She stiffened and turned away from him. The coffee was percolating rapidly. She moved it to the back of the stove.

"Hi, Unca Colin," said Zoe.

He squatted down to kid level. "Hi yourself."

"Do you wanna peach, Unca Colin?" she asked.

"Okay, sure. Peaches are my favorite."

"Do we have peaches, mama?" said Zoe getting off her chair and tugging on Naomi's jeans.

"No, Zoe. Just apples now."

"Where's Unca Peter?"

"He'll be back soon," said Naomi. "Here, Zoe, come sit and have some bread."

"And a peach, too? Mama, can I have a peach, too."

"We don't have any peaches, Zoe."

"Then a apple?"

"Okay, an apple."

"I like apples better than peaches, but sometimes I like peaches better, don't I, Mama?"

"Yes," said Naomi.

When Naomi had poured two coffees, she and Colin sat down facing each other across the table.

"Naomi..." Colin paused. "Chris told me the police are going to be asking you all sorts of personal questions, things about you and Philip, about how you met him, those sorts of things. They won't hold back."

"Why is that important, how I met Philip?"

"They'll be looking for any leads."

Naomi looked down at the table. "I just wish things could go back the way they were."

"Things weren't so hot the way they were," Colin said quietly.

"Philip could be in danger..."

He sighed.

"You want to know how I met Philip, Colin? Okay, I'll tell you."

"You don't have to."

"No, I want to, just to make you understand what a nice and gentle person he is. And how he loves me and Zoe more than any-thing. When they find him, that's what he'll say."

Colin looked at her sadly, said nothing.

Naomi met Philip in northern Maine where she had worked as a cook in a logging camp. The very first time she saw him was during a midweek lunch. He was sitting at the table with the foreman and a couple of big shots in the forestry camp. She watched him for a while, noting the easy way he spoke and smiled, the way he pushed his blond hair out of his eyes. When he saw her looking his way, he winked. She had looked away shyly.

Later, when she was peeling potatoes in the kitchen, he came in and straddled a stool with his long legs.

"Hi," he said.

"Hello."

"I came to tell you how good your lunch was. You're a good cook."

"Thanks."

"Been here long?"

"Few months."

"You like it here?"

"It's a job."

"Yeah. A job."

"Aren't y'all supposed to be working?" She cocked her head at him.

"It's my break."

"Don't give me that, you guys don't take breaks." He didn't look like the regular logger who came through here. His jeans were clean and his pale yellow cotton shirt looked brand new.

"I like your accent," he said.

"I guess it's pretty hard to hide where I'm from."

He asked her how a pretty southern belle ended up in the bush in northern Maine. She shrugged and said it was a job and that she never intended to go back south again. Never. He asked why and she didn't tell him.

After she finished the potatoes they went for a walk. Like children, they played a guessing game with each other's names. Starts with an *N*. Noreen? No. Norma? No. Nancy? No. And they had gone on like this until he had guessed her name.

"That's an exotic name," he told her. "Naomi. For an exotic woman."

She laughed. "The one thing I'm not is exotic."

"Yes you are, the mystery woman from the south. Won't tell anyone why she's here."

"It's none of anyone's business."

Two days later he left for another logging job. As soon as he left she realized she hadn't guessed his name. She didn't know who he was. Two weeks later he was back and when she told him this he laughed. "I can't believe I didn't tell you my name. Why didn't you ask?"

"I guess I forgot."

"It's Friend, Philip Friend."

They saw each other regularly. He visited on his days off, and they spent two or three days together before he was off to another job. On one of their times together, the first time that he had an entire week off, they travelled in his truck down to the coast. Used to the bush, they didn't mind sleeping in the truck along the road or camping in his ripped little pup tent. It was all an adventure to her, even when it rained and the bottom of their tent flooded.

Travelling down back roads is how they discovered Lambs Island. They camped in the church. It was empty and not even locked, with a woodstove, firewood, and even a cot.

During that full week on Lambs Island she truly fell in love with him. They would sit side by side on the rocks down by the water and talk. She told him things she had never told another living soul. And he would put his arms around her and tell her none of that mattered. None of anything mattered. They wrapped a blanket around themselves and sat in the wind beside the lighthouse where they watched the sea for hours.

At the end of that week Philip told her he had to head to the mainland, that he'd be back in a couple of days. She asked to go with him, but he said it would be a lot of boring running around, and she would end up sitting in the truck most of the time. It had to do with work, he said. She said she didn't mind. She would wait on the island. It was a nice place to wait.

Two months later she was still waiting. When he finally did return he was full of apologies and love and flowers and gifts and money. He'd taken another job and had no way of letting her know. He promised that in the future he would either take her with him or find some way of letting her know where he was. She accepted that. It was enough to have him back. He brought flatware with him and dishes, blankets, and a second cot. The church would be a perfect place for them to stay, he said.

"No rent," he told her. "We can afford this. It's just temporary, of course. Just until I can get a full-time job somewhere. Until we can get a house or an apartment. You don't mind, Naomi, do you?"

He stayed for two weeks, time enough to dig out a garden patch beside the cemetery. Then he had to leave, he told her, a quick job up near Houlton. Just wait for me here, I'll be back, he told her.

He came and went and came and went and still she believed him, that each time he came he would stay for good. When she told him she was pregnant, they drove into Bangor and were married at a justice of the peace. Then he left again, but started sending her money every week. At first she had to get Jules to take her across the channel to the bank to withdraw it. Eventually, Jules offered to pick up her money for her.

"I go to the bank for lots of people," he said.

That became the pattern of her life. Waiting for Philip. Caring for Zoe. Planting the garden. Harvesting. Then Colin showed up. Then Jeremiah. Then Jo. Then Peter.

She told most of this to Colin, though, not all of it. She kept some of the things to herself. At the end of her story, Colin said, "I'm sorry all this had to happen."

She wiped her eyes and began gathering things into a box: a loaf of bread, a thermos of coffee, some preserves.

"Where are you going?" he asked.

"I'm taking some food over to Jules."

"I'll stay with Zoe if you want."

"Thanks."

There were several people waiting at the ferry terminal when Naomi arrived. A man named Joel was leaning against his car, arms crossed on his chest. "You any idea where Jules is?" he called.

"No. I brought him over some food."

"Well, he's not around," added a foot passenger named Brett. "And a bunch of us need to get across. He's never been this late before."

"Where is he?" called another. "Where's he staying now? In town?"

Naomi pointed to the ferry. "That's where he's sleeping now. Up there."

Joel and Brett followed Naomi out onto the ferry and up the ladder to the pilothouse, staying behind her, right on her heels. The two were going on and on about where could he have gotten to. Brett was late for work three times last week, and if he didn't make it on time, he was going to lose his job.

Naomi slid open the metal door to the pilothouse. The two men behind her bounded in. Jules was there. He was lying against the far wall, eyes and mouth open.

"What the?" said Joel pushing past her. "He have a heart attack or something?"

"He still alive?" asked Brett rushing forward. "Hey Jules! Someone get some water."

But Naomi knew he was already dead, and she backed down the ladder and raced through the woods, scraping past branches and rocks.

When she arrived at the church breathless and sobbing, Colin reached for her, held her, as she sobbed out her story.

Colin was right. The police came that day, great groups of them with flashing lights and uniforms and guns on their hips. They parked near the back of the church and asked her again and again where Philip was. She kept shaking her head, but they kept persisting. I don't know. I don't know where he is. Why can't you believe me? They asked about the Friday deposits Philip made. They called someone on their cell phone to check the bank. They asked to see deposit slips. She didn't have any and told them so. They asked to see any of Philip's clothing that he may have left. She pointed to a jacket, and they went over it inch by inch, finally taking it with them. She heard them debating on the usefulness of taking fingerprints. They didn't ask about her marriage license and she didn't tell them that Jeremiah and Peter had gone to get duplicates.

They also asked her about Jules. When was the last time she had seen him alive? What did he seem like to her? They asked Colin that, too. Then the red-headed cop Virginia sat down across from her at the table, and Naomi went a little bit into the story again of where she met Philip, leaving out even more details than she had left out with Colin. Naomi watched Virginia's freckled fingers write all of her answers down in a book.

By evening the police had left, and Colin made tea and went and got Zoe from Martha's, laid her on the cot, and covered her with a blanket. Naomi avoided sleep, certain that as soon as she closed her eyes, she would see the twisted face of Jules there, eyes staring, mouth partly open. Or Jo lying on the beach—a limp, wet, rag doll.

When her eyes became so heavy that she couldn't keep them open, she lay down on the other cot. By now she had convinced herself that the note in Philip's truck was from a girl who lied and made up stories. Hadn't that been proven? By the kind of questions Jo had asked, Naomi knew that Jo had never met Philip. What does your husband look like? she would ask. What kind of a person is he? How tall is he? What color hair does he have? Jo, for reasons that had died with her, had chosen to pretend that she knew Philip by writing that note. But why?

Something woke her, and she sat straight up in bed clutching her blanket to her chin. A falling branch? The wind? It was a heavy sound, like falling ice in the winter. What had she been dreaming about? The night was clear, and through an opened edge of burlap, she could see faint light from the stars.

And then she started screaming.

Colin rushed into the room, pulling on his sweater over his jeans. All Naomi could do was to point. Words wouldn't come. Her mouth refused to make the sound of them. He looked toward the window. "What is it?" he asked quietly. "What did you see?"

"A face." She was sobbing now, and her shaking fingers covered her face. "A horrible face. I know you're going to say it was a dream. But I woke up and saw a face there. I did. Right in the corner of the window. Looking in at me."

"Did you see who it was?"

"No, it was a face with a long nose. Like a mask."

"It wasn't anyone you recognized?"

"No."

"It wasn't Philip?"

"Of course not."

Colin went outside then and Naomi could hear him calling Philip's name, over and over. "I know you're out there, Philip. Show yourself, you blistering coward."

And Naomi looked down at her hands shaking in her lap, wondering why everyone was blaming Philip.

FORTY-SEVEN

WHEN JEREMIAH AND PETER ARRIVED at the ferry the following afternoon, Jules wasn't there. Instead, a large, broad-shouldered man wearing an orange jacket and wide pants waved them on with sweeping movements of arm and shoulder. When the orange-jacketed man walked past them on the ferry, Jeremiah rolled his window down.

"Jules taking some time off?"

The fellow turned his jowly face toward them. "You haven't heard?"

"Heard what?"

"Dead," he muttered. "Died right here on this ferry. Right on this very ferry. Right up there in the pilothouse." The man pointed.

"Jules is dead?"

"Deader'n a doornail."

"How'd it happen?" asked Jeremiah.

"They're talking murder. That's what they're saying. They called me in from Bar Harbor. I just heard about it today, myself. Jules was a nice fellow. Kind of quiet, if you ask me, but nice. Wouldn't hurt a fly. Man didn't have an enemy in this world." He shook his head and lumbered back to the lines. "A terrible way to exit, I would say."

Jeremiah was frowning and shaking his head. Peter looked ahead of him to where the water of the channel met the land in a line of black. He said, "Man, I can't believe that."

"I wonder what really happened," said Jeremiah.

Peter looked down at his lap, his loose corduroy pants, bunching at the knees. He said quietly, "It might be Roos."

"Roos?" Jeremiah looked over at him.

Peter nodded.

"Why would Roos kill Jules?"

"I don't know. Jules made up scrapbooks about everyone. I saw

Jo's. There could be lots of reasons."

The rest of the fifteen-minute ride was spent in silence. But Peter thought about yet another death, about Jo's note, about the scrapbooks Jules had, about Roos, about the threats. A gull landed on the railing of the ferry, and Peter watched it, very still in profile.

When they arrived back at the church, Colin was chopping wood.

"What happened to Jules?" Jeremiah asked Colin.

"Naomi found him," said Colin. "He was murdered."

"Who would do that?" asked Jeremiah.

"I don't know what the police are thinking, but I'm thinking Philip. I won't tell Naomi that, though. But it has Philip's name all over it."

Then Colin went into one of his tirades against Philip. Peter had heard it all before. "No one has any proof of that, Colin," Jeremiah said.

"What about the marriage license?" Colin asked. "You've got it?"

"Naomi isn't going to want to hear, but there is no marriage license. The whole thing is probably some sort of computer error, but they couldn't find any record of that marriage. They had a birth certificate for Zoe but it was in Naomi's maiden name of Forrest and not Friend. We got a photocopy here." He reached into his pocket.

By now Naomi and Martha had come outside. Naomi walked toward them and grabbed the photocopy out of Jeremiah's hand.

"It's wrong," she said. "The one I had specifically said Friend. Under 'father's name' it had Philip Friend. I know that for sure, because I used to look at it from time to time. In this one the father's name is left blank." She looked up. "So this one's obviously wrong."

Jeremiah took his glasses off and was opening and closing them nervously. He cleared his throat. "They promised they'd get in touch as soon as they found anything. The Zoe Forrest birth certificate is coming by mail. We already paid for the duplicate, so at least you'll have that."

"But I don't want that," she said. "I want the real one. The one I had."

Naomi looked terrible, thought Peter. The jeans and T-shirt she wore today accentuated her thinness, giving her a hollow look, like a branch ready to snap. She kept running her long fingers through her thick, pale hair which stood out like an untamed bush.

"What about the insurance policy?" asked Martha. "Did you get that?"

"There's no record of a person named Philip Friend ever taking out an insurance policy."

"You probably went to the wrong place," said Naomi.

"We went to the one you wrote down. But then we also went to as many other insurance companies as we could find. And then did some phoning to the others. One of them did a computer search."

"This is ridiculous."

Jeremiah turned to her. "We'll get to the bottom of this, Naomi. We will. Don't worry."

She turned and went back inside the church.

"Something's happening here," said Colin. "Something big. First there's that note from Jo and now this."

"What note?" said Peter.

"Jo left a note in Philip's truck. You didn't know?" asked Colin.

"I can't believe we didn't tell you," said Jeremiah.

Peter shook his head. Then he cleared his throat. "I got a note from Jo too."

All of the faces turned to him.

"You got a note?" asked Colin.

"What kind of a note?" asked Jeremiah.

He went inside to his mattress and retrieved the note and locket he had hidden underneath it.

"Why didn't you tell anybody until now?" Colin said when he returned.

"The note said not to. So I didn't." He handed it to Colin.

"Green ink," said Colin.

"Yeah, so?" asked Peter.

"The note in Philip's truck was written in green ink. That's what Chris said."

"What does that prove?" asked Martha.

"Maybe nothing. Probably nothing. What's in your hand?"

Peter held up the locket letting it dangle by the end of the chain. "Her note was wrapped around this."

"What is it?" asked Jeremiah.

"A necklace, a locket," said Peter. "But, I have no idea who those girls are inside. I thought they might be relatives of Jo or something, but they don't look anything like her."

Colin took the locket and opened it. All of them looked down into the faces of the two round-faced little girls, obviously twins, light hair combed back with blue barrettes on the right sides of their faces.

Martha turned to Colin. "Do you know who they are?"

Colin shook his head.

Martha was holding the locket now and shook her head and frowned as she peered down at it. "I don't know," she kept saying. "There's something about them."

"Maybe Naomi knows who they are," said Colin.

Inside, Naomi was sitting at the table, Zoe on her lap.

"Naomi." Colin laid the locket down on the table in front of her. "Do you know these girls?"

Naomi picked up the locket and looked at the girls closely without saying a word.

Colin turned to Peter. "When you talked with Jo she didn't mention anything about this locket?"

"We never talked about that."

"Or little girls?"

"Nope."

"So you have no idea why she left this with you?"

"Nope."

Naomi put a hand to her throat and began coughing.

OCTOBER 1, 1998

FROM THE JOURNALS OF MARTHA MACGREGOR

The girl, Jo, is dead. Her body washed up on the shore down by the church today. When I got up this morning the sky was that awful red color, the color that reminds me of blood, smears of it, as if a murderer has wiped his fingers off on the sky. I looked out my window and knew that something awful would happen today. I lit the fire, made my tea, and sat down to write. Then Colin came and we raced, the two of us, down to the water and watched the police retrieve her body.

Oh, how can I write this without it sounding like the ramblings of an old woman, a still-grieving mother? But this death today has brought Andrea's death back to me. The sky was this color the day she died too. Those striations of red, it was the same way then.

I knew there would be storms that day and told Andrea so. She laughed and said she wasn't going far, just out to her traps and back in, and that the Andrea C. *was the best boat in the harbor and could handle just about anything. So she left.*

I stood at the window that day, the one I look out of now as I write this, and watched her move out. But then she did a curious thing. She turned north and began heading toward the cliffs. What on earth? I put my pen down and called Colin at Bill's, and he met me at the cliffs. Down below was Andrea, trying to free one of her traps that had gotten caught in the reef. I put my hand on his arm and said, She will make it, Colin. She will get that trap and get around to safety. She has done this before. You watch.

But she didn't. We could hear the engine of the Andrea C. *sputter and die. And there we stood, looking down, watching her vain attempts to get the engine going as the boat edged closer and closer to the rocks. The sky was dark, then, almost black, and the wind came up suddenly. Colin gripped my arm.*

And now Colin is weeping, standing beside my woodstove, telling me about Jo, making no move to wipe away the tears that wash down his fine cheeks.

I killed her, he says. Oh Martha, I killed her!

I stand up immediately, stunned, shocked to my very core, my pencils dropping to my desk because, of course, you know what I'm thinking. I have no words. My hands will not obey my command to lie still, but flutter at my side. I fear I will faint.

Colin is still crying, uncontrollably; wrenching sobs, emanating from some place deep within him. He collapses to the floor, puts his face into the afghan on my sofa. I watch. I am mute. I am not sure I have ever seen him cry. He didn't even cry when the two of us stood on the top of the cliff and watched Andrea die, but stood grim-faced and silent. He didn't cry at her funeral.

The police, I think, they will come soon. Oh, what is to become of him? Of us? I come to my senses long enough to say, Colin what happened? Tell me what happened. I sit on the floor next to him.

He says one word to me. Andrea. He is thinking about Andrea.

Not Jo.

Do you wonder, he asks, why I have sought shelter in the church all these years? I shake my head. He continues, I am seeking redemption. I have offered myself as a sacred oblation, an offering. I have lived the life of the monk, the martyr, all to atone. But nothing has changed. The guilt is still there.

I am looking across at him now; the sky outside my window is still striated with blood.

He draws in a deep breath and then says, I am responsible for Andrea's death.

I have found my voice. I say, Oh, Colin, you are talking nonsense. You talk such foolishness. It was an accident. But he is shaking his head, shaking it vigorously and the fine hair moves from side to side. Did you ever wonder why the engine died? he asks. No one asked that. No one questioned that. Not one person at the inquest.

He tells me then, through his tears, that he was supposed to have done repairs on the diesel engine of the Andrea C., *something to do with a plugged air filter. But because he was behind on another boat, he left the* Andrea C. *for later. He is talking, his voice raspy. I strain to hear.*

I guess I didn't think it was as dirty as it was, he says, but I'm just making excuses. I should have gotten to it, Martha. I should have. Andrea was my wife. She didn't know it wasn't fixed. I told her it was. I told her it was! I was upset with her that morning for nagging me about it. I had a million things to do that morning, another boat to work on, plus that college business which was making me crazy. It's fixed, Andrea, *I said,* It's fixed! Just leave me alone about it!

If the boat had been in perfect working order she would have beaten the tide. She always did.

I sit there for many minutes after he tells me this, staring at the pattern of the afghan he holds to his face. I don't know what to say. Finally, I put my hand on his shoulder. Colin, it was an accident. She took chances that even Manny or Dob wouldn't take. No one would do what she did. No, Colin, it was an accident. You can't blame yourself.

Foolish words, I know. But I don't know what else to say.

I killed her, he says. I didn't mean to. I loved her, you know I did, Martha.

He gets up then and walks out the door. I watch him go, slowly making his way down the wharf heading on the road that leads to the path toward the church. As he goes I think, all this time. He has held this to himself all this time.

FORTY-EIGHT

NAOMI WAS LOOKING DOWN AT HER BARE FEET, at the way they grasped the rocks like fingers. If she concentrated on her feet she wouldn't have to think about Philip. She wouldn't have to think about the uncertainty that was beginning to gnaw at her. It was Colin's fault, all his doing, his incessant questions, planting all that doubt into the minds of the police officers, putting all these doubts into *her* head. *If he loved you he wouldn't leave the way he does. What kind of a husband does that?* But Colin didn't know Philip the way she did. That's what she said to herself over and over again. But even that thought was mocking her now. Did she really know him? Can one person ever really *know* another person? She realized with a kind of horror that if she doubted Philip, doubted their love, her whole life lost meaning. She had nothing else on which to plant her feet. No other foundation.

She was walking past the cemetery now, and the late afternoon sun was casting oblong shadows on the ground from the white grave markers. People dead and their secrets buried with them. She thought of Jo.

"What does Philip look like?" Jo had asked one evening when the two of them sat on their cots. Jo was holding Curtis in her lap, feeding him with a bottle. Zoe, on the cot, was wearing one of Philip's T-shirts as a nightgown. It was big and clownish on her and Zoe laughed and fluttered her arms, and the sleeves flapped wildly. This got Curtis laughing in that gurgling, giggling, hearty way that babies laugh. This got Jo and her laughing as if they would never stop.

Naomi longed for laughter now.

"He's tall and big, broad shouldered," she had said after the laughter had died. "But not fat. Muscular. Not an ounce of fat. Zoe takes after him."

"Can I see a picture of him?"

"No. Isn't that funny? I don't have any pictures. He's not one for pictures. Says he's not photogenic."

"Not even a wedding picture?"

"No."

"Tell me what he's like. His personality."

Naomi had laughed. "Why are you so curious?"

"That's just me," said Jo. "Curious. Lots of people say I'm too curious for my own good."

Curiosity killed the cat.

And now people were asking her a whole lot of questions she didn't have answers for. Naomi broke a dead twig from an overhanging branch and twirled it in her hands as she kept walking. She kicked a stone in the path, not even minding that it hurt. But it was those two little girls in the locket that caused her to gasp. That's when she had gotten up to leave, when she had come out here.

"No," she had said to them around the table. "I've never seen these little girls before." Why, then, did those little girls fill her with such fear? Why did they seem so familiar to her? Why had she put her hand to her throat? Why had she come out here, leaving so suddenly?

She sat on the stoop of the first little cabin and picked at the bark on the stick she held. She peeled away strings of it like wallpaper, smoothing it the way she had seen Colin do. If she had a knife she'd whittle at it, the way Colin did. A deep fear was tugging at her; she no longer felt safe in this place. This island was the one place where she had felt safe: the cabins, the island, the church, the sea, her garden. It was the one place where no one from her childhood would come and hurt her. But now, she didn't feel safe anymore. The sun went behind a cloud. She shivered in her coat.

FORTY-NINE

IT WAS MORNING. The twins had left for school, Paul had left for work hours ago, and Margot was going through Paul's things. Carefully, methodically she was reaching her hands under the socks in his sock drawer, putting them back exactly as she found them, side by side, folded in upon themselves, a row of black and a row of brown. His white socks he kept in another drawer, the ones with the red stripes never getting mixed up with the ones with blue stripes.

Margot felt between layers of his T-shirts. Why was she doing this? Did she really want to know who *she* was? Or should she, like Paul seemed so desperate to do, put it all behind them? "With God's help we can do this, love," he had said the previous night. "We can put it behind us. We can get on with just being you and me. I'm ready to do that."

She had to admit that he had been awfully nice to her the past few days. On Friday night they had gone out for a long dinner and a walk. He had tried to hold her hand; she had withdrawn hers. He didn't press. On Saturday he had taken the four of them out for a long drive in the country to look at the fall colors. They had driven up to the mountains and stopped at a cafe for lunch. His face was beaming. My little family, he said over and over, I've come home to my little family. On Sunday they sat together in church. Afterward, after most everyone had gone, he spent a long time standing in the church parking lot talking to Chuck, their minister. She had waited in the car with Pam and Sara trying not to think about what the two were talking about.

Later, when she had asked him, he said, "I told him that lately I had strayed far away from God, and I was trying to find my way back. I asked if I could come and talk with him about it, maybe get him to pray with me."

"Did you tell him you had an affair?" Margot whispered, hardly able to say the words.

"I thought we would tell him that together."

Margot felt relieved. It seemed awfully important to her that no one know about this. Especially not Sara and Pammy. Oh, dear God, may they never find out. She knew that if it wasn't for the girls, she would have gone away for a while. Just to be alone, just to sort it all through. Paul was pressuring her to call Chuck. But she could never do that. What would she say to him? She and Paul had visited in their home. The four of them, Chuck and his wife and she and Paul had gone out to dinner in restaurants, for coffee after the evening service. They had worked on committees together. Once, she had even sung a duet with the pastor's wife. He would be the last person she would call.

My husband had an affair. She said the words out loud into the empty space of the bedroom. It happens all the time. There are even books written about it. People go on talk shows and talk about it. Famous people do it. Sixty percent, if you believe the statistics, have extramarital affairs.

But now on Monday morning, Margot felt hurt and bruised and very alone. There was nothing in his sock drawer. There was nothing in his T-shirt drawer. There was nothing in the pockets of his suits and jackets.

On his bedside table was a half-eaten roll of Tums, a few paper-back mysteries, assorted keys, an old watch of his that no longer worked, a couple of pairs of sunglasses, one with the earpiece broken off, bits and pieces of things, notes which she read, pennies, old Visa receipts which she examined, and other oddments. But no long, perfumed love letters, no matchbooks with phone numbers on the covers, no handkerchiefs with lipstick. She shut the drawer. She walked out of their bedroom, carefully closing the door behind her.

The door to Paul's office was locked and she looked down at the knob in her hand, surprised. He never locked it. Always before she would come in here to answer the phone, opening up the window for air or to vacuum.

Back upstairs she grabbed the handful of keys from his bedside table and went down again. She fumbled with several until she found one that worked. She was in. Feeling like a trespasser, she carefully closed and locked it behind her. She dropped the small pile of keys on the corner of the desk and stood briefly in the shaft of sunlight. It was a lovely room, really, a showplace of an office, with its fireplace, dark wood, stained glass in the windows, and a deep plush oriental carpet on the floor. And of course the African violets.

She stood for a moment in the stillness. What kind of man occupied this space in his off hours? His desk was neat, with a square marble desk set in the corner, two pens upright like goal posts, a brass desk lamp, a pad of empty paper embossed with his name. His computer sat on a small desk extension. It occurred to her to turn it on, see if she could find anything on it, but knowing Paul, it would be guarded by all sorts of passwords and codes.

She turned. There were the bookshelves with the books arranged by height, not by author, not by subject matter, not by their availability for service, but by height! Next to it was a wooden filing cabinet. Locked. And none of the keys worked. She sat down in his leather chair. Paul always had to have the best—the fastest sports car, the biggest house, the most expensive leather couch, the most powerful computer.

She pulled out the large center desk drawer. It contained neat rows of pens and pads of paper, staples in a small box, a box of paper clips, a box of blank computer disks, a scattering of rubber bands.

The topmost side drawer contained African violet fertilizer and watering utensils. The middle one held paper and more pens. It was in the bottom one that she found the only evidence that anyone did any real work in this place. She lifted out a manila folder of what looked like a stack of invoices to Paul Douglas, Computer Consulting. Absently, she began shuffling through them. Names and addresses of companies she didn't recognize. She knew Paul did consulting on the side, apart from his job. Maybe these were invoices from his own business. Maybe there was a very good reason he had his office locked. Maybe he didn't want the IRS people to find these. Or maybe she was letting her imagination run wild and these were perfectly legitimate, honest receipts.

Near the bottom of the pile a name caught her eye. Philip Friend. She pulled out that invoice and smoothed it on the table. No address or phone number. Philip Friend had purchased a computer program from Paul, something called LI Data Base, whatever that was. Paul had said he had never heard of Philip Friend.

And then Paul unlocked his office door and walked in.

She could see shock in his eyes as he stood there. She could see his mouth working. She remained at the desk, holding onto the invoice.

"What are you doing here?"

"I was just going to ask you the same thing."

"This is my office, Margot." He was trying so hard to keep his voice even that it almost amused her. Funny, she didn't feel all the things she thought she would feel. She didn't quickly jump up, hiding the folder and claim she was in here to dust. She did none of those things, but sat there, calmly holding onto the invoice between her thumb and forefinger.

He said, "I came back home to remind you of the dinner tonight, and I find you going through my desk drawer like a jealous fishwife! How'd you get in here in the first place?"

She nodded toward the keys, then stood. "I could ask you the same thing, you know. How could you dare to violate our sacred marriage vows said before God and all our family and friends? I could ask you the same thing, Paul. Turnabout is fair play. I just wanted to find out who she is."

"Was."

She glared at him.

"It's no longer an *is,* it's a *was.* I told you. It's over. How many times do I have to say I'm sorry? Do I have to get down on my knees and beg?"

"Did she break it off? Is that why you're running back to me? And if she hadn't broken it off you'd still be there, driving around California with her—"

"Stop!"

But Margot could not. She got up, reached for an African violet from the window sill and threw it hard against the fireplace. She took great pleasure when she saw the clay pot break into a hundred pieces, the dirt and roots and little blossoms scatter across the plush carpet.

He grabbed her shoulders. "Stop it!" he yelled. She pulled away from him.

"That's it, isn't it? Your mistress broke it off with you, so since no one better has come along yet, you come back to your fat wife! How was she in bed, Paul, was it worth it?" She grabbed another African violet, but he lunged at her and held her shoulders in his hands. There was a rage on his face, an expression she had never seen before; his grasp tightened on her shoulders and it frightened her to her core. She wondered if she had gone too far.

"How many times…" His voice broke, his grasp on her weakened. "How many times do I have to tell you that I'm sorry? How I don't want to keep secrets from each other any more? How I want to start over?"

She backed away from him, staring at his face. "Okay, if you don't want to have secrets, how come your office was locked?"

"Force of habit."

"It's not your habit. I can't remember it ever being locked before."

He put his hands up. "I have no idea why I locked it this time."

"And who *is* Philip Friend?"

"I told you, I never heard of him."

"He's a friend of yours."

She handed him the invoice which she had crumpled into a ball. He straightened it out and looked at it. "I have no idea." He turned it over. "This was probably a long time ago. Let me check my computer records. If I've done business with him it'll all be here," he said patting the computer. He sat down in the leather chair and she watched while the computer screen lightened.

"I have to go to work, Paul."

He put up his hand. "No you don't. You're so curious, have a seat, we'll clear up this Philip Friend mystery once and for all."

She watched him do a search for Philip Friend. It yielded nothing. He tried again. No record found.

"I don't get it," he said. "If I have that invoice, his name has to be here. Yet it's not. I don't know why."

"Would it be on your computer at work?"

"No, I don't think so, but I'll check. But I think he was a private client of mine. I don't understand it. Name doesn't ring a bell. Nothing."

FIFTY

By MIDMORNING MICK AND VIRGINIA were back on the island. They had driven in behind the church just as Peter was walking out the front door to go to the lighthouse. They motioned for him to come back inside. So he shoved his paperback book into his pocket and followed them. Jeremiah, Martha, and Colin were sitting at the table and Naomi was sitting on the edge of the cot cradling Zoe in her arms, looking down at her.

The room was stifling, as Peter knew it would be, with Jeremiah adding more wood even as they entered.

Colin rubbed his hand over his beard. "To what do we owe the honor?" he asked.

"We're still looking for Philip," said Virginia.

Naomi looked up expectantly as Virginia approached her. "Mrs. Friend, if you have any idea where he is, would you please tell us? This is very important."

She shook her head. "I already told you. I don't know. I keep telling you."

"Are you sure? Are you positively sure?"

"Naomi said she doesn't know," added Colin from across the table.

Mick said, "There is some speculation that Mrs. Friend here may be hiding him. That's one theory. I don't believe it because I've been out here, because I've met you folks. I'm just telling you what they're saying down at the station."

Colin picked at his teeth with a toothpick. "Well, that's a wrong theory."

"We also want to know about the bank account," said Virginia.

"Please," said Martha. "This has been hard on her, having Philip go missing and finding Jules and all."

"What about the bank account?" Naomi leaned forward. "Is there some money in it now?"

Virginia pulled up a chair beside her and said gently, "Can we see your bank records?"

"Jules had all of those." She was fiddling with the frayed ends of the blanket which rested in her lap.

Virginia looked helplessly up at her fellow officer, then to Naomi.

"I want to get this straight, every Friday your husband deposited fifty dollars to your account and Jules went to the bank for you and took it out with your ATM card?"

"Right."

"How long had he been doing this?"

"About four years. Before I had the card Jules would just go into the bank for me."

"How long have you had the card?"

"Maybe two years."

"And it's the bank in town? The one on Main Street?"

"Right."

There was a silence. Virginia turned pages in her notebook. Mick coughed and shifted his position. Colin and Jeremiah waited. Peter leaned against the doorjamb.

Finally Mick said, "Mrs. Friend, that just doesn't add up." He looked around the room. "Okay folks, did any of the rest of you ever pick up Mrs. Friend's money on a Friday?"

No one said anything.

Naomi said, "Jules did this for me. I never wanted to bother anyone else with it. Jules offered."

"And now Jules is conveniently dead."

Peter could see the color drain from Naomi's face.

Virginia turned to her. "Mrs. Friend, it's so important that you tell us the truth. So much is riding on this."

"I am telling you the truth."

"Could you please tell us what is going on?" Colin said.

The officer said, "There is no record of an account anywhere in any bank in the entire state of Maine in the name of Naomi Friend. There was never any account, no record of any deposits ever being made from the account of Philip Friend into his wife's account. Oh, and no record of any account belonging to anyone named Philip Friend, either."

Naomi rose. "But that's impossible. I got money. Every Friday. Fifty dollars." She turned to Colin, to Jeremiah, to Martha. "Tell them that. Tell them that Philip sent me money."

"But do you have proof?" asked Mick. The husky officer went over to Naomi, towered over her, stared down at her. "Mrs. Friend, I have to ask you one more time. Are you protecting your husband?"

"Absolutely not."

"This is serious," Virginia said. "If it were only the bank records our problem wouldn't nearly be so grave. But there is no record anywhere of Philip Friend. No Social Security number, no income tax, no record of employment, just a driver's license with no address, just a place of birth and a date." Virginia was shaking her head. "As far as we're concerned the man doesn't exist." Virginia looked at Naomi who was shaking violently.

She put her hand on Naomi's quivering shoulder and said gently, "Do you by any chance have a photo of your husband?"

She shook her head.

"Wedding pictures?"

"Philip didn't like getting his picture taken."

"Since we don't have a photo," Mick said, "we've got a fellow in Bangor who does these composite sketches. Would you agree, Naomi, to come down and help us with that?"

She nodded.

"There's more," Virginia said. "Remember that logging camp where you said you met your husband?"

Naomi looked up and nodded. Peter could see the fear in her eyes.

"Well, they have no record of any Philip Friend ever working for them."

"I don't understand. That's where I met him. I'm not crazy, and I'm not hiding him."

"We believe you," said Virginia. "Do you know any other places where your husband worked?"

She shook her head. "He was going to get a job in New Jersey. On the waterfront. But I don't know the name of the company."

"We're checking into that now. Anything else?"

She shook her head again. "I'm sorry, I just don't know." She was still shivering, and Jeremiah took the coat, Jo's coat, from the hook and placed it around her shoulders.

"Did he leave anything here of his?"

"No."

"No clothes, no effects?"

"Not really. Just his coat that you went through."

"Nothing else? Think hard."

Naomi pointed. "Just his daughter!"

Everyone looked at Zoe, who was sitting happily on the cot coloring on the inside of an open paper bag, large swirling masses of reds and greens, a tree, a house, the ocean. She was singing while she worked and seemed oblivious to all that was going on around her.

"This is his daughter," Naomi said it more quietly now and then stroked Zoe's hair.

Zoe, aware that the attention was now focused on her, smiled at them, held up her picture and said, "See what I made?"

OCTOBER 19, 1998

FROM THE JOURNALS OF MARTHA MACGREGOR

Colin came to see me today. It was low tide and we walked along the rocky, muddy shore together. That Colin still comes to me, still talks with me, still confides in me about the hard things in his life, a dottering old woman, is remarkable. He says that I am anything but dottering. You have more energy than ten people, he says, and you are good to talk to. That's kind of him.

We have not spoken of Andrea's death since the day Jo died. It, like so many other subjects, will not be spoken of. A part of me thinks that Colin must work these things out for himself. But, oh, he has carried this pain for twenty years! I need to help him, but what to say.

He told me that Philip left. He arrived a couple of weeks ago, right after Jo died, if I remember correctly, and now he has gone. He does this, comes and goes at will. I have tried to talk to Naomi about it, but it's a closed subject with her. I understand that. There are closed subjects with Colin. There are closed subjects with everyone.

Colin's hatred for Philip is another matter. I don't understand it. As soon as Philip comes back, Colin immediately retreats either to the Andrea C. *or into moody quietness. When I have asked him about it in the past, he says he hates the man and doesn't trust him. I say, Why, what business is it of yours? Answer me that. But he doesn't.*

The tide was very low when we walked and the wharf sat high on its pilings. How odd this is, I said, that we can walk on sea bed which in just a few short hours will be flooded with water. I wonder if this is how the Children of Israel felt when they crossed the Red Sea? And Colin said, No, it's not like that at all. That was a miracle of God and this is just nature. I was surprised at this answer and looked over at him. Colin has never used the words miracle *or* God *in the same sentence. I said, Well, nature is a miracle of God, if you ask me. Look at all the little sea creatures who depend on the tide pools. If that isn't a miracle of God, I don't know what is.*

We walked east out toward the point. If Colin realized this, he said nothing about it. If we were to keep on going we would soon be at the base of the cliff. It would be safe there now and enchanting with the rock shapes, but I knew the two of us would not venture that far. We would go so far, then by some unspoken agreement, we would turn around and head back.

Ahead of us was Jules's old dory, tied by a long line to a rock. It rested on the dry sea bed. Isn't that Jules's dory? But what's it doing way down here? No, that isn't Jules's boat, I'm sure of it, said Colin. And he should know.

We walked over to it. No, it wasn't Jules's. I saw that now. It was a large rowboat, maybe eighteen feet long, the outside was a faded black. I had never seen it before. And I know every boat on the island. Maybe one of the children has a new boat, I offered. Colin shook his head. They wouldn't dock it this close to the cliff. They would tie it up at the townsite. You'd have to be crazy to let your child row way out here, Colin said.

Just after we passed the boat we turned around.

But I began to wonder about that boat. I'll have to ask Jules about it.

FIFTY-ONE

At the shop, Margot could not keep herself from crying. She would be cutting a piece of fabric for a customer and her eyes would brim with tears. Jane would take the scissors gently from her and whisper to go to the office. Margot would then lock herself in the bathroom and sit and wait until the tears stopped. Then she would slap cold water on her face, dry it, and emerge once again. Jane kept looking at Margot in a solicitous sort of way, not understanding, probably presuming it had something to do with fatigue or illness or something the matter with one of her daughters.

"Is it your mother?" Jane asked at one point.

"My mother?" Margot looked up in surprise. "What about my mother?"

"Well, is she ill? Is that why you're so upset? I remember last year when she was so sick." And she had looked at Margot with such a look of concern that Margot almost laughed.

"Oh no, nothing of the sort. Not that. No, my mother's fine. She walks five miles a day now. No, she's fine. She's in better shape than I am."

"Then what?"

"It's fatigue. I'm tired. So much to do."

Jane had looked at her, puzzled.

At one point Jane said, "Margot, why don't you just get away? I can't remember the last time you took a vacation."

"I was just away."

"That was business. That doesn't count. You and Paul both need a vacation. What I prescribe is for the two of you to get away. For a week. I'll mind the store. He's looking as dour as you are these days."

Margot hugged her arms around her chest. "That's all I need," she said. "Right now I've got a mountain of sewing to do. If I started

273

now I could sew all day twenty-four hours a day and still not get everything done that needed to be done. Instead, I can't concentrate, I think of Jo, I spend precious days running all over the countryside visiting her parents and her foster parents and the people she worked for. Heavens knows why I did that." Margot sat down on the stool behind the cash register and began hooking paper clips together. "And I never did find the locket. Paul doesn't even know it's missing."

"That reminds me," said Jane. "Did you hear the news?"

"What news?"

"I heard it on the radio this morning on my way in. The police are looking for that Philip Friend person that I was called about."

Margot felt a shiver begin somewhere deep inside of her. "The police are looking for him?"

"A manhunt involving all the New England states, New York, and even Canada now. He's feared armed and dangerous and anyone with information regarding his whereabouts is not to approach him but to call the police. Sounds pretty scary."

"Are you serious?"

"I keep wondering if I should call the police."

"Yeah, I think you should."

That evening, wearing one of her own designs—an ankle-length knit dress in pale mauve with a hand-painted bodice—Margot held onto Paul's tuxedoed arm and walked around the grand ballroom of the Sheraton amongst other couples also arm in arm, also clad in their finest. Serious looking waiters in red bow ties carried trays of tall glasses of champagne and plates of oysters, tiny cheese balls, shrimp and pieces of smoked fish on crackers.

Paul was subdued, quiet, and patted Margot's hand. Margot wasn't altogether sure she liked her hand there, so close to him, but whenever she tried to withdraw it, he took it and firmly placed it back in the crook of his arm. For show, she thought. He's doing this just for show.

They were standing near the entrance to the ballroom when Margot turned to him. "Did you hear about Philip Friend?"

"What, love?" he bent down to her.

"The police are looking for him."

"Where'd you hear this?"

"Jane told me. Then I heard it on the news myself on the way home. He's armed and dangerous and people with any information about him are supposed to call the police. Did you check the computers at work for his name?"

"Sure did. Nothing." He sighed. "I wish I could place him. I just can't remember him."

"Maybe you should call the police."

"You know, I believe you are right. I'll do that when we get home."

They were interrupted by an associate of Paul, a slim woman in her midthirties named Bonnie. She was with a man she gushingly introduced as Lorne, the new programmer. Lorne was medium height, with straight hair, thinning on top, which brushed the collar of his jacket.

"Lorne, meet Margot, Paul's wife."

"Nice to meet you." He extended his hand.

"Hello, Lorne," she said.

Bonnie wore a floor-length black dress which showed a lot of cleavage and was slit halfway up the side. Margot wondered idly how sitting down was accomplished in an outfit like that. Bonnie carried a tall champagne glass in one hand and began touching Paul with the other, pawing at his arm with her long red fingernails, stroking his shoulder. In the presence of small, thin women, Margot always felt large, like a jellyfish in a school of minnows.

"Margot, have you tried the shrimp balls? They are to die for."

"I'm not very hungry, thanks."

"Well, I never knew you to pass up food! Margot, do you mind terribly if I steal your handsome husband for a teensy minute. I hate to talk shop, but there's something I need him for."

"Be my guest."

Bonnie took hold of Paul's arm and led him away. Margot

watched them, the casual way they talked, the glances, the smiles, the easy familiarity between the two of them.

"That's a beautiful dress you're wearing."

Margot turned. She had forgotten Lorne was there. "Well, thank you," she stammered.

"You're a dress designer, aren't you?"

"How did you know?"

"Paul mentioned it."

In the corner Bonnie Bimbo was looking earnestly up into Margot's husband's eyes. They were standing too close, and Margot felt as if she couldn't breathe. She would go home and crush every one of his African violets. She would unfold all of his black socks and scrunch them into his drawer in a big lump. She would take his package of Tums out of his bedside table and grind them all up and sprinkle them all over his leather books.

"Is the painting yours too?" he asked.

"Oh. What?"

"The painting on your dress, is that your design too?"

She touched it absently with her fingers. "Oh, yes. I guess."

"Well, that in itself is beautiful. You studied art?"

"I did, yes."

"And what made you get into dress design rather than painting pictures?"

Margot warmed to him. "I guess when I kept painting all of my T-shirts, I realized that maybe clothing was my forte." He chuckled. She said, "And you're a programmer?"

"Yep, just moved here from California."

"Oh."

He smiled.

"Quite a change I would imagine," she said.

"Yeah, there are definite differences between the casual, laid-back atmosphere of the West Coast and the truly stuffy New England East Coast."

She laughed. "Oh, it's not that bad here."

He grinned. "I was surprised, that's all, when I got here and was expected to wear a tie to work. I didn't even own one. Had to go out and buy one."

Margot feigned horror. "Imagine! Well, I could have designed one for you." She paused, said carefully, "So I guess going back to California last week was a welcome change. You didn't even pack your tie, I bet."

"I didn't go back to California last week."

"Oh, you didn't go with Paul?"

He looked at her oddly.

She said, "Paul went to California last week on some education thing. Some course or something. Meetings."

"Margot," his voice was quiet. In front of her, Bonnie was gazing up into Paul's eyes and laughing, a flirty little laugh, showing a lot of teeth and cleavage. "Paul didn't go to California last week. There was no company trip last week."

She backed away from him slightly, and he must have read her thoughts because the expression in his eyes said, "Sorry."

Paul and Bonnie returned. Paul was smiling broadly, and Bonnie walked beside him, her arm in his, eyelashes fluttering. Margot stared at them. Of course, he wasn't in California. She had tried phoning, remember? And the receptionist said no one from East Coast was there. He wasn't driving around in a taxi. She had called him on his cellular. She had no way of knowing where he was when he picked it up. He could say he was anywhere, how would she know the difference?

On the way into the dining hall she took his arm, looked up into his eyes and said sweetly, "Where did you go if it wasn't California?"

He stopped in his tracks, looked down at her grim-faced. "I told you about that already. That it's all over. I don't understand why you just can't let it go!"

"It's not that easy, Paul."

"Have you called the minister?"

"The minister? Since when is he 'the minister'? He's always been just Chuck."

"Don't harp, Margot. Try to be pleasant for my sake tonight. This dinner is important to me."

FIFTY-TWO

A FRESH SALT BREEZE WAS WAFTING ACROSS THE ISLAND the following morning when Virginia came back to drive Colin and Naomi to the mainland. A police artist had been summoned and was waiting for them. "He's got his sketchbook, his computer, and he's ready and waiting." She chatted on about police sketches and their validity and why this artist was so good, and how they were lucky to get him on such short notice.

"Naomi, we'll want you to come, of course, but does anyone else know Philip equally well?"

In the end it was Jeremiah who suggested that Colin accompany her. "Except for Naomi, you know the face of Philip probably better than anyone around here."

Naomi wasn't sure how she felt about Colin coming, but she went along with it.

Naomi sat in the front seat of the patrol car and watched Virginia's hands. Her right one was on the wheel and her left one punctuated her conversation, like a conductor of an orchestra.

"It's really nothing to worry about, this sketch artist business. It's even quite fun in a way. And you'll love Al, he's the artist. He's so good, and he'll put you right at ease. There's really nothing to worry about."

Naomi rubbed her hands and listened, nervously fingering her ring finger and the whitish line where her wedding ring was supposed to be, her hands tanned except for that place.

Colin was in the backseat, and Naomi was quite certain he was not listening at all to Virginia. She could picture him looking out at the passing scenery, lost in his own thoughts.

If Virginia noticed the strain between the two of them, she chose to ignore it. Ever since Naomi had found Colin's little box of rings, things had changed between them. And it was her fault entirely. She should never have gone into his private place. It was inexcusable. Yet, why had he snatched those two rings away with such a fury? Why were they so precious to him? *I was married once.* When he had said that to her, he had surprised her to the core. She always had Colin pegged as a wanderer, a gypsy, not willing or able to get close enough to anyone.

She knew so little about him. No one did. Except, perhaps, Martha. Those two had a closeness she could not understand. When Naomi first came to the island she had the idea that Martha was his mother. When she asked him if this were true, he had laughed, "Oh, that's a good one. I'll have to tell Martha that one."

Yet he knew just about everything there was to know about her. He overheard every argument. He was there when Philip chided her for losing the ring. He was there when Philip complained of the filthiness of the place. Now he even knew how she had met Philip.

When they arrived at the police station, Virginia led them into a small office in the back of the building. She and Colin walked side by side behind her, not touching, not talking. They entered the room which contained a computer on a table surrounded by several wooden chairs. They were introduced to a man in baggy gray sweats, longish hair, and a drooping mustache. This was Al Wood, the artist, Virginia said proudly.

For the next hour, she and Colin talked about Philip, about the shape of his face, the spacing of his eyes. They compared picture after picture to try to find a close match to his. Was his nose like this? Or this? No, thinner. Sort of a Grecian, Roman nose, but not pronounced. "He's a very handsome man," said Naomi at one point. "No," said Colin. "He is profoundly ugly."

Al would draw something, look at them, and they would confer and decide whether it looked like Philip or not. All this talk about Philip was somehow comforting to Naomi, and it felt good to be doing something concrete to find him. Al scanned the picture into the computer and then made even more changes. His eyebrows, are they more like this or like that? Like that. No, wait, more like this one. His ears? It's hard to say. In the end they produced a portrait of Philip that was more than passable, it really looked like the guy.

"What are you going to do with this picture?" she asked Virginia when they were finished.

"We're going to circulate it. Get it on television. If someone out there has seen Philip Friend, we'll know. We'll find your husband, Mrs. Friend."

"Thank you."

They were about to head back to the island when Chris and Mick walked in hurriedly.

"So glad you're still here. So glad you haven't left."

Chris's face was grim. He didn't look at Naomi, but headed over to Colin, where the two of them began talking in the corner. Colin kept glancing over at her.

Mick said, "Mrs. Friend, we've found some information that is really important."

"Something happened to Philip."

The officer cleared his throat. There was a pause. "Maybe you better sit down." Virginia put an arm on Naomi's shoulder and led her to one of the wooden chairs against the wall. She sat. Mick and Virginia sat with her, one on either side.

"Is he dead?" She barely whispered.

The officer grunted. "Well, yes, I guess you could say that. He died in 1954."

She stared at him, at the deep set eyes blinking at her, like two black marbles, the wiry mustache above his thick lips. She felt as if she couldn't breathe. She put a hand to her neck.

"What do you mean?" she asked quietly.

"Okay, well, remember when Virginia said there was no record anywhere of anyone named Philip Friend?"

"Yes."

"Chris corrected us on that. Prior to us looking, Colin had him do a search of Philip Friend's driver's license and he came up with something. Chris faxed those papers to us, with his birthday and birthplace and so forth. Turns out there really was a Philip Friend. He was born in Freeport, Maine, in 1953 and died a year later."

Naomi felt her skin grow cold. Her throat felt constricted. She began to cough.

"Would you like a glass of water?" asked Virginia.

She found her voice. "No thanks."

He went on, "I've got a copy of the death certificate right here. The same date of birth as your Philip Friend, the same birthplace he gave on his records."

It gave her an odd, eerie feeling to look down at the death certificate and read her husband's name. "There's a mistake. I don't understand."

Mick looked at Virginia. Chris and Colin were now standing beside her. Chris said, "What we're saying Naomi, is that Philip Friend, the Philip Friend that is your husband, doesn't exist. He took the name of a dead child to get a driver's license. But now," Chris looked at Colin. "Now, it looks like he is methodically erasing every trace of Philip Friend, or trying to, from the face of this planet."

Virginia caught her as she fainted. They laid her on the hardwood bench of the police station. Colin stayed with her until she recovered.

FIFTY-THREE

MARGOT DECIDED TO GIVE PAUL A SECOND CHANCE. She would trust him. She would forgive him. She had come to that conclusion last night after Paul's company dinner. And this morning as she talked business with Jane, as she conversed with customers, as she met with the suppliers, as she perfected her designs, as she sewed, her thoughts were never very far from Paul. *How many times do I have to beg your forgiveness?* he had asked. Thinking about it, it truly seemed that he wanted to come back to her. Perhaps his overzealousness at wanting to start over again had more to do with actually wanting to start over than with anything else.

After he had said, "Don't harp," she had begun to cry, "Paul, I'm having such a hard time with this. Don't you realize?" He looked down at her and seemed, then, to understand. Finally. A change came over him. Throughout the dinner his eyes had only been for her. He ignored Bonnie, who had managed to seat herself next to him and who kept pawing at him with her long fingernails. He bragged to those at the table about his wife's artistic talent, her designs, and the success of her business. His eyes really did seem full of pride when they looked at her.

So, perhaps she had been wrong. Maybe the problem was hers. Maybe she needed to forgive. Maybe God had put this awful thing in her path so that she would learn how to.

When they had gotten home, they had stood in the darkness of the kitchen and held each other for a long time. He was weeping then, and she knew—she didn't know how she knew but she knew—that this time it was genuine. She had taken a tissue and tenderly wiped his eyes. He told her that he loved her, had always loved her, and that if he could change the past he would in an instant. If he lost her now, life would have no meaning for him. "I've done some terrible, terrible things, Margot."

"I forgive you." She had said it with all the meaning she could muster.

"I don't deserve you," he had said, weeping. "I don't deserve someone as good and wonderful as you. I've committed the sin of David, and yet you're still here with me."

"I am and will be forever."

She had not gone to bed right away. She told Paul she had to work on some new designs. In actual fact she had decided to pray. Paul went upstairs and she sat at the dining room table without turning on the light. An almost full moon sent splinters of white light into where she sat, head bowed into her folded hands. What did Jesus say about forgiveness? Seventy times seven. She hadn't even given Paul one chance. Not one. She hadn't even attempted to forgive, so engrossed was she in her own hurt. She also thought back to the final chapters in the book she had bought. It was possible to go on after adultery. It was possible to forge an even better relationship than before. That's what her book said. "God, help us to do that," she prayed.

When she had finally gone up to bed, Paul was already asleep. She lay down beside him and put her arms around him. They lay that way until she fell asleep.

This morning she felt better, infinitely better. It wasn't a gushy kind of elated happiness. It still hurt, but she would get past it. Her marriage was too important to throw away.

At one point in the morning Jane turned to her and said, "You're different today. Serene."

"Have you ever forgiven someone for something they did which was so outrageously bad that you thought it was beyond forgiveness?"

"What are you talking about?"

And then she told her best friend about Paul, leaving nothing out. It felt good to share it with a friend. *That's the first step in healing,* the book said, *talking it over with someone, admitting there is a problem.*

Jane stared at her.

"I know it's hard to believe, and it was so hard for me, and still is, but I honestly think he wants to change. He's been so nice to me lately."

"And Margot, he came back to you. You have to remember that."

Jane had gone over and hugged her. They stood that way for a long time. When they released themselves from the embrace, both were crying.

Margot went into the office and called Chuck.

FIFTY-FOUR

PETER NEVER HAD MUCH TO DO WITH CHILDREN. He had a few cousins younger than him, but he never paid much attention to them. So it surprised him that Zoe was so readily latching onto him. Peekaboo Zoe, he called her. Her favorite game consisted of running and hiding behind the gravestones, then giggling until she fell to the ground when Peter approached, crouching, making gorilla sounds.

Jeremiah told him that the name Zoe meant "life" in Greek. She was aptly named, thought Peter. When there seemed to be so much death and darkness on the island, so much sadness, Zoe continued to laugh in spite of it all.

It was Zoe who made him start thinking about his own mother. He would look at the way Naomi read to her, helped her draw pictures, and write her name in big letters—ZOE. A long time ago he had sat at the kitchen table in Red Deer writing his ABCs on lined paper, under the watchful eye of his own mother. A long time ago he would lean up on the kitchen counter asking to lick the beaters. A long time ago she would rush home from her job in the lawyer's office in time to drive him to soccer or baseball. A long time ago she sat on the little chair next to the piano and patiently listened to his scales, over and over. He would read his poetry to her, and she would comment on it, praising the imagery, pointing out the errors. And when teachers would write on report cards that Peter needed to "buckle down" and "spend less time day dreaming," his mother would defend him. "That's the artist in you, Peter, don't let anyone steal that from you." Afterward she would help him work out a schedule of study.

A few days ago Jeremiah had said to him, "Why don't you call your mother?"

"If you call your wife, then I'll call my mother."

"Touché," said Jeremiah winking at him.

Zoe was with Peter in the sanctuary reading to her about the adventures of Peter Rabbit when he heard Naomi say loudly, shrilly from the back room, "But Philip washed everything!"

"Mama," said Zoe scampering down from Peter's lap.

Peter followed the little girl into the back room where the two cops, Mick and Virginia, were unloading the contents of a black bag onto the folding table. Colin was there along with Jeremiah, Martha, and the private detective named Chris.

Naomi's hand flew to her mouth. "There won't be any fingerprints here because Philip washed everything."

"What?" asked Virginia.

"He washed everything."

"What do you mean he *washed* everything?"

"Just as I said, he washed everything. I came in here; it was the day before he left. He was quite grouchy and said that nothing here was clean enough for his daughter, and he was wearing these long yellow rubber gloves, the kind the fishermen use, and he had every plate and cup out on this table. He was washing them and putting them away. He had buckets of water all over the place. Then he washed down the table and the walls and all the windows."

"Neat freak, our Philip," said Colin. Martha gave him a look.

"So you came in here, and he was methodically washing down the entire place," Mick said.

"Yes."

"What about the sanctuary?" asked Chris.

"He washed that too. Washed all the pews in the church."

"A busy man," muttered Colin.

"The outhouse?"

Naomi shook her head. "I don't know. I saw him out there. He might have been washing that, too."

"Can we hire this guy full time?" asked Colin.

Mick and Virginia looked at each other. Colin, eyebrows raised, looked over at Chris. When Naomi finally spoke it was in a voice so quiet that Peter barely heard from where he stood. "I know of a place," she said. "The cabin in the woods. We had some wine, celebrating his new job. I left the glasses there."

"What are we waiting for?" said Mick, rising.

"Can I come, too?" asked Zoe. "To the cabin?" But her mother seemed not to have heard her. Peter sat Zoe down in her wagon and pulled. He was on the path directly behind Naomi and Colin who walked side by side, keeping step with each other but saying nothing. Peter remembered what Jeremiah had said, that these two were in love. He wondered at that.

Just before they got to the cabin he heard Colin say to Naomi, "I'm sorry, Naomi, about all of this."

She seemed not to have heard him.

When they entered the cabin, there were two wine glasses and an empty bottle leaning against a log. Mick said, "Bingo!"

He put on a pair of rubber gloves and then took both wine glasses and the empty bottle and put both in a plastic Ziploc bag.

"Let's go," said Virginia, but Naomi had placed a hand to her mouth. She stumbled and would have fallen had not Jeremiah caught her. He sat her down on one of the log chairs.

"Naomi? What is it?" he asked.

"I need to say something. I need to tell everyone something now." Colin was immediately at her side. "Those two girls in the locket." Her voice was barely above a whisper. "I know who they are. I've known since the minute I saw them."

NOVEMBER 4, 1998

FROM THE JOURNALS OF MARTHA MACGREGOR

Jeremiah is a very wise person. I learned that today. In the midst of all the trouble—the police officers here and that whole fingerprint business and the trek to the cabin and then what Naomi told us about the twin girls and how little sense that made—all of us ended up in the sanctuary. I don't know how that happened, but something made us gather there, and so here we sat in the front pew, all of us, all in a row. Next to me was Colin, next to Colin was Naomi, and then Jeremiah and then Peter. Zoe sat on Peter's lap.

The police officers and Colin's friend Chris were in the kitchen of the church talking about things, taking notes and poring over their papers and that locket and the note they found in Philip's truck, talking on cellular phones to people. There was no need for us to stay there, we were just in the way, so we filed into the sanctuary as if by some curious preordained order. It was silent for a moment as we sat there; it felt like ten minutes that we sat there, but probably more like a minute had passed.

It was Colin who spoke first. He turned to Jeremiah and said something like, Jeremiah, can you help us? I think that is what he said, although his back was to me and his voice was muffled. What I saw is Jeremiah looking at him, raising his eyebrows at him. Help you? Jeremiah asked. How?

Colin then motioned with his arm to all of the books at the front. If you are a minister, surely after studying all of those books, surely by now you must have some words for us, by now you must have learned something?

He got up, Jeremiah did, and walked slowly to the front. I was surprised at this. I thought Jeremiah would balk, would say something like, Oh I have nothing to say. But he rose from the pew and walked to the front. A pair of his jeans lay drying on the railing, and he slid them over and leaned against it. He looked at us and then pushed those crooked glasses of his up onto his nose, tried to straighten them around his ears.

I have often written that Colin has an angelic face, that his small and perfect features remind me of an angel's. But as Jeremiah stood there, I have to say that about him. He looked like an angel. Even though he is rougher looking, his hair wilder.

He reached behind for a book, which I could see was a scuffed spiral notebook, and opened to somewhere in the middle. He began reading:

These are my memoirs. This is what I have written. This is what I have discovered in my studies. This is what I know now. (He cleared his throat, looked up at us.)

I have categorized life into three compartments: things that are not important, things that are a little important, and things that are the most important.

Here are the things that are not important. (He shuffles his paper, hops up on the railing, crosses his ankles.) Money, control, a big house, fan mail. (He coughs.) Here are things that are a little important: good food, clean water, having enough firewood and blankets to last the winter. Here are the things that are the most important: making sure other people have good food and clean water, making sure other people have enough firewood and blankets to last the winter.

He closed his book.

Is this it? Are these the profound words of the man who has spent the last number of years reading all the books in this place? All of my grandfather's books? Clean water, firewood, and blankets? We looked at each other. Jeremiah hopped down from the railing, smiled and said, That's it.

We continued to look at him. I could see that Colin was about to say something. Jeremiah raised his hand to silence him. He turned to another page in his book and began:

I was hungry and you gave me something to eat. I was thirsty and you gave me something to drink. I was a stranger and you invited me in. I needed clothes and you clothed me. I was sick and you looked after me. I was in prison and you came to visit me. (He pauses) Those are the words of Jesus Christ from the Book of Matthew. It sums up the entire gospel of

Christ. If everyone did that, if everyone looked after another, if we loved each other absolutely, looking past race and gender and a myriad other things that get in the way, we would fulfil the gospel of Christ on this earth. If we made sure other people had enough firewood and blankets to get through the winter. If we made sure other people had fresh water and good food....

He coughed, shuffled his pages. From the back room I heard conversation. It sounded like Chris's voice. I hoped that we would not be interrupted.

He read:

Like Job, I have sat among the rubble cursing the day I was born. God has dealt with me bitterly. I was pointing my finger at God, blaming Him, enraged that He would do this to me, pluck me out of a successful career, take me out of my family, place me here on this desolate island, my only companions these dusty books. (He looks behind him.) But what my accusers meant for evil, God meant for good. This place has enriched me. I have learned much from you, all of you. I was a stranger and you invited me in. (He looked at us then), you have given me cups of water, bandaged my wounds. Without question, you did all of this for me. And I thank you.

This island, too, has enriched me. I have seen the hand of God in the tides, the waters, the creek, and the seasons. The silence has enriched me. The books have guided me, made me realize that I was not alone in my struggles; others have struggled before me. This church building has made me see that God, though He may be silent at times, is still there. Of my accusers I can finally say, forgive them, Father, they didn't know what they were doing.

Before I came here, I was not too concerned about the gospel of Christ, about making sure people had blankets and food. I was more concerned about ratings, and receiving enough donations by mail to keep the radio program on for another month, and would the next royalty check be big enough to buy that car I wanted. Sometimes I did a bit here and there, casting my little daisies of goodwill and then expecting everyone to tell me what a wonderful person I was. I was in need of the mercy of God, the grace of God. The salvation of God. I needed Him to forgive me and to change my pitiful daisy-casting life into a work of God. And He has done that. He has forgiven me for my pride, and only now can I forgive others. Only now do I care about the blankets and food of others. On my own, I would not care. Only through Christ.

He closed the book. Then he sat down in the front pew next to Peter. For a long time no one moved. Even Zoe was quiet. Colin placed his hand on top of Naomi's. She didn't withdraw it, but let it remain there. Her head was bowed, her long hair falling forward. I don't know how long it was before we got up and filed out of the sanctuary, but by the time we were in the back room of the church, the fire needed stoking and the police officers were gone.

FIFTY-FIVE

"Hello."

"Hello."

"Hello, who is this?"

"This is Peter, Mom."

"Peter?"

"Yeah, Mom, it's Peter."

"Peter? Oh my goodness, Peter! Where are you? Are you okay? Peter! Is this really you?"

"Yeah, it's me. I'm fine, Mom."

"Tell me where you are. Are you home? Are you calling from Edmonton?"

"I'm in Maine, Mom."

"Maine!"

"Yeah."

"You mean the state of Maine?"

"Yeah."

"On the east coast? Way out there?"

"Yeah."

"But that's so far! How did you get there?"

"I drove. When I left I drove, and now I'm here."

"You're in Maine right now?"

"Yeah."

"Are you all right, Peter?"

"I'm fine."

"Are you sure? Are you absolutely sure?"

"Yeah, I'm really fine."

"You have no idea how worried I've been."

"I'm sorry for that."

"Peter, everyone's been so worried about you. We even had the police looking. Blair calls me every second day. Have you talked with her?"

"No."

"All your stuff is at my place. Your landlady called when you didn't pay your rent. So Blair and I packed up all your stuff. It's all safe. It's all here. Are you coming home? Are you? Is that why you're calling?"

"Maybe soon. I just wanted to call and let you know that I'm all right. Everything's fine now. I'll be home soon."

Suddenly, more than anything else Peter wanted to be home. Wanted to be in his little apartment on Stony Plain Road, wanted to drive over to Jasper with his friends on the weekends, wanted to walk along the river with Blair, wanted to go down to Red Deer every second weekend to visit his mother, wanted to mow her lawn for her, wanted to sit by himself in his apartment and work on his poetry, wanted to rent movies and watch them with his friends. Wanted to be home.

FIFTY-SIX

IT WAS WARM FOR NOVEMBER. A freak front of warm air was being carried north by the Gulf Stream. It had been like this for a couple of days now. Naomi, Colin, Peter, Jeremiah, and Martha were sitting outside the church on logs watching Zoe play in the dirt at the edge of the cemetery. No one was talking much. Naomi sat very still, her long skirt tucked in around her ankles. The little girls in the locket, the blond twins—she had told them they were Philip's daughters. That's what she had said to them in the cabin, "These are Philip's daughters." Jeremiah had stared at her, eyes wide. Mick and Virginia had looked at each other. Chris got out his little notebook. Colin had made a sound in his throat, and Martha had put her hand on his neck.

But she knew this and had known it the minute she had seen their pictures in the locket, so closely did they resemble Philip, Zoe. Colin hadn't seen it. Jeremiah hadn't seen it. Neither had Martha or the police. But she had. Maybe that's what Jo was trying to tell her.

She was sitting like this, leaning forward, drawing lines in the dirt with a stick and thinking about the two girls when Chris drove up in his little blue Chevette. He parked it beside Peter's truck and walked toward them. He carried a sheaf of papers. He wasn't smiling.

"We've got something," he said. "A match."

Colin raised his eyebrows.

"The fingerprints from the glasses in the cabin match the fingerprints taken at the scene of Jules's murder. They also match the military record of a person named Paul Douglas, last address Boston, Mass."

"What are you saying?" asked Colin.

Chris pulled up a log and told them that when Mick and Virginia had left the previous day, they ran the prints through a computer search. The first thing they found was that the prints matched the ones found at the crime scene in the ferry. Which meant that the same person who had drunk a bottle of wine in the cabin was probably the same person who had murdered Jules. They were still working on the Jo angle. Chris was there when the computers found a match, and Mick had again yelled, "Bingo!"

The match they found was for a Paul Douglas who had served for one hitch in the military. His date of birth was March 13, 1952, and his place of birth was Boston, Massachusetts. His discharge address only read Boston. His eye color was blue, his hair color blond, and he stood 6'2." No other information on his current whereabouts. "Here's the kicker," Mick had said. "Oh boy, here's the kicker. You want to know what this guy did in the service? Computer programmer!"

When Chris told this to the group, Naomi said, "That just proves that Paul Douglas did this, not Philip Friend."

Chris looked at her. "Naomi, Paul Douglas *is* Philip Friend."

FIFTY-SEVEN

PAUL WAS NOT AT HOME WHEN THE POLICE CAME. Margot had just come back from a morning appointment with Chuck and was unloading a small bag of groceries she'd picked up on the way home. The session with Chuck had gone well, she reflected, as she put away the milk, the jar of pickles (Paul liked the dills with extra garlic), the loaf of rye bread, and the cream for coffee.

She had been nervous when she first walked into his office. Some of the church staff were there when she arrived, but if anyone knew the reason for her visit, they greeted her cheerfully and said nothing.

Margot had sat down in the chair across from him and began by saying, "There are some things happening in my life that I need help to get through."

He had looked at her, paused, seemed to want to say something, then didn't.

"It's Paul," she said.

"I know."

She softened. "You know?"

"He came to see me."

"What did he tell you?"

"I got the impression that there was more than what he was telling me."

"Let me guess—he told you he had strayed away from God and wanted to find his way back."

Chuck nodded.

"Did he tell you he had an affair?"

"Not in so many words. He told me he had committed the sin of David. He said he wondered if God could forgive him and restore him like He did David. I told him, yes, He could." He folded his hands on his desk. "Paul is a very troubled man. He was terribly agitated."

"Things should be better now."

He raised his eyebrows.

"I've forgiven him. I want to start over."

On the way home Margot puzzled over the conversation. Then the police came to the door, two grim-faced, uniformed officers asking for Mr. Paul Douglas.

"He's at work."

Outside another two sat in a second patrol car. One of them at the door radioed the one down at the street, and that car drove off.

"What's this about?" she asked, fear clenching at her stomach.

But they didn't answer her. Instead, they produced an official looking piece of paper saying it was a search warrant. They told her they would be searching the premises. Not, would she please allow them to look through the house, but that they would be searching the premises.

"You can't just come in here." But they were already walking past her into the house. "I have to call Paul, you just can't come in here."

She made for the phone, but an officer stopped her. "Please don't phone your husband, ma'am."

"I can phone him if I want."

"No, I wouldn't do that, ma'am. Please."

She backed away. They had showed her identification, sure enough, but what if these people weren't police officers after all, what if they were impersonators, people dressed up as police officers? She'd heard of that happening.

They asked her if Paul had a home office and where was it. She pointed to the end of the hall, and then followed them in. One of them went immediately to the computer and unplugged it.

"What are you doing?"

"We'll be taking this with us."

"His computer?"

"We will give you a receipt for everything we take."

She watched them pull open the desk drawers she had so recently rifled through herself. There were the little jars of African violet fertilizer, the pads of paper, the staples. They found the file that contained the invoice for Philip Friend and placed it in a box. They tried the wooden filing cabinet. When it wouldn't open they asked her if she had the key. She shook her head, so they broke it open with a screwdriver. Wearing rubber gloves, they laid file folder after file folder in the boxes they brought. The cabinet was jammed with them. In the bottom drawer the file folders were stacked one on top of each other and not neatly lined up. On the bottom of the stack was a small package wrapped in brown paper, opened at one end. When the police lifted out the files, it slid to the floor. Margot heard something clink and bent down to pick it up. It was a woman's silver wedding ring. And not a very expensive one by the looks of it. Also on the floor was a piece of paper she was able to read before the officers took it. It was a certificate uniting Philip Friend and Naomi Forrest in marriage. She looked at the date. She watched the officer place it in a box they brought. Also in the bottom drawer was a pair of old-fashioned horn-rimmed glasses.

Something twigged in her memory. Last night, watching the news with Sara and Pam. "Look at that picture, Mom. It sort of looks like Dad, doesn't it?" On the television was one of those police sketches of Philip Friend, the man they were looking for, considered armed and dangerous. Do not attempt to approach him. Phone the police immediately.

"Oh, a lot of people have similar face shapes. And your dad doesn't wear glasses."

One of the officers had placed the pair of glasses in a plastic bag. *Sort of looks like Dad, doesn't it.* Suddenly the enormity of it became a physical weight and Margot slumped into Philip's chair. *The sin of David.*

"Mrs. Douglas?" A woman police officer placed a hand on Margot's shoulder. "Is there someplace you can go, someone you want me to call for you?"

Margot nodded.

A few minutes later, Jane had put up a makeshift sign in the shop window, "Closed for family emergency" and had driven to Margot's. She helped Margot pack a small bag, then went to take Sara and Pam out of school. They spent the rest of the day at Jane's.

FIFTY-EIGHT

"You came."

Margot picked up the handset. "Yes."

The skin of his face was loose and bagged, as if you could grab handfuls of it. His eyes were sunken and unfocused, and his blond hair was dull and stuck out in tufts all over his head. He didn't smile at her the way he normally did, just stared through the meshed window in the prisoner visiting room. A guard lounged against the wall, watching them. This was the first time she had seen him since that morning ten months ago when he was arrested for the murders of Jo, Beth, and someone named Jules. Since she didn't have to testify, she hadn't gone to the trial, not once. She and Sara and Pam had stayed with Jane.

And then the trial was over and Margot had to figure out what she was going to do with the rest of her life. She started seeing a counselor, someone that Chuck recommended. She started attending a support group. She had begun taking very long walks in the early morning, trying to figure out how things had gone so terribly wrong.

And now she was leaving. She had sold the house and her half of the business to Jane. They were packed up, and in two days she and Pam and Sara would be living in Washington state. Her mother had urged her to move "home" to Kansas. But Kansas was not her home anymore. At her age she couldn't move in with her mother. She needed a clean break. A new start. For a couple of years now a small boutique in Seattle, Washington, had been very successfully selling her designs. There was a thriving fashion industry out there and a market, she was told, for her kind of eclectic clothes.

She had come to say good-bye to Paul.

And also there were a few things she had to know.

She gripped the handset. He looked small, shrunken behind the mesh. "I'm leaving. I just came to tell you."

"Where are you going?" His voice was raspy. He coughed several times.

She took a deep breath. "That doesn't matter, Paul."

"But my daughters…"

"I have to know a few things. There are a few things I need to ask you. How did it start, this so-called marriage you had with that woman on the island?"

"It was in all the papers."

"I didn't read too many papers at the time. I want to hear it from you."

He rubbed his left hand over his stubbly head. "I met her when I was working out some bugs on a computer program we sold to a logging company."

"And?"

"I was," he paused, looked down at the fingernails of his left hand, "attracted to her."

She stared hard at him.

"So, I kept seeing her. Every chance I got. She didn't know I was married."

"And you never enlightened her to that little detail of your life."

He shook his head. "I had to see her. She was like a drug…"

She held up her hand. "Spare me."

"When she became pregnant, well, I had to marry her, didn't I? You have to understand about Naomi, she's very sensitive. She's been hurt a lot in her life. I couldn't hurt her more…"

"Well, you've done a fine job of that now."

He sighed. "I never meant to hurt her. So I had to fake a marriage to her."

Margot peered at him through the glass. "And then you began sending her, what, fifty dollars a week? My goodness, Paul, did you think you could afford that? I mean, you spend more than that on fertilizer for your African violets!"

"Naomi's quite good at making do with a lot less. And I couldn't create suspicion."

"You kept her a virtual prisoner on that island. That poor woman…" Margot bit her lip. She had thought of trying to meet Naomi, but several friends including her counselor advised her not to. What purpose would it serve? Both of you have suffered enough. So she didn't. But Margot looked at her on the news sometimes, a thin, sad-looking woman with lots of long, light hair, who looked pale and terribly frightened. When she appeared on camera she was always flanked by the same people: a gray-haired man who wore little John Lennon glasses, and another man, slightly shorter, with fine straight hair. These two always held onto her, one on either side. Also in the little group was a thin young man who didn't look more than eighteen and an elderly woman whose steel gray hair was cut like a dutch boy's. There was a child, too, a pretty little girl named Zoe who was sometimes seen holding onto the hand of the elderly woman. Or the young man.

Margot paid particular attention to the little girl, who looked so like Sara and Pam that it made her heart pang. So far, her daughters hadn't made the connection, hadn't asked about that little girl. She wondered if there would come a time when the two of them would ask about their sister.

Margot turned her thoughts back to Paul. "And then what?"

"What do you mean and then what?"

"Beth found out and so you had to kill her."

Paul nodded.

"How did she find out?"

"You remember the summer she worked for me? She got into my hard drive. She was looking for something else. She was very smart. She found out about Naomi and confronted me with it. I had to…I had to…"

"Glenna *stayed* with us. For two months. Both of us helped her, prayed with her, sat with her in the night!"

Paul shrugged.

"How did Jo find out?"

He grimaced. "With Jo it was different. Jo was a schemer and a liar. Her coming to us was no accident. She was looking for her baby…"

Margot stared at him. "Were you the father?"

"Oh, please!" He leaned back in his chair and rolled his eyes and Margot saw a little of the old Paul in his grin and ready laugh. "Give me some credit. No, I was not the father, I don't know who was. No, her foster mother told her that her baby was adopted into a good home, and Jo got it out of her that her baby was adopted by two doctors in upstate New York. She found out that East Coast Group sold and serviced the lion's share of the medical office computer programs in New York, so she got my name and showed up at your shop."

"I don't believe that!"

"That part's true, Margot. I easily discovered where her baby was. But in the meantime she discovered about Naomi."

"You found Jo's baby, and she found out about your secret life."

"She didn't keep her part of the bargain. She didn't play fair. I made a deal with her. I told her I'd tell her where her baby was if she wouldn't tell you about Naomi, and then first thing I know she's run off to Lambs Island. Well, I was frantic! What was I to do? I had to get there before she told Naomi about you. That's when I faked that trip to California."

"And you got there and killed her. But why that poor ferry operator?"

"Same reason. That little weasel knew everything about everyone. Kept tabs on absolutely everyone on the island. Nosy little bugger. I knew it would only be a matter of time until he found out about me and you and Naomi and Jo. Besides, he saw me, the first night I came rowing to the island. It would be only a matter of time before he remembered and recognized me. From then on, I tied up my boat farther up the island toward the cliffs. I was in the store when I heard that little weasel saying he'd seen someone rowing across the night Jo died. So, I planted the hat I wore on someone else's bed so I wouldn't be blamed. I had to do that, you see."

She stared at him. "I have to ask you one more thing."

"Go ahead."

"What was I to you, Paul? Did you ever love me at all?"

"Of course. I loved you. In the end I chose you. Don't you remember?" He stopped, looked at her, and then smiled. "I never told anyone this, not even my lawyer, but I'll tell you now. I went back to the island once. I knew I had to kill Naomi, either that or frighten her so badly that she went nuts. Which wouldn't be too hard to do since she was on the verge. Well, when I got to the church, I just couldn't do it. I wore a mask and looked in at the window, but I just couldn't do it." He looked down at the table in front of him. "I loved both my wives, but in the end, when I had to make a choice, I came back to you."

Margot felt sick. Her voice carried no emotion when she said, "The divorce should be final soon. My lawyer will get you the papers. I'm leaving now."

He looked at her, a pitiful expression on his face. "Oh, Margot, don't go. Please don't go. Don't leave me. You told me that you would stay with me forever. Don't you remember you told me that?"

But she had already risen and had turned her back to him.

EIGHTEEN MONTHS LATER
FROM THE JOURNALS OF MARTHA MACGREGOR

COLIN AND NAOMI WERE MARRIED YESTERDAY, in a quiet, sweet ceremony in the small open garden behind my house. Zoe was the flower girl and quite charmed the guests, which included almost all of the islanders. Naomi was beautiful. She has lost that fearful look, that darting look in her eyes that had been so much a part of her during the trial and before. As I sit at my writing table now I can see them, the three of them, Colin, Naomi, and Zoe, walking along the pebbly beach. Zoe is between them, and they are holding her up by her hands, one on each side, lifting her over the rocks as they walk. All three of them are laughing, Zoe giggling the way she does. They have walked over to the breakwater and are sitting there, Zoe on Colin's knee. He and Naomi are in conversation, I can see that. He points at something in the distance, but from where I sit I cannot see what he is pointing at.

Naomi and Colin will live in the little house that used to be the church manse. Manny moved out some months ago and is renting a trailer from Dob. He said there was too much upkeep on that little house. Well, upkeep is just what Colin loves! He says the first thing to go will be the kitchen cabinets. He's already working on some in mahogany. I tell him, Colin, you'll have that place looking like the inside of a boat! But I am glad he has a project now that he sold the *Andrea C.*

He is working for Bill—working for—no, that is incorrect. He and Bill are partners now. A month ago *WoodenBoat* magazine came to the island and did up quite a story on their business. It was a good write-up and mentioned none of the bad business that happened so long ago. Hopefully that business is long forgotten by everyone. It's my opinion that Colin will eventually take over the business. Bill's arthritis is making a lot of the work difficult for him.

A few weeks ago Colin told me that he will never go north again during the summer. He will stay here, he said. He will never leave Naomi, even for a day. Colin has finally forgiven himself for Andrea's death. Once during that awful time during the trial I saw Colin and Jeremiah in the graveyard. Both were sitting on grave markers, with heads together, closely, as if praying. Colin was different after that.

Almost a year ago, just after the trial, Jeremiah and Peter left in Peter's truck. We have received three letters from Peter. He is doing well. He is in his last year at university and is having some of his poetry published in a book. He says he will send us one when they come out. Hooray for Peter is all I can say! We haven't heard from Jeremiah.

There is some interest in trying to find a minister for the church. I write this with happiness, wondering why this wasn't the first thing I mentioned. Yes! People are definitely interested. As islanders can spare time away from their traps, they drive over and work on the church. The roof was the first thing fixed. Then the window. The folding table in the back has once again become the place where the laborers gab and eat their lunch.

Down along the beach I see Zoe scampering in front of Naomi and Colin, splatting her booted feet in the puddles as children do. She runs to the edge of the water and walks in as far as her boots will allow. But it is Colin and Naomi that I watch. His arm is around her, and he has turned to look down at her and she looks up at him. I see the look that passes between them. She places her head against his shoulder. They stay this way, close, as one, until Zoe comes splashing back. Colin and Naomi rise from their place, and taking Zoe's hands again, they walk up toward the wharf, toward my place. I imagine they will drop in for tea, so I shall put my writing things away.

A MYSTERIOUS DISAPPEARANCE…A FAMILY IN TUMULT…VOLATILE SURROUNDINGS…CAN ONE WOMAN CONNECT THE PIECES IN TIME?

When nine-year-old Ally Buckley turns up missing, fear spreads throughout the New England fishing village where Sadie and her family live and worship. But when Sadie discovers one of Ally's drawings among her husband's possessions, she suspects danger may be closer to home than she had ever known.

ISBN 1-57673-659-8

DISCOVER THE SECRET OF THE SEASHORE

While investigating a long-unsolved murder, mystery writer Sharon Colebrook and her husband, Jeff, find unexpected secrets, startling revelations, and dangerous truth within their own family tree.

ISBN 1-57673-614-8

THE JOURNEY TO PEACE...

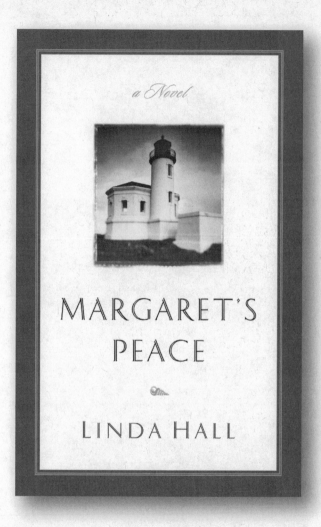

a Novel

MARGARET'S PEACE

LINDA HALL

Margaret returns to her family home on the Maine coast in hopes of finding peace and the God she has lost. Instead she must relive the death of her sister and face long-buried secrets.

ISBN 1-57673-216-9